THE CHELSEA CHOKER

SNAPPED

THE CAMERON COOPER SERIES

C.S. DODDS

CEDAR HILL
BOOK GROUP

Contents

For Mom -

Thank you for the countless trips to the library and for instilling a love of books and reading in me.

SNAPPED

CHAPTER 1

Max

I WAS ON A mission that night to do the bidding of my mentor, my champion, my hero, the only person in the world who understood me and listened. He has taught me everything I know: patience, skill, persistence, and the most important factor—no remorse.

Nash knew me before we even met. He knew my loneliness, my desperate need for attention and love, my yearning to belong somewhere, to someone. He had appeared when I was at my lowest. Homeless, living on the street, afraid every night, and hungry.

It was a simple gesture. He'd asked if I wanted to join him for dinner at a diner around the corner from where I hid in the shadows. I'm not even sure how he saw me. I'd thought I had done an expert job camouflaging myself from the strangers who passed by every day, but he'd looked right into my eyes as I peeked through the cardboard box I called home.

Famished and stretching my dollars, I'd agreed to go because I knew he couldn't harm me in such a public place. Besides, we were about the same size, and I thought I could handle him if he got any ideas. I'd heard people on the streets sometimes did favors for money or food or just a human touch. I wouldn't go there. Prostitute myself out of need. I was on the street because I sought my independence. I wanted control of myself, not constantly doing what others told me to do.

So, I went with him, but I made sure the terms were clear.

"Just dinner, right?"

"Yes, just dinner. And conversation. Is that okay?" he'd asked.

"I guess it depends on what you want to talk about. I don't answer questions I don't want to, got it?"

"Agreed."

We'd gone around the corner to the diner, where we sat in a corner booth. Nash hung his jacket on a hook on a post separating the stalls, and there we sat, looking one another over.

"My name is Nash. What's yours?"

"Max." I'm not sure why I'd told him the truth. I glanced around. There were enough people in the diner that I'd felt safe if this guy was a perv.

"Hello, Max. It's very nice to meet you. Would you like to hang your jacket up?" He'd motioned to where his own black jacket was hanging.

"No, I'm good. I'll just put it here." I nodded to the red vinyl seat next to me as I wiggled my arms free of my jacket sleeves.

The waitress had come over with two glasses of ice water, tossed two straws on the table, and handed a menu to each of us. She didn't seem to care that I wasn't exactly the cleanest looking person in the place. "You need a minute?"

"Yes, thank you," Nash had answered.

He'd opened his menu and looked it over. I opened mine and pretended to read it, but I was looking at him. There was nothing special about the guy—middle-aged, white, gray in his hair and beard—with more gray sprinkled in his beard than his head, small, black-framed glasses that sat right at the bridge of his nose, which was straight and proportionate to his face. Just your average guy. He dressed well, probably had money, and had a soft, southern drawl when he spoke. I couldn't figure out what was happening. Was he just a friendly guy doing his good deed for the week, or was there something more dangerous happening and I just couldn't see it yet?

"What looks good to you, Max?" Nash had put down his menu, slid the paper off a straw, then placed it in a glass and taken a sip.

I did the same. Picked up a straw, stripped it of its paper wrapper, plopped it in the other glass, and took a long, steady drink. I was thirsty and the icy water felt good going down my throat.

I'd asked, "Is there a limit?"

"What do you mean?"

"To how much I can spend?"

Nash had laughed a little. "That's very considerate of you, Max, and no, no limit. Order whatever you like."

The waitress came back just then.

"Are you ready, or do you need a few more minutes?"

"I believe we are ready. Right, Max?"

I'd nodded yes.

"I'll have the turkey dinner special and a cup of coffee. Max?"

"I'll have the cheeseburger deluxe with regular fries and a Coke."

The waitress took our menus and trotted off.

He'd sat there looking at me with a grin on his face. I have to admit it was a little creepy, but I was used to creepy. People called me creepy.

"Would you mind telling me about yourself, Max? Where are you from? How did you end up living in a box on the street?"

"I don't know," I'd said, shrugging my shoulders.

"You don't know what? Where you're from or how you ended up homeless?"

I didn't want to answer a bunch of questions. For all I knew, he was a cop or a private detective sent by my crazy father to find me. That thought had made me smile. My father couldn't give a shit where I was—he would never spend money to find me.

"I choose to live on the street. It makes for good people-watching."

"It must get scary sometimes, not to mention cold and… lonely."

"I have plenty of friends. The homeless are their own community—we look out for each other." I'd lied. I didn't talk to anyone, make eye contact with anyone, or accept anything from anyone unless they dropped it at my feet. Like this one time, this guy was going around handing out socks and baggies filled with toiletries to all the vagrants. When he got to me, he'd squatted down in front of me and tried to start a conversation. I didn't even look up. He gave up and left the stuff on the ground next to me. When he was out of sight, I grabbed the baggy and socks and put them in my secret hiding spot.

"How long have you been here in the city?"

"Long enough. How long have you lived here?" *Let's see how he likes a million questions—I'm full of them.*

The waitress had come back with our drinks and dropped another straw on the table for my Coke. That one I didn't open. I'd save it for another day, another use. Nash took his coffee black, which hadn't surprised me. His slim physique made me think he watched what he ate, so no sugar in his coffee.

"I just moved here recently from the South. My work has brought me here rather unexpectedly."

"What do you do?" I didn't care what this guy did, but if I asked the questions, I was in control of the conversation.

He'd sat looking at me for a few seconds, which made me uncomfortable, and then he answered.

"I'm an appraiser."

"What do you appraise?"

"I can appraise almost anything, but I work mostly in the arts. Specifically, medieval paintings and sculptures...weapons."

"Oh." My disinterest had oozed from every pore.

The waitress slipped our plates in front of us and asked if we needed anything else. Nash answered no, and she moved on to the next table. My empty stomach grumbled with hunger, but I didn't show it.

I'd inspected my burger—lifted the bun, took off the tomato and lettuce, added some ketchup, replaced the bun top, and cut it in half. I'd taken my time savoring that first incredible, delicious bite. The juice and grease from the meat ran down my chin, the gooey cheese mixed with the bread and burger in my mouth—it was heaven. And it was all I could do not to moan as I'd washed it all down with a slurp of my soda. *My God, this might be the best damn burger I've ever had*, I remembered thinking.

"How's your food?" he'd asked. "Any good?"

"It's okay," I'd said, my mouth full of ketchup and French fries perfectly cooked, as only diners seem to know how to do—crunchy on the outside and tender on the inside. I'd looked around, feigning boredom with the entire scene, but really, I'd been excited to be having my first hot meal since I couldn't remember when.

He'd seemed amused as he ate his own dinner. I'd observed how he'd cut his meat, piled some stuffing on top, added a little cranberry sauce, and finally impaled a green bean with his fork before stabbing the neat stack of food and eating it. The perfect bite. He did that with every mouthful until he finished the last morsel.

Conversation was sparse while we ate. Nash tried once more to get me to spill my guts, but I'd share nothing personal with him. I still couldn't tell if he was some kind of freak or not.

Now I realize how lucky I was that night.

The waitress came back and asked if we wanted dessert.

"Chocolate cake," I'd said. She nodded as she wrote. "To go. And a tuna sandwich," I added. I'd glanced at Nash to see his reaction. There was nothing, not even a blink.

"And you, hon? Refresh your coffee or something else?" She nodded her head in Nash's direction.

"Yes, a little more coffee, please. But no dessert."

I'd wanted to get out of there, but I wanted that chocolate cake more, so I sat fidgeting, waiting for the cake. I slipped my jacket back on so I could make a fast exit when the waitress came back. This guy knew where I slept, and I was antsy to move somewhere else. It was easy to move when your home was already in a box.

The waitress returned, but only to refill his coffee, and she waddled off again. I couldn't help but stare at her colossal ass. It was some behind she had. It seemed to move separately from the rest of her body as it jiggled and wiggled under her waitress uniform, contrary to the rest of her body. Momentarily, it amused me, but then I sat, impatient, trying not to make eye contact with Nash, wishing the food would come already.

He sipped his coffee and peered over the rim at me. I'd felt his eyes on me, examining me, trying to pry into my brain.

"Thanks for dinner. It was good," I'd offered.

"You're welcome. And thank you for joining me. I don't enjoy eating alone; it was nice to have a sinner companion."

"What?"

"It's nice to have someone to eat dinner with."

Oh, dinner.

The waitress had returned with a brown bag. I'd stood, taking it from her hands, and looked at Nash. "Yeah, it was cool. Well, bye." I headed for the door before he could say another word.

That was months ago, and since then, things have changed. Nash gave me projects to undertake at his command. The current mission was a soccer chick.

I was watching her play on the brightly lit field down by the piers. She was number seven and moved well; the muscles in her legs defined, her dirty blond hair pulled back in a ponytail, her face pink from exertion. Her team was winning, thanks to a goal she'd just scored. My job was to swap my Poland Spring bottle, which I held with the sleeve of my sweatshirt so as not to leave any fingerprints, with her identical bottle. Nash had spiked the water in my bottle with a sedative.

Patience was the first thing Nash had taught me. I paid attention like any good fan as I inched closer and closer to Seven's gym bag, thrown on the ground next to the field. Mimicking the action of the game, I moved to either side of the bag. No one paid any attention to the lone figure cheering the team on at the sideline. The other spectators concentrated on the fast-paced game.

Her team was about to score again, and I prepared to swap the bottles. I stepped closer to her bag, and it happened. They scored. I threw my hands up in the air, pretending to cheer, and "accidentally" dropped my bottle on top of her open bag. I bent over and picked up Seven's bottle instead. Standing, I clapped my hands for the team and took a swig from her bottle, just as if it were my own. It was too easy. Keeping my head down to avoid any cameras, I retreated to the fence and found a place to wait for her near the exit.

The game ended, and Seven headed to the sidelines. She sat down on the turf next to her bag and took a quick sip from the bottle I'd dropped before replacing her cleats with a pair of flip-flops. She chatted with her friends as they gathered their belongings and then she took a nice, long drink. The women walked casually toward the exit as the next game got underway. A few hung back to watch the game start, two others headed toward the porta-potty as my intended walked toward the gate alone.

Seven exited onto the sidewalk, took a left, stopped for a moment as she finished the water, and threw the empty plastic bottle into the trash. I stood in the shadows as she searched in her bag and pulled out her phone. She started down the sidewalk again as she checked her messages.

I followed a few feet behind, knowing the drug in her water would hit her hard and fast, and it did. She swayed and staggered to the chain-link fence that surrounded the field, dropped her phone and almost fell over when she attempted to pick it up. No one else noticed the woman having a hard time standing. I stepped in quickly.

"Hi—are you okay? I'll get that." I bent down and picked up her phone.

She looked at me, her eyes half-closed, watery. Her chapped lips parted as her jaw slackened and she struggled to draw air. She leaned against the fence to keep herself upright, her body betraying her, morphing from solid muscle to a fluid mass.

"Here, let me help you." I took her arm around my neck and pulled her close. Her feet dragged along the cement. "Let's find someplace for you to sit." I helped her along the dimly lit sidewalk. Bystanders paid us no mind. People in cars passed us, clueless as to what was happening.

We came to the corner, where there was a small park area at the end of the stadium. I steered her into it and over to some full bushes. She could barely stand as I eased her onto the ground and laid her on her back.

It was so easy. So much easier than Clara and Wayne, which was messy, even though I don't remember whacking at them. I remember what it looked like when I was done, so much blood everywhere, on the floor, the couch, the ceiling... everywhere.

And it was easier than my first with Nash. The nerves were calm. The doubt eased. The guilt quieted. I knew what I was doing now as I donned a pair of kid leather gloves and slipped the silky blue ribbon around her neck, and knew how to do it efficiently, quickly, silently.

CHAPTER 2

Hunter

THE DEATHS OF FOUR women along the riverbanks of lower Manhattan revived not-so-old feelings in Hunter Finnegan and his team of New York Police detectives. The wounds were still healing from the last killing spree, just a little more than two years ago, that had hit too close to home in every conceivable way.

Not only were their own people targeted and murdered, but it had turned out that one of their own, someone very special to Hunter, was behind the killings. There wasn't even time for the police community to move on before they discovered the first victim of a new psychopath.

Hunter leaned into his steel-gray desk as he read through the files on the victims, one large hand holding his head up. The first victim of the murderer the press was calling The Chelsea Choker was Brittany Davidge, a thirty-two-year-old chef who worked on private yachts.

An event planner had hired her to prepare dinner on a vessel docked at Pier 59 for a private party. The yacht captain had discovered her body when he went to the galley for a drink and found food burning in a pan on the stove. He called for her, and when she didn't answer, he searched the ship.

He'd located her lying on a bed in a dark cabin and thought she was sleeping. When he couldn't wake her, he realized she was dead.

An asterisked note at the bottom of the report stated that the poor guy appeared visibly shaken as he tried to explain to the police how he had come across her body.

Hunter flipped the page to the forensics report. It was determined that someone had spiked her wine with ketamine, a powerful anesthetic-turned-party-drug. She wouldn't have been able to fight back and was most likely unconscious when her attacker struck. Her hands rested on her abdomen, and a blue ribbon, the murder weapon, was wound tightly around her neck and tied in a bow. The determined cause of death was strangulation.

In the color photo stapled to the page, Brittany Davidge looked as if she was napping. Her pristine chef's coat didn't have any evidence of foul play, not even a stray hair, but the blue ribbon, Hunter thought, was telling its own story.

Since that first discovery, three more women had died and were left in the same position, lying peacefully on their backs, hands on top of their abdomens, a blue ribbon tied in a bow around their necks. All the bodies were found within a one-mile radius of each other along the Chelsea Piers.

"The chief wants to see you in his office, Hunter," Rhonda Saintil, Detective Third Grade, said, as she sat down at her desk, opposite Hunter's. The new case didn't thrill her, since the last serial killer, Cameron Cooper—aka The Stealth Stalker—had nearly murdered her. A single mother of two, Rhonda was mentally still recovering and not cleared for anything that didn't involve sitting at her desk. Everyone knew she was grateful for the reprieve from active duty.

"Thanks." Hunter closed the file he was reading and sat staring at it. Michael Dwyer, the chief of detectives, had been aloof since The Stealth Stalker case closed and Hunter knew he was on the chief's shit list after he'd brought in a consultant on the case. It turned out that Dr. Cameron Cooper, the consultant, was the very serial killer they were pursuing. Or rather, an alternate personality of hers was the killer. And his frequent visits to Cameron at St. Christina's State Hospital for the Criminally Insane only made the situation worse. He should have known he wouldn't be able to keep the visits a secret.

Rumor had it that the police commissioner, Olivia Tate, was breathing down Dwyer's neck to catch this new killer wreaking havoc in her city, which gave Dwyer a reason to come down hard on Hunter.

He took a deep breath and stood up from his desk. *Better not keep him waiting. It'll only make him angrier.* Walking through the station and up the stairs to the chief's office, Hunter couldn't help but think about how much had changed in a year, at least for him. He'd fallen in love while hunting a killer, only to realize he'd fallen in love with the killer.

Hunter knocked on the chief's open door and stood waiting for the invitation to come in.

"Are you going to stand in the hall all day?" That was the closest thing to an invitation the chief offered.

"You wanted to see me, sir?" Hunter said, walking into the spacious corner office of Chief Dwyer.

"Yes, I did. Have a seat, Hunter. The commissioner is on her way here, and I think you should join us and be just as miserable as I am." He leaned back in the large, black leather chair that creaked slightly every time he moved. "I figure if she sees you here, she'll chew you out too, taking some of the heat off of me." He folded his hands on his round belly, pleased with himself.

"I assume this is regarding The Chelsea Choker?"

"Yeah, The Chelsea Choker. What a stupid name." He rotated his chair, so he was looking out across the city he'd sworn to protect. An angry frown clouded his expression as he shook his head. "Where do these people come from?" Dwyer mused out loud.

"Good morning, Chief, Detective Finnegan," Olivia Tate said, entering the room and extending a hand to Hunter and then to Chief Dwyer.

Commissioner Tate was the city's first Black female commissioner. She was tough as nails but had a reputation for being fair and wise—Solomon-wise. She was sixtyish and had devoted her entire career to the NYC Police Bureau. Nationwide, she had a reputation for being a leading innovator in advancing police policy and procedure. Police forces around the country implemented her model for an effective police/community relationship.

The two men stood. "It's good that you're here, Detective," she began. "I would like to hear your report firsthand, especially since you seem to be our in-house expert on serial killers."

Hunter took a quick glance at Dwyer, who was turning red—a bad sign—and back to Commissioner Tate, whose expression was ambiguous.

"Let's sit over here." Commissioner Tate motioned to the round mahogany table and chairs in the corner. "Gentlemen, I'm sure I don't have to tell you that the mayor is extremely concerned about the newest serial killer to hit our city. He's so concerned that he calls me every morning just to yell about it. It's all I can do to not hang up on that man! But I don't. I wait patiently until he finishes venting, and then I wait some more for his apology. You see, I understand how he feels. Frustrated, angry, frightened for our citizens, because I feel the same way. Now my question to you two is: what are we doing about it?"

Dwyer responded, "Commissioner, we concur with you, of course, and we are just as deeply troubled by this killer as you and the mayor. My people are on top of this, and we are closing in with every passing second. There are undercover cops all over the piers—it's only a matter of time before this creep fu...uh, screws up, and we have him. Isn't that right, Detective?"

"Yes, Chief, that's right. And Commissioner, I want to assure you and Mayor Wallace that we are working on this twenty-four seven. We've set up new surveillance cameras, and our undercover team is determined to bring an end to these killings." Hunter felt satisfied with his answer. The chief and commissioner seemed less so.

"Detective, I think you should bring Commissioner Tate up to speed on the latest progress."

Hunter knew Dwyer was going to make him squirm as much as he could. "Of course, sir." *Asshole.* "We have four victims, all women, white, in varying ages and appearance. They were all incapacitated in some way. Either through their own volition, like by drinking too much alcohol, or because the killer presumably drugged them. The killer then took them into a remote area where he strangled them with a satin ribbon, tied it in a bow around the neck, and left them, hands folded on their abdomen as if they were sleeping."

Hunter thought this was a satisfactory response but could tell by the expressions of Tate and Dwyer that they required more. "All the incidents occurred in the Chelsea Piers area, and that is where we're concentrating on our surveillance. There have been four murders to date, as you know. The latest victim was found just this morning."

"Tell me about her," Tate said.

"Her name was Michelle Roberts. A man walking a dog found her lying in a small enclave at the end of the soccer field on Twelfth and Twenty-Fourth."

"What were these women drugged with?"

"He drugged three of the victims with ketamine. Autopsy discovered that the second victim, Jessica Ericssen, sustained serious injuries after a push down a flight of stairs outside on Pier 61. She was attending a corporate event there and had had a couple of drinks, according to witnesses. She went outside to have a cigarette with a friend. The friend left her alone to go to the lady's room. When Jessica didn't come back inside, the friend searched for her and found her body under the stairs behind a vending machine. He left her just like the others...on her back, hands folded on her abdomen, ribbon tied in a bow around her neck, the ribbon being the murder weapon."

"Forensics checked the latest ribbon for evidence?"

"We just got the report back. No fingerprints, no DNA, nothing. It was fresh off the spool. The killer is meticulous."

"So, what's your take on this guy, Detective?" Tate asked.

"I think we're dealing with someone on a power trip. Maybe he's on the weak side and isn't confident about his abilities to take down a woman on his own, so he drugs her first or pushes her down the stairs to incapacitate her so he can dominate. We think we have a video of him captured at the soccer field. Very nondescript. Gray hoodie with the hood pulled up, baggy blue jeans, Van sneakers, always keeps his head down and face out of view. He's conscious of the cameras. We think he's a young white male based on his hands, which are visible."

"It's not a lot to go on, is it, Detective?" Commissioner Tate seemed irritated with Hunter's report.

"No, Commissioner, it's not, but that's all we have right now." Then it occurred to him. This conversation with the commissioner was the golden opportunity he'd been waiting for. "We could use another viewpoint, someone who can give us some insight into a guy like this. I'm not a profiler or analyst, but I know where we can find one."

Chief Dwyer, who'd been half-dazed, enjoying the attention placed on Hunter instead of himself until this point, suddenly realized what Hunter was getting at. He sat forward in his chair, leaned in on the table, and pointed one pudgy finger at Hunter.

"If you think I'm going to let that psychopath ex-girlfriend of yours anywhere near this case, you are out of your fu—... out of your mind!" His bloodshot eyes were bulging, and the vein in his temple was protruding, pulsing and purple.

"What are you suggesting, Detective?" Commissioner Tate's brows rose high, and her own eyes were wide with concern.

"Why not use Cameron Cooper? It would be good rehabilitation for her. She was an analyst with the FBI, a psychologist, and who better to give us insight into a serial killer than someone with her unique situation?" He had already proposed the idea to Cameron. He just needed to get it past the chief. But the commissioner, he realized, was much more open-minded and forward-thinking than the chief. If she gave her okay, the chief would have to concede.

"You mean another serial killer?" Dwyer hissed at Hunter.

The commissioner studied Hunter, her brows furrowed, her dark brown eyes probing his.

"Chief, you know she's not a serial killer. The doctors have explained it to you several times. Cameron has no recollection of The Stealth Stalker killings and was not in control when they happened. She would be perfect for helping with this case. I already have an established relationship with her, and I know she has incredible instincts. Her record as an FBI agent alone qualifies her for this case."

"Yes. Yes, it does. And she's in a state forensic hospital for the insane because she's a killer!" The chief's baritone voice was getting louder with each word, and he was on the verge of berating Hunter. His secretary stuck her head in and pulled the door to his office closed. "What the hell is wrong with you? You want a profiler? How about we hire one that's not in prison for murder? I'm sure we can get you one of those!"

Chief Dwyer stood up and paced the office, his face nearly purple with anger. Hunter knew if the commissioner wasn't sitting right there, he really would have laid into him and possibly would have gone after him physically.

"What insight do you think she could offer?" Commissioner Tate asked.

"What? You're not seriously considering this, are you?" The chief stood with his hands out and his eyes popping again.

"Just a minute, Mike. I think Detective Finnegan makes a good point. Ms. Cooper has a unique point of view. It's not unheard of, you know...that law enforcement turns to criminals for insight on how the criminal mind works. Tell us how you think she can help."

"I think Cameron can tell us more about this guy based on his method of killing, the area, the way he dresses. She's studied this.

Cam knows a lot more about it than any of us and could probably tell us the kinds of places a guy like this likes to hang out in and maybe answer questions we don't even know we have." Hunter felt hopeful that Tate might actually agree to let Cameron in on the case. His pulse quickened at the prospect of working with her.

Commissioner Tate studied Hunter and then looked to the chief, who was now leaning his big ass against his desk, shaking his head, arms folded across his broad chest, as the bulging vein in his temple rhythmically humped his skull. Hunter could see she was contemplating it, weighing the pros and cons of reaching out to Cameron. It would be career suicide for her if something were to go wrong. Or, if Cameron's help led to The Chelsea Choker's arrest before he could strike again, she could be the innovative hero of the day for setting one serial killer loose on another.

"All right, Detective Finnegan, I'll allow it, but there will be strict rules, or it will be your ass on the line. Understood?"

"Yes, of course, Commissioner, your rules all the way." Hunter couldn't believe it—she had agreed to let Cameron work on a case! It didn't matter to him what the rules were. All that mattered was that he was going to get to see Cameron more than twice a month. Internally, he was smiling, laughing, handing out high fives. To Tate and Dwyer, though, he appeared stoic and professional.

"You have got to be kidding me!" The chief pushed himself away from his desk. "Please tell me you are not letting that murderer out of prison?"

"No, I'm not. Detective Finnegan will go to her." Commissioner Tate stood to leave. "You can bring her the files and a laptop. You will have open access to her within reason, and I'll allow her to call you if she needs to. I have to talk to the D.A. and the Corrections

Department about all of this first, of course, but I don't see why there should be a problem. I'm depending on you, Detective, to make sure there are no problems, because all our careers will be on the line. Understand?"

"Yes, ma'am. And thank you. You won't regret this."

"I better not. Goodbye, gentlemen."

Hunter and Chief Dwyer stood in silence as the commissioner left the office. Hunter was ecstatic, and it was all he could do not to smile. But if the chief even saw a hint of happiness in Hunter at this moment, it would be a death sentence for him. Reluctantly, Hunter turned and looked over to Dwyer, who was frowning, head tilted down, eyes up, his tell for being truly pissed.

"Do you remember our deal, Hunter?" Dwyer's voice was low and rough, anger resonating with each word.

Hunter remembered the deal to be more of a threat. "I do." He was to always maintain Cameron's guilt in The Stealth Stalker killings, or the chief would find a way to fire him and make life hell for him. That was the chief's "deal."

"I feel like you just reneged on our deal when you stated, in front of Commissioner Tate, that Cameron Cooper was not responsible for the deaths of five police department personnel. You said, and I quote, 'Chief, you know she's not a serial killer.' I thought I made it clear to you, Hunter, that I don't know that, and no matter how many times you or her doctors say it, it will never be true to me."

"You did, sir."

"And to top it off, instead of coming to me directly with this lamebrained idea to read Cameron in on the case, you sidestepped me and went over my head to the commissioner. And you had the audacity to do it right in front of me." The chief's voice was getting deeper and sounded more like a growling animal than a human being.

"I apologize, Chief. I didn't mean to do that," Hunter lied. "The idea came to me as we were discussing the case. I never intended to go over your head. It just came out of my mouth."

"Is that right? Well, guess what, Hunter? You've put yourself and the commissioner in a very precarious position. Cameron is unpredictable at best. I will make sure the mayor and everyone else who matters knows that this deal with Cameron is between you and the commissioner. And when this thing goes south, and I predict it will, I will just as easily sidestep you as your career dies a miserable death and you take the commissioner down with you. Hell, maybe if I play my cards right, I can step right into her job when you're both fired!"

The chief sat down on his chair and leaned back, hands rubbing his protruding belly, a smug smile curling at his lips. "You know, Hunter, I'm beginning to like this deal. I just realized I no longer have to find a way to get rid of you. You just did it for me."

Hunter walked back to his desk. His feeling of elation had become slightly subdued with the chief's sobering remarks. Had he just committed career suicide? He shook it off. It didn't matter. Cameron was far more important. He would find a new job if the chief finally had his way and canned his ass.

He sat back down at his desk and jotted down a list of items Cameron would need and want. Checking the list, he leaned back, a tight-lipped grin inching across his lips.

"For someone who just came from the office of the man who hates him, you look very pleased with yourself," Saintil said.

"That I am. I just hope I don't regret it."

CHAPTER 3

Cameron

Looking through the barred window of her room out onto the park-like surroundings, Cameron Cooper reflected on the past twelve months and how time really had flown. It had been a little more than two years since the former FBI analyst and profiler had first met Detective Hunter Finnegan, fallen in love, been convicted of murder, and ultimately been incarcerated at St. Christina's State Hospital for the Criminally Insane—a maximum-security forensic psychiatric center.

Diagnosed with Dissociative Identity Disorder, or D.I.D., she had multiple personalities or alters hidden within her psyche. One of them was a killer.

Her mind had fractured several times throughout her life, beginning with the traumatic abuse she'd suffered at her stepfather's hands when she was a child. The alter who surfaced then was Angel, a child herself, who took over Cameron's mind when her stepfather beat her. Angel took the abuse for her and stashed away the memories to protect Cameron.

After months of intensive therapy with St. Christina's resident psychiatrist, Dr. Reid Heisser, Cameron had a better understanding of what had been happening to her mind. The last time it had fractured was while she was working as a consultant with the NYPD, hunting a serial rapist.

The criminal had trapped her in his latest victim's apartment. He had killed the woman during his attack on her, and as officers searched the building, leaving the profiler alone with the body, he pounced. As they fought, he slammed her head against a table. The attacker thought he had knocked her unconscious until she crawled to a kneeling position, stood, and came at him with the methodical ease of a trained assassin.

But, as Dr. Heisser had discovered during hypnosis, it wasn't Cameron Cooper who had crawled off the floor. It was someone new.

When her head struck the table, in extreme fear for her life, her personality had splintered again. The identity formed was a man who called himself Jason Jonette, a tribute to the serial killer who had nearly killed Cameron and a co-ed named Lisa Allen more than ten years earlier.

Jason was angry that the rapist could have killed Cameron by bashing her head against the table. If anyone was to kill Angela Cameron Chadwick Cooper, it would be him.

He lunged at the rapist, and punched him in the throat, incapacitating him just long enough to grab a lamp wire, wrap it around the man's neck, and choke him until he fell to the floor. Not satisfied that he was dead, Jason picked up the lamp and smashed the murderer's face and head with it.

A serial killer was born.

Jason Jonette, aka The Stealth Stalker, had a draconian persona and wanted to be Cameron's dominant personality. It was his mission to kill Cameron Cooper. In misguided attempts to do so and gain control, the personality known as Jason Jonette went on a killing spree. He had murdered five NYPD female employees and nearly a sixth before he was stopped.

When he attacked Detective Rhonda Saintil, plunging his knife into her body, she fought back, driving her own knife into his thigh, nicking the femoral artery. Jason Jonette limped away and Cameron Cooper awoke severely wounded.

Hunter and Detective Glen Levine had found Cameron screaming and covered in blood in her bedroom. They rushed her to the hospital, and afterward, they'd discovered a secret apartment connected to hers and in it, the possessions of a serial killer.

Photographs of the victims hung on a closet wall, and their shoes, the killer's trophies, sat neatly lined up on the floor under each photo. Strewn in the bathroom were a wig, beard, mustache, and a bloody knife used in five murders, still coated in Detective Saintil's blood.

Cameron had nearly bled to death. When she awoke in the hospital, she had no memory of how she'd sustained her injury.

The person Rhonda Saintil had driven her knife into to save her own life may have been Jason, but the meat and bones body was that of Cameron. It was her flesh that was cut, her artery nicked, and to the people who knew her and worked with her, it was Cameron Cooper who doctors had rushed into emergency surgery and who lay recovering in the hospital.

The heavy stress of the situation, combined with the injury and medications, was enough for the alters to reveal themselves to hospital staff and eventually to Hunter Finnegan.

At the hospital, Hunter stood, shocked, as he listened to the woman he was falling in love with state that her name was Jason

Jonette. The pieces came together for him at that point. Cameron Cooper was The Stealth Stalker. Forensics would later confirm Cameron's fingerprints and DNA covered all the items from the secret apartment.

The head nurse ordered a psych evaluation and as the hospital's resident psychiatrist tried to evaluate Cameron, alter Jason took control and attacked her. The doctor's assistant captured the incident on video as police officers swarmed the room, guns drawn, and Jason made demands. Police officers and hospital staff had subdued and sedated the alter known as Jason Jonette before the doctor was seriously hurt.

The next morning, Cameron watched the shocking video of herself attacking the smaller woman. She'd had no idea she was so sick, and it devastated her to learn that her hands were those of a murderer, or more precisely, of The Stealth Stalker.

The killer she had been pursuing, she realized with horror, lived in her own mind.

The courts remanded her to St. Christina's until the day doctors diagnosed her mentally fit to stand trial for murder. Cameron had told Hunter to forget about her, move on with his life. She didn't want him visiting her, seeing her incarcerated in a place where insanity ran hand in hand with evil.

She wandered down the light-blue-and-white hallway of St. C's highest security ward, processing her thoughts. Hunter hadn't given up on her, she acknowledged. He was determined to be a part of her life, even inside a hospital for the criminally insane. He'd kept in touch with Dr. Heisser, and finally arranged bi-monthly visits in secret, knowing that if Chief Michael Dwyer discovered his covert visits, he'd make life miserable for him and probably fire him.

But he'd said he wanted more. Hunter told her he wanted her well and whole again; he wanted more time with her; he wanted a life with her. He was determined to continue to see her. He needed her.

So, Hunter found a way into the inner chambers of the giant, clanking beast that had gobbled Cameron up and would never release her from its clutches. The beast whose insides were sterile white and where the cries of the insane reverberated off its metal bones.

She'd deserved it, she thought, as she stood in the doorway to the common room where patients, a nicer word for inmates, could roam free. She deserved to be trapped in the bowels of the beast for the rest of her life. And she'd learned how to be at peace with it, as did her alters, including Jason Jonette—most of the time. But under the right circumstances, she had found it was easy for her to lose control and for Jason to take over.

Two and a half months after Cameron had arrived at St. Christina's, there'd been an incident.

An orderly, Myra Gordon, had taken it upon herself to play disciplinarian. She was a sadistic bitch who Cameron was sure got off on seeing her in pain.

Myra was about the same height as Cameron, but she had a good eighty pounds on her. The excess fat puckered her face and made her blue-shadowed eyes appear small in comparison. Her hair was an unattractive shade of yellow, cut chin-length, and styled with what Cameron could only assume was a home perm, badly done. There were dark gaps in her mouth from missing teeth. She was slightly bowlegged and her uniform looked physically uncomfortable, as it strained and pulled against her many rolls of excessive flesh. And she was surprisingly strong.

She had taken to calling Cameron a faker and a liar. The first time Myra had abused Cameron, she'd pushed her to the ground with one of her big, meaty hands. Then she'd kicked Cameron and demanded that she stand up, but before she could, she'd grabbed her hair and pulled her across the floor by it, slamming her head against the wall.

"Where's your other personalities, Cameron? Huh? Why don't they come out and help you? I know why—because you are a lying bitch. There's nothing wrong with you. You just like to kill other women. You aren't sick, like the other poor bastards here. You're just a murderer," she'd hissed, and kicked her again.

Cameron's alternate identity, Jason, didn't care for Myra. It was his job to torture Cameron, not hers.

After a rough afternoon suffering from a stress-induced migraine brought on by Myra's abuse, Cameron had finally fallen asleep when Myra paid her one last visit before she left for the night. No one was supposed to be in any of the patients' rooms after eight p.m. The guards locked the doors down, and, as most of the inmates were medicated for the night, the guards relaxed, hoping for a quiet and uneventful evening shift.

Myra had snuck into Cameron's room as the guards were indulging in a homemade coffee cake—a gift from one of their wives—and some freshly brewed coffee, a nightly ritual before their rounds. Myra had taken advantage of the distraction and the opportunity to torture Cam a bit more before she went home.

The portly orderly unlocked the door and silently closed it behind her. She approached the bed and dumped a mug of hot coffee on Cam's face. Cameron sprang up as she howled out in pain, but it wasn't Cameron Cooper that Myra had roused. It was Jason, and now it was his turn to have a little fun.

By the time the guards had heard the screams, unlocked the doors, and figured out which room the noise was coming from, Jason had done a number on Myra. The guards stood in the doorway, unsure of what they were looking at, and then drew their tasers.

"Cameron, back away from...who is that?" Grey Turner, the head guard, asked Petey Johnson, whose mouth hung open as his finger rubbed the side of the taser's trigger guard.

"I'm not sure," Petey whispered back.

Another guard with a stun gun and a nurse with a syringe full of droperidol appeared. The nurse gasped as he looked over Turner's shoulder.

Myra was unrecognizable. Her pudgy face oozed blood from the nose and mouth. More blood covered her face as it ran down from a raw spot on top of her head, saturating her hair and turning it a repulsive red.

Jason had slammed Myra's face against the wall, breaking her left cheekbone, shattering her nose, and knocking out two more teeth. He'd torn a chunk of yellow hair from her scalp, repeatedly stabbed her with the leg broken off a chair, and by the time the guards opened the door, he had her on the floor with a foot on her throat, ready to crush her windpipe, yellow hair held high in a tight fist. She was no more than a bloody lump of moaning flesh.

When Cameron awoke in the morning, she was in a padded cell, tightly wrapped up in a straitjacket, no memory of what had happened the night before, or why she seemed to be covered in blood, and why her face and left hand throbbed.

Dr. Reid Heisser was the first person she had seen that morning. He explained that she, or Jason, who was left-handed, had attacked an orderly named Myra Gordon and nearly killed her.

Cameron described to Dr. Heisser Myra's physical and verbal abuse. She really couldn't say anything in her own defense except, "She wanted to meet my alters. Unfortunately for her, she met the violent one."

After Dr. Heisser had heard Cameron's side of the events, he had her brought to the infirmary, where he treated her burned and blistered face and x-rayed her hand for broken bones. There was enough evidence that Myra had provoked the attack and that Cameron, or Jason, had acted in self-defense.

Heisser sent her back to her room, which comprised of nothing more than a mattress on the floor now, a wardrobe, a sink, and toilet in the corner. The smell of bleach lingered in the air. She had lost the privilege of a desk and chair.

The attack on Myra was a monumental setback. It was the first time that Jason had manifested since Cam's diagnosis, and it meant that the staff would watch her much more closely, especially at night. Nighttime was when Jason had always been the most active—hunting his victims in the cover of darkness.

The hospital had a camera installed in her room, and the guards watched nightly for any movement. It didn't bother her. She was curious herself to see if Jason was pacing the room at night, strategizing an escape or planning his next violent attack.

She was hoping for an escape, but there was very little activity. It mostly depended on how stressful Cameron's day or week was. When Jason appeared, he mostly stood looking through the small glass window in the metal door that separated him from the rest of the world.

Cameron wandered into the common room. Most of the other patients were having lunch, and it was quiet. She hunkered down in her usual spot, a worn and stained green couch pushed into the corner just under the window.

As she gazed out through the bars, she could see Hunter making his way across the property to the parking lot. He had just left Cameron and St. Christina's after their regular bi-monthly visit.

But this visit was surprising.

His green eyes had shone with excitement as he'd offered a solution to their separation.

"I have a new case," he'd said. "The Chelsea Choker. He's drugged and strangled three women along the piers. I think you can help. This is your area of expertise and I think you can give us a unique perspective into a psychopath's mind...and help us catch a killer."

Cameron had suggested there were other experts he could and should turn to—not a convicted killer serving a life sentence in a hospital for the criminally insane.

"Remember what Dr. Heisser and his colleague, Dr. Franzen, had both said? It would be detrimental for me to return to police work in any capacity. It could set me back and undo any progress that I've made in the last few months."

She knew he was desperate to see her, and this case was just an excuse. But it was a poor excuse, and Hunter was irresponsible in asking for her help.

On the other hand, Cameron *could* help. She could do some good in the city that she'd hurt so gravely, and there was the bonus of getting to see Hunter more than twice a month. She could correspond with him on an actual computer, meet with him at least once a week, and have access to files. She could do research.

Rather than being the one under scrutiny, she would be the one scrutinizing. She would actively engage her mind and perhaps, by assisting in finding this killer, she could find a small sense of redemption, a foundation to prove that she was not a lost cause but a person capable of healing, contributing to society, and potentially reintegrating into society someday.

Seeing Hunter left her sad, yet hopeful. She'd been sure that he would have given up on her by now, but instead, he'd devised a way to visit her twice a month. Those visits were all she had to look forward to.

Cameron lived in a new world where she had very little control over her life or even her day. The people who inhabited that world were not friends, they were caretakers. She liked Dr. Heisser, and their therapy sessions were going well. Most of the guards were okay, although Petey Johnson was still a little spooked by her.

Word had spread to the other orderlies about what happened with Myra, and most of them treated her with kid gloves, never sure of who they were really talking to, Cameron or an alter. The nurses were always on their guard, not just with her, but with everyone. They maintained a professional demeanor and a guard at their sides. If the inmates did as they were told, there was no problem. If they acted up—spit, hit, bit, screamed, refused medication or food, crapped on the floor, then there was trouble.

But even with all of those people and their daily interactions, she'd felt lonely and sad until Hunter had visited. Hunter was the only real friend she had, and his was the only relationship worth working for.

The new world confined her to a handful of rooms—the room where she slept, the recreation room, Dr. Heisser's office and the cafeteria, and a small room at the end of Corridor A, next to the guard's room. She'd lost cafeteria privileges after the Myra incident, but Dr. Heisser had recently reinstated them for good behavior.

The Myra incident had also added another five years to her life sentence. She imagined her spirit trapped and wandering the halls of St. Christina's until those five years expired.

It sounded hopeless, yet she hadn't lost hope. She held onto it because Hunter did.

She worked hard every day to understand why all of this had happened. The fractured identities, the internal struggle, the killing spree. Therapy with Dr. Heisser had been eye-opening for her. Cameron hadn't realized how much her stepfather had traumatized her as a child or how her mother's death had left her feeling even more out of control. She then chose a career where she had to confront real-life monsters, as if it were normal for them to exist at all.

And there it was—she'd chosen that career for a reason. So no one else would feel helpless the way she did when she was a child and her stepfather had terrorized her. Or when her mother died or when the actual Jason Jonette kidnapped her and Lisa Allen. She chose that career to make a difference, to protect the vulnerable, to save them, to help those who couldn't help themselves.

Cameron needed to do this. She needed to help Hunter track this killer. It was what she had sworn to do. Protect the innocent from monsters...like herself.

CHAPTER 4

Max

Nash wasn't as creepy as I'd imagined the first time I'd met him. After that first night at the diner, I'd gone back to my box and fed Sammy Cat the tuna sandwich while I ate the chocolate cake. Then we moved. I'd picked up my cardboard box, bolted out of there, and found a new place closer to the park to call home.

One week later, there was a voice outside the box. It was Nash.

He had found me and asked if I would like to have dinner with him again. The insurance money that I'd taken from my mother hadn't lasted as long as I'd hoped it would. New York City was crazy expensive.

When I'd first arrived, I'd found a one room "loft," as the landlord had called it, with a shared bathroom in a very questionable neighborhood. It was a thousand dollars a month! I'd realized I'd run out of money if I kept on living there much longer and I also wanted to eat, so when the warmer weather arrived, I made the move to the street until I could find a job and budget my money better.

Then Nash invited me to dinner, and, trying to spend as little of the remaining money as possible, I agreed.

Afterward, I moved my box again. And he'd found me—again.

He must have watched me closely because this went on for several weeks, and slowly, we forged a sort of friendship. Finally, as fall approached, he asked if I would like to stay in his spare room. He promised no funny stuff and I could leave any time I wanted. He'd said he liked me and enjoyed my company, and he worried about me living on the streets. I agreed to check out the apartment, but wasn't making any promises.

When I saw the enormous, four-story, nineteenth-century townhouse he lived in on a tree-lined street, I couldn't say no. It was the most beautiful home I'd ever seen. And it was getting cold out.

In exchange for a bedroom of my own, and all the food I could eat, I had chores to do. Clean the house, go to the grocery store and pretend to enjoy listening to Nash go on and on about his work as an appraiser. It seemed like almost everything he showed me was some kind of ancient weapon. If it could kill another person, he was an expert in it.

He was strict in following a schedule and overly concerned with cleanliness and order. If he didn't like the way I cleaned something, I had to do it over, and I had to do it the way he wanted it done. He spent most of his time in his office on his computer, hardly ever leaving the house. And on the rare occasion he went out, he didn't allow me to go with him.

But one day, out of curiosity, I'd followed him. He had gone to the museum. He'd told me he conducted most of his work at museums. I lost him when I got inside. It was like he'd disappeared into an exhibition. I thought there must be a secret door that only employees knew about. I hurried home, afraid that he'd doubled back and was waiting for me, which he wasn't.

During dinner one evening, just a couple of weeks after I'd moved in, Nash broached the subject of death.

"Have you ever killed anyone, Max?"

At first, the question shocked me, mostly because I *had* killed someone, two someones exactly. But it wasn't a normal question, and I didn't have a normal answer. Of course, I wasn't about to tell him that.

"Why would you ask me something like that?" I'd asked, with the best look of surprise I could fake.

"Just making dinner conversation," he'd said. "Aren't you going to ask me if I've ever killed anyone?"

He seemed amused as he daintily cut his steak, dipped it in a fancy steak sauce, and placed it carefully in his mouth.

I rolled my eyes. This was the game he liked to play. "Sure. Have you ever killed anyone?" I'd asked, certain that the snob of a man sitting across from me had probably grown up with a servant to kill his spiders, never mind a human being.

"This is a serious discussion, Max. No eye-rolling, please." Nash had placed his sterling silver fork and knife onto the side of his silver-trimmed china plate. "I have, in fact, killed another person. Does that shock you, Max?"

Yes. "Nah—not really. I guess under the right circumstances, anybody can kill." I tried to remain cool. Maybe it was accidental—a hit-and-run or some weaselly accident like that.

"What do you consider to be the right circumstances?"

"I don't know...self-defense?"

"What about in defense of someone else? What if you believed someone killed someone you cared for, and you killed them for revenge? Would that be alright to you?"

I wasn't sure what this guy was playing at, but that was a question that hit too close to home. "No—the right thing to do there would be to call the police and turn them in." I threw up the old three-finger scout salute with my right hand for the "on my honor" and all that crap symbolism.

Nash seemed amused again.

That was the Nash I was starting to like. A pleasant southern gentleman who was eccentric, obviously rich and probably just as lonely as me. He often asked odd questions, as if he were feeling me out. Looking back, I think it was more of him leading me somewhere dark. Very dark.

That same night, just before dinner, I'd met the other Nash, who was the scary opposite of the southern gentleman.

Nash didn't know about Sammy, so I had snuck her into my room and kept her out of sight. I wasn't sure what Nash would say about a cat, but I couldn't risk asking if she could stay and him saying no. I cleaned up after her daily so there would be no telltale odor and kept her well-fed to keep her quiet and happy. He did not know she was there until she escaped from my bedroom one night and ran past him.

As I flew down the stairs after Sammy, I heard the words, *What the fuck was that?*

It didn't sound like Nash's voice. It sounded...evil.

The look in his eyes and the way he spoke when he'd spotted her actually scared me. His eyes turned black, or at least that's what I thought I saw, and his face, ears, and neck turned a dark red, as if all the blood in his body had rushed to his head. If he'd grown horns at that moment, he would have looked just like a picture of the devil MeeMaw had shown me once. Right down to the goatee.

His voice sounded demonic, low and husky, not at all like the southern gentleman who'd befriended me. When I landed at the bottom of the steps with a thump, he stared at me with those black eyes.

He had pushed past me into his office, emerging with a large knife. It featured the ridges and pointy tip of a hunting knife, like the kind my father kept in a sheath attached to his belt.

Nash was going to kill her.

He'd followed her trail through the living room, and I'd run down the hallway, cutting him off in the kitchen. I spotted her hiding under the kitchen table and grabbed her by the scruff as she hissed, expressing her displeasure. I quickly pitched her out the back door into the garden before he could hurt her. I slammed the door and blocked it with my body so he couldn't follow her out. He looked like he knew how to handle that knife. He didn't need to catch Sammy to kill her. He just needed to aim and throw.

Before I said a word, that's exactly what he did—he threw the knife right at me.

I watched in horror, paralyzed by fear, as the knife flew directly at me. I squeezed my eyes shut, grimacing, and held my breath, waiting for it to plunge into me and feel the shocking pain that would follow. For just a moment, I'm sure my heart even stopped.

The knife landed with a thud and a twang, embedded in the door, just missing my right ear, but catching some hair. I was stunned by the violent act as I glanced sideways at the polished black handle of the blade mere inches from my face.

His anger filled the room, terrifying me as I stood frozen, pressed to the door. A single tear made a beeline down my face and dropped off my chin. I blinked away more tears as I tried to catch my breath, my heart pounding, my mind filled with panic. I was the deer in the headlights, too afraid to think straight, never mind move.

"What do you know about that...creature?" He didn't yell or scream the words. He'd said them with malice, each word spoken with hatred. The voice of a demon.

I couldn't breathe. I wanted to run. I wanted to open the door, grab Sammy and run. I just couldn't will myself to move.

He took a few steps closer to me and with each step, panic grew in me and spread through me like fire, stripping my muscles of the ability to move freely. I felt myself shaking.

Even with all the horrible things my stepfather had done to me, I'd never been this afraid. He'd never thrown a knife at me or tried to kill me. He may have used his size to overpower me, but I never felt like my life was in danger... until now.

"I asked you a question."

His voice was calmer and more human. He was so close to me I felt the warmth of his breath on my face and detected the faint scent of the minty candy he sucked on after each cigarette.

The blood drained from Nash's face and his pallor returned to normal. As his pupils constricted, his eyes appeared hazel again. He was reverting to a human being, but his anger was still palpable. He pulled the knife free from the door and my hair. Newly sliced strands drifted to the floor.

"Shh, relax Max. I'm not going to hurt you."

I'd flinched when he rubbed the back of his fingers on my cheek.

He'd taken me by the hand and nodded his head toward the living room. I'd followed behind him, not because I wanted to, but because he willed me to. We'd sat together on the sofa next to the brick-and-tile fireplace and I stared out in front of me, afraid to move because he held the knife in his left hand and my hand in his right. I figured if I moved quickly enough, I could break his hold on me, smash his head into the fancy coffee table sitting at my feet and run like hell to get out of there.

"Max, look at me, please."

I turned toward him but kept my gaze on the blade.

His eyes had followed my stare down to the knife, which shined with the flames of the fire reflected off of it. I imagined if the devil owned a knife, it looked like this one. He'd let out what sounded like a sneer, or possibly a soft chuckle. I was a little panicked, so it was hard to tell. He pulled open the drawer of the antique table next to him, placed the knife inside, and closed the drawer.

"Better?" he'd asked.

It was only slightly better. My mind raced as I imagined how I was going to grab Sammy Cat and get out.

He'd shifted on the sofa so that he was facing toward me.

"Max, I am so sorry about what just happened. I lost my temper. It was inappropriate and I can see that I've scared you." The gentleman was back. He'd brushed some hair from my face, letting his fingers rest on the side of my jaw. "I overreacted when I saw a cat, which I did not expect to find in my home, run past me. I was brought up to believe animals belong outside, not in a well-kept and clean home. I can only assume the cat is yours? Hmm?"

Afraid to speak, I nodded.

"Please believe me, Max, when I say I would never do anything to hurt you. You're my friend and I care very much for you. Can you forgive me, please?"

He'd sounded so sincere. And there was something about the way he'd looked at me—with love and tenderness. He'd taken both my hands in his and stroked them. This time, I didn't flinch at his touch. I relaxed, and he knew it.

"What the hell was that? You threw a knife at me. You could have killed me."

He'd shook his head and put a hand to his forehead. "I know, I know...and I apologize. And just to be clear, if I really wanted the knife to hurt you, it would have. I have a terrible temper. It's true. I suppose it is best you understand that sooner than later, when our relationship is even more...evolved. I am thinking about the long term here, Max. That's how much I care about you. When I return to Georgia, I am hoping you will consider accompanying me. Would you like that, Max? Move to Georgia with me. Get away from this dirty city and its nasty cold weather?"

That would be nice. "Do you swear you will never threaten my life again?"

"Yes, I swear it on my mother's grave. I wouldn't say that if I didn't mean it—Mother was a saint, and I loved her very much."

"Sammy Cat too?"

"Is that the kitty's name? Sammy Cat?"

"Yes. And I don't go anywhere without her."

"That's a shame. I'm afraid the cat will have to go. She can't stay here. Not in my house."

"Fine." I'd broken free of his clammy grasp and stood. "If she goes, I go."

I climbed the stairs two at a time, headed to my room, slammed the door, and thought about how easy it would be to get rid of him. He didn't drink himself into a stupor like Clara and Wayne did nightly, but he did need to sleep. My heart was still pounding from running up the stairs as I paced in my room, contemplating what had just happened. *What the heck was that whole scene with the knife and looking like an escapee from hell?*

I'd lain down on my bed. My bed. It was a queen, all for me, with a fluffy down comforter and sheets scented with lavender. They were silky and clean and didn't have any holes in them like the ones on my bed back home. A pretty rug partially covered polished wood floors and matching dark wood furniture—a nightstand, wardrobe, and a dresser with a mirror over it—adorned the room. I had a private bathroom and a television. It was a far cry from the way I lived with Clara and Wayne.

This was the best I'd ever lived in my life. A warm bed and a full belly. And Nash had never treated me badly...until he did. Technically, he didn't touch me, at least not abusively. He'd never laid a hand on me like my stepfather, Wayne. And I liked Nash...a lot. He was kind and very generous—most of the time, and he was good-looking for an older guy. Our relationship was growing...we were becoming closer. He was all I had in the world. Him and Sammy Cat.

I wouldn't hurt him—I had to make it work. I also needed to get Sammy back in the house. She wasn't used to living outside in the cold weather.

I'd quietly opened my bedroom door and listened for Nash. The soft music he listened to while he dined drifted throughout the house. Creeping down the stairs to the second floor, I stopped at the landing that led down to the main floor. The mouth-watering scent of garlic and wine wafted up to me. Nash was also an excellent cook. He was full of all kinds of surprises. My stomach gurgled as the aroma of food instantly made me hungry.

I'd slowly descended the staircase. The double doors to the living room were open wide, and I spotted the table where Nash had stashed the hunting knife. The fireplace had a fresh stack of wood burning bright orange and yellow in it, the flames dancing above the logs. I rounded the doorway of the living room and spied Nash in the adjoining dining room, happily eating, as if nothing had happened earlier.

I'd approached him cautiously as he ate his dinner.

"Nash, can I please bring Sammy in? I'll keep her in my room, and I promise to clean up after her. You won't even know she's here." I said, in the sweetest voice I could force.

"No."

"Fine. I'll take Sammy and leave."

"If that's the way you want it."

"First thing in the morning, we are out of here. And don't bother looking for me again. Even if you find me, I won't come back."

"Why not go tonight?"

Shit! I didn't want to leave. I just wanted Sammy to stay. For the first time, I felt like I had a home. A real home. With someone who actually wanted me there. Someone I actually liked.

"You're being unreasonable. She's so small, she hardly takes up any room. And she's quiet. You didn't even know she was here until tonight."

Nash seemed to contemplate the fact that he wasn't aware that a cat had been living in his house.

"Please Nash—I'll do anything. I'll clean up the backyard or ...or, I don't know. Anything."

Nash sat back in his chair. His expression suddenly relaxed as he gazed up my body until his eyes locked onto my own.

"Anything?" he'd asked.

Hmm, maybe I shouldn't have said anything. "Within reason...sure anything."

He motioned for me to sit down. That was when he'd hit me with the question—had I ever killed anyone? And I, of course, said no. And then *he* admitted to killing someone.

"It wasn't in self-defense or an act of revenge," he'd said. "I see myself as a warrior."

A warrior? I almost laughed. *Sure, if Pee Wee Herman were southern and a psycho, then I guess I could see where he was going. Besides, I thought rich people had other people to do their dirty work.* "Did you hire someone to do it for you?" I asked, amusing myself.

"No. I preferred doing it myself. It's a rush like no other." There was a glint in his eye that reflected the flames from the fireplace. "Max, who loves you?"

The question threw me. My MeeMaw had told me she loved me, but she was the only one who'd ever said those words. "Lots of people," I'd lied, but only because it was part of the game.

"What if I told you *I love you*? I consider you my friend. I'm willing to provide a home for you, food, clothing...and I would love to make you my protégé."

What he eventually asked me to do was not within reason, but he had just said he loved me...hadn't he?

CHAPTER 5

Hunter

Hunter Finnegan and Glen Levine were en route to St. Christina's Hospital for the Criminally Insane. Levine smoothly weaved an unmarked Ford Explorer Hybrid through traffic on the FDR Drive along the East River. The chief had reprimanded him for using his personal vehicle for work, so he'd grudgingly started using the NYPD vehicles, but only the unmarked SUVs. This one was fully loaded, just the way Levine liked it, with all the latest equipment, including a computer tablet for real-time updates and 360-degree cameras.

"I can't believe you BS'd the commissioner into agreeing to let Cameron Cooper in on this case. The chief must have gone ballistic," Levine said.

"Yeah, he did," Hunter replied with a chuckle. "I thought he was going to lunge across the room and tackle me. If the commissioner wasn't standing right there, I might be a missing person right now."

Levine smiled, "So how did you do it?"

"Dwyer, Commissioner Tate, and I were in Dwyer's office. Tate wanted an update on The Chelsea Choker and the chief wanted me in the hot seat. I saw an opportunity to request additional help in the way of a profiler, and I mentioned I knew where we could find one. By the time the chief realized what I was doing, it was too late. The idea intrigued Tate. She liked the thought of using a criminal to catch a like-minded criminal. He bellyached, of course, and that vein in his temple—it was twitching and pulsing. I thought it was going to burst at any moment, but it was too late. She was all in."

"You've got balls of steel, my friend," Levine declared with a laugh.

Hunter stretched his long legs out in front of him. One perk of traveling with Levine—plenty of leg room. "Well, it's not all good. Dwyer realized this could be his opportunity to get rid of me if this goes south. If Cameron embarrasses the department and the commissioner, he's hoping she fires me. And if things really go to hell and The Choker kills again, he thinks he'll step into Tate's job. Two birds, one psychopath." Hunter held up two fingers with a smirk.

"And what happened to 'Cameron is innocent? Not a serial killer, but a wounded, traumatized victim?' Or do you plan on bringing out her alter Jason somehow and asking for his advice?"

"Come on, Glen. We've been over this enough already. She is innocent. You heard the doctor's report, same as I did. She wasn't cognizant of what was happening. She was just as shocked and angry as the rest of us. Can you imagine what that must have been like for her? She'd devoted her life to law enforcement, only to develop another personality that was a killer. And all of it stemming from abuse and trauma? She's had a rough life...I marvel at how much she accomplished given the circumstances of her past. Abused as a child, witnessed her mother shoot her stepfather to death, kidnapped by a serial killer and nearly killed herself. There might be more we aren't even aware of. Not the picture-perfect childhood or life I've had."

"You've had your own traumas, and you didn't turn into a murderer." Levine retorted, alluding to Hunter's wife, who was murdered—strangled to death during a home invasion, and to his first partner, who was killed in front of him when he was a rookie cop.

"No, but my so-called traumas happened when I was an adult. Not when I was five or six."

"Uh-huh—I guess." Levine, along with many other members of the NYPD, privately questioned the wisdom of Cameron being in a hospital rather than a maximum-security prison. "I still struggle with the psychology of it all. I understood what the doctors said, but it just doesn't seem plausible to me."

Hunter shook his head. "I know you understand the human mind is complicated. I know you've delt with people who are completely psychotic, and you accept their diagnoses. Maybe you struggle with this because it happened right in front of you, and you were as clueless as the rest of us. We're only human, right? We can't read minds or predict what's in people's hearts."

"You would think after all these years we could."

Hunter pressed the seat-warming button on the dash in front of him and almost instantly felt the black leather warming against his tired and sore muscles. He glanced over at his friend, one of the few confidants he had, and knew he was simply being honest about his feelings and not argumentative. Even if it felt like he was disagreeing just for the hell of it. He also knew Glen Levine would always have his back and support him, even when the rest of the world would not.

He'd proven that when Cameron was revealed as The Stealth Stalker. What a shit show that was. The entire department questioned Hunter's dedication to the job and whether he was complicit in Cameron's activities, while the chief wanted his head. But not Glen Levine—he stood by Hunter.

"So, I guess I can safely assume you still have feelings for Cameron? Beyond an investigative capacity?"

Hunter thought for a moment before he answered that bomb of a question. "I can't help myself." He sank down into the warmth of the seat, closing his eyes, relaxing for as long as he could before they arrived at St. C's. "I fell in love with her before I knew she was..." His voice trailed off; he was uncertain how to finish the sentence. Hunter gave Levine the side-eye, checking his expression. It was surprisingly blank.

"Don't you ever think about what lies beneath?" Levine asked. "What if you say something wrong one day and the alter Jason takes over and tries to kill you? Jason is a psychopath, so doesn't that mean Cameron is as well?"

"I haven't mentioned this before, but I've been going to therapy," Hunter said, again stealing a quick glance at Levine for a reaction. But he was still unreadable. "I had my own questions regarding that very subject. Is Cameron a psychopath because she has D.I.D. and one of her alters is a killer? After months of poring over her case, and with the help of Dr. Heisser and my therapist, I know she's not.

"Serial killers who are psychopaths show a lack of empathy for their victims and no remorse for their crimes, and while that may describe the alter, Jason, it does not describe Cameron. She's overly empathetic and beyond remorseful. If she could go back and undo everything that happened, she would in a heartbeat.

"Dr. Heisser is confident that they're going to purge her alters and make her whole again. The part of her fractured mind that was Jason Jonette will no longer exist. It's a long and painful process for

Cameron. Not only is she facing what she endured as a child, but she's also facing the murders committed by the alter Jason. I can't even imagine. Heisser feels that if she can find the strength to face and move through what happened, then she can be whole again, with hope for a normal future. It won't be easy, but so far, Heisser says she's doing exceptionally well."

"That could take years, Hunter. I'd hate to see you waiting for something that might never happen. And when she faces the events of last year, it could end up breaking her permanently. I've done my research, as well. The mind, as they say, is a fragile thing. She's already broken, more than once, and facing, *remembering*, the severity of what happened might be too much and send her over the edge. I just don't want to see you get hurt. You've been through enough already."

"I was concerned about that as well," Hunter said as he reclined the seat back a few inches. "We've discussed it—Cameron, Heisser and me. Since Cameron was so intimately involved in the case, she knows what's coming, but knowing what happened is a different beast from remembering as a person who was there. That will be devastating. When Heisser thinks Cam is ready, they'll explore those events through hypnosis. He'll create a safe place where she'll know she's in the present and the memories are just that—memories. Still, remembering yourself thrusting a knife into an innocent person who's done nothing to you will be extremely difficult and traumatizing all over again."

Levine nodded; his brows furrowed. "And you'll be there for her, and I'll be here for you, but to be clear, that doesn't mean I'll be there for her. I still have my concerns about Cameron, and I can't forget that The Stealth Stalker murdered a good friend of mine."

"I understand. You're a good friend," Hunter said, looking out over the East River as they drove along the esplanade. He'd offered to help in any way he could and Heisser had agreed he could be useful in Cameron's recovery, but a tiny part of Hunter regretted making the offer.

"So, what's the plan when we get to St. C's?" Levine asked.

"We're going to meet with Cameron and catch her up with what we already have on The Choker. Hopefully, she'll have some insight for us that will at the very least steer us in the right direction to catch this guy."

"Do you really think she can help from inside St. C's or is this more like—I don't know—an opportunity for you to see her more often?" Given Hunter's feelings for Cameron, Levine accepted Hunter visiting her twice a month, but he didn't want his own time wasted.

"I actually think she can help. If I didn't, I wouldn't have suggested it to the commissioner, thereby putting my ass on the line with the chief. Look, she's a psychologist and a former FBI analyst—she's experienced with these kinds of cases. It won't hurt to pick her brains and see what she has to say—will it?"

"Okay. I just don't want to waste time and resources. And I don't want to end up as a chaperone for the two of you."

"Our meeting will be strictly business, okay?"

"Okay."

Hunter stared out the window as Levine drove over the bridge to the island where Cameron would most likely spend the rest of her life. The twenty-story-high yellow brick building that housed St. Christina's loomed in the distance. Through a clearing in the trees, Hunter could just make out the razor-wire fence that surrounded the main hospital building and several other buildings that together formed the state hospital complex. But even as they drew nearer to the foreboding-looking complex, he couldn't help but think to himself, *And I get to see Cameron.*

CHAPTER 6

Cameron

Chief Security Officer John Mercedes led Cameron into a small conference room where she would meet with Detectives Finnegan and Levine. It was a new room for her. In the last year, she had only been in six different rooms at the hospital—her own room, the cafeteria, Dr. Heisser's office, the general recreation room, the small exercise room on another floor and the infirmary. She was the only patient on her floor allowed to go to the exercise room, and only when no one else was using it, for everyone else's safety. Cameron Cooper, aka Jason Jonette, aka Stealth Stalker, was an anomaly at St. C's, and no one was taking any chances as to what could happen or who might appear at any given moment.

There were two windows in the conference room, larger than the one in her room but covered with the same gray, steel-meshed bars. A large, brown wooden table sat dead center, with three chairs on either side and one chair at each end. Cameron sat on the middle chair of one set of three. It seemed like a safe choice.

She felt stressed and had concerns that Glen Levine was joining them. The last time she had seen him, he was pissed at her. She couldn't blame him. She had accused his best friend and partner of being a serial killer. *It turned out he was right when he told me I was wrong, and I was crazy*, she mused. She didn't know what to expect, certainly not forgiveness, but perhaps the understanding that she would never willingly or intentionally hurt someone, never mind commit murder.

The longer she sat there, the more anxious she became. She sat back in the chair, closed her eyes, and tried to meditate, going to the imaginary beach house in her mind. She needed to appear calm, in control, and above all else, professional. One little mistake and Levine would drag Hunter out of there and with him, her opportunity to show them how much progress she'd made since being incarcerated.

She could hear voices outside the door and immediately recognized them as Hunter's and Levine's. Her stomach clenched; she drew in a deep breath and slowly released it. *I can do this*. When the door opened, she stood to greet them. John Mercedes entered the room first, then Glen Levine and finally, Hunter. John caught her eye and gave her a discreet thumbs-up. Cam gave him a subtle, grateful smile.

"Hello, Detective Levine." She didn't offer her hand; she was afraid he wouldn't take it. "Detective Finnegan—it's always nice to see you." She tried not to smile at Hunter but was too excited and nervous to contain a tight-lipped smirk. Levine caught it and gave Hunter a disapproving glare. The two men sat across the table from her, Hunter directly across and Levine next to him.

"You can reach me on the intercom if you need anything or if you're ready to leave. And just a reminder, there are cameras in this room that will remain on the entire time you are here. Hospital rules." John stepped out of the room, closing and locking the door behind him.

"Cam, you're looking well." Hunter smiled. Levine rolled his eyes.

Impatient, Levine commented, "Let's get started, okay?"

"Yeah, okay." Hunter opened a black leather satchel and pulled out several files with names on each one.

"Did you bring the map of the piers?" Cam had asked for a map and some colored markers so she could make a visual outline of where the murders had taken place.

"Yes—right here." Hunter unfolded a large paper map of the Chelsea Piers area and took a brand-new package of colored markers out of his case, handing them to her. A trace of his boyish grin graced his handsome face. Levine sighed, obviously displeased.

"How do you want to begin?" Cameron asked, looking back and forth between each man.

Levine answered, irritated, "Let's begin with the first woman murdered."

Hunter commented, "Good idea, Detective Levine. And let's remember, we're here to solve a case and work together calmly and professionally." Hunter directed the comment at Levine, but it was a friendly reminder for Cameron, too. He opened the cover of the top file on the pile and turned to Levine first.

"I already gave Cameron a synopsis of what we're dealing with—a serial killer preying on women in the Chelsea Piers area. The press is calling this guy The Chelsea Choker." He directed the last part at Cam. Hunter held up a photo of an attractive brunette. "This is Brittany Davidge. She worked as a chef on private yachts. She was preparing a meal for a private dinner party on a super-yacht moored at Pier 59. The captain of the ship went down to the galley for a drink and found a pan of food burning on the stove. He called out to Brittany; when she didn't answer, he went looking for her and found her lying unresponsive on a bed in a stateroom. He called nine one one immediately and started CPR, but it was too late."

"How was she killed?" Cam's nerves were getting to her. Hunter had already told her they were all strangled—a word that conjured up Jason Julian Jonette, aka The J-Bird, who had kidnapped and nearly killed her during her tenure as an FBI agent.

"Strangled with the blue satin ribbon I mentioned left tied in a bow around her neck. There was a nearly empty glass of wine in the galley with only her fingerprints on it. Forensics discovered that the wine contained ketamine—a powerful anesthesia, also known as Special K on the streets. After drinking it, she would have been helpless to defend herself."

"So, you think this guy climbed aboard a docked ship with people on it, found his way to the galley, spiked a glass of wine, and killed a woman with no one seeing him or hearing anything?" She made notes on a yellow legal pad as she spoke. It felt so good to be working, to use her mind and skills again, that she didn't care that Levine seemed to wish her dead. "You don't think it could have been someone already on the yacht?"

"We interviewed everyone on the scene. The people on board the yacht all seemed pretty shaken. Brittany was well-liked. Everyone said her chef skills were superior, and they couldn't imagine anyone wanting to hurt such a sweet young woman."

"Whaddaya think, Doc, we don't know how to eliminate suspects?" Levine leaned back in his chair, frowning.

"No—that's not what I think, Detective Levine. I know first-hand that you are very good at your job." Cam needed to get this over with, clear the air with Levine, or at least allow him to lash out at her. "I also know and understand that I am the last person you want to work with. I don't blame you. I get it. If I were you, I probably would have fought this opportunity given to me all the way to the top.

"I also know that I owe you and everyone else on the other side of these bars an apology. I cannot begin to tell you how sorry I am that five of your colleagues...friends, lost their lives because of me. Even though I don't remember any of it, I know I am responsible, and I've accepted that I'll remain incarcerated for the rest of my life. If I could change any of this, I would. The only thing I can do is put my skills to use and maybe save someone else from dying. I'm paying my debt to society, but I want to do more. I want to contribute. I want to help. This is me, Glen—Cameron. We were friends. I'm not asking you to forgive me. I'm just asking you to let me help. Justice has been served. This is my chance for redemption."

Levine stared at her, arms crossed in defiance across his chest, his face slightly red. She couldn't tell what he was thinking. Cam glanced at Hunter, who gave her a slight nod and a wink. Non-verbal encouragement. The tension strained her neck, causing a sharp pain to shoot up the back of her head. A feeling of panic crawled inside her mind. The last thing she needed right now was a migraine.

She took a deep breath and let it slowly escape through parted lips, a relaxation technique Dr. Heisser had taught her. She was about to give up on Levine and go back to the case when he leaned forward, hands folded on the table.

"Your apology will never be enough because it can never bring those women back." He spoke in the calm, assertive way that was all Levine. "However, I believe that justice is being served here and that you are where you belong. I also believe that you have something to offer, that you may give us some insight into this guy and maybe even help us—a little. If I didn't, I wouldn't be here today. I may never trust you again. We may never be friends again, and I think you are sincere when you say you're sorry, but it isn't up to me to forgive you. That's up to the people you hurt. I can handle this situation here as long as it's kept professional—that goes for both of you. Got it?"

Hunter and Cameron nodded in agreement, and Cam didn't know about Hunter, but she was relieved and encouraged that Levine was willing to accept her help.

"Agreed," Hunter said, opening the next file. "Let's move forward."

He went through each file the same way, holding up a photograph of a woman robbed of her life, describing where she'd died. "Jessica Ericsson was attending a corporate event at Pier 61 when she stepped outside for a cigarette. The coroner's report found injuries supporting a fall down a flight of stairs before being strangled and left behind a vending machine.

"A jogger discovered Nicole Williams's body on Pier 63, lying in the grass between two fat evergreens, as if she had fallen asleep looking up at the stars. No one in the area that night recalled seeing her, much less seeing another person. Toxicology also showed ketamine in her system." He placed the photos of the three women in a row.

Hunter picked up the next photo for Cameron and Levine to see. "A man walking a dog found Michelle Roberts's body under some bushes in a small enclave at the corner of Twelfth and Twenty-Fourth near the Chelsea Waterside Park Field, where she played soccer. Videos of the game posted on social media showed someone hovering near her bag. We think The Choker swapped her water bottle with one laced with ketamine. Witnesses said they saw her walking down the sidewalk with another person. They didn't notice the person she was with because they focused on Michelle, who appeared to be drunk and staggering—the other person seemed to help her walk."

Levine added, "There's a pattern to the killings—the days between double each time. The first two happened two days apart. The second and third happened four days apart. Third and fourth, eight days apart. We assume the next one, if there is a next one, will happen on day sixteen."

"So that means we have a few days to get ready for this guy," Cam added. "The predictable timeline indicates he's sure of himself, confident, and perhaps taunting us."

"Yeah, we have people setting up more cameras on the piers and undercover officers will be in place," Levine added. "All the murders happened between five and nine p.m., after work, when the piers are most crowded in the evening. If the weather is good on day sixteen, it'll be challenging to cover the piers, even with extra officers on patrol."

"What do you think? Do you think we have anoth—" Hunter caught himself and shifted uncomfortably in his seat.

Cameron knew what he was going to ask—if it was another woman out there killing. It was the same thought she had. Sedating the victims first would indicate the killer was too weak to strangle them outright using their own strength. It could be a woman, a small man, or someone with a handicap.

Levine added, "We don't have any results from Michelle Roberts or the crime scene yet. We have asked that anyone who was at the field that night contact us if they remember seeing the person in the hoodie."

"Can you show me on the map exactly where each woman was found?" Cam asked, pushing the map into the middle of the table. Hunter pointed to the exact location for each victim, and she marked the spot numerically in order using a red marker. It surprised her to see how they lined up in a perfectly straight line along the river until the place where Michelle Roberts was found. From there, the location turned inland. "Have you found a connection between any of the women? Could they have dated the same person? Or go to the same grocery store? Anything at all that would link them?"

"We haven't found any links yet. Saintil and Barone are working on it, but so far, nothing." Levine frowned as he looked over the map.

The mention of Rhonda Saintil's name tempted Cameron to ask how she was doing, but she knew better. If she asked about the detective that her alter, Jason Jonette, had attempted to murder, Levine would go ballistic and most likely walk out. Hunter had told Cam during another visit that Rhonda Saintil had made a full recovery but was staying on desk duty for the time being. She unconsciously rubbed her hand over the thick scar that ran down her thigh, a reminder of that day.

"Do you have the victim's ages, home addresses, and where they worked?" Cameron asked instead.

"Yes—we have bios on each one for you right here." Hunter handed her a manila folder with several sheets of paper inside. She opened it and found a report on each woman featuring a photograph in the upper left-hand corner, and a map next to it with markers showing where she lived, worked, and was killed, each spot color-coded—blue where they lived, orange where they were employed, and red where they were murdered. The victim's pertinent information was listed below: age, address, marital status, employment, where they were born and grew up. "I remembered how you like to work—with all the information on a physical file you can touch."

Cam smiled at Hunter, recalling how observant he was of everyone and everything around him, and how methodical he was in his work. She turned her attention to the information in her hands. Nothing was jumping out.

"I doubt these are random killings. Usually, serial killers have a reason for choosing their victims. It appears this killer is someone young, maybe in their twenties, based on the style of dress you mentioned. The hoodie and jeans also signify a young male. Do you have any video or pictures of Michelle walking along the sidewalk?"

"Yes, it's a little grainy, but here's one you can have." Levine handed her an eight by twelve still from a street cam. "I also have the video on my laptop. Just a second while I open it." He tapped away and then turned the laptop around to face her.

Cam could see Michelle staggering along the sidewalk outside of the stadium and being helped by another person, who kept their head down and turned into Michelle's shoulder.

"We can estimate how tall this person is by using Michelle's height. You can see they're about the same height. Michelle has on flip-flops, and the person with her has on sneakers. If you can tell me more about those sneakers, I can tell you more about our mystery person."

"I'll get Murphy on it right away." Hunter jotted down "sneakers" on his note pad.

"Also, find out if the women went to church or synagogue or any communal places like that, what hair salons or nail salons they frequented, maybe doctor's offices, or gyms. There has to be something linking these women together, and we will find it."

Hunter and Levine both took notes as she spoke. Cam felt like her old self as she flipped through the pages Hunter had given her, studying each woman's profile. It was invigorating after months of not using her brain for anything but self-reflection, therapy, and healing. She decided that putting her mind to work was the best therapy she could get.

"I have a surprise for you," Hunter said, smiling outright this time. "Here."

He pulled a laptop from the bag he had carried in and put it on the table in front of Cameron.

"This is for you to do research. It's already connected to the Wi-Fi here. The guards at the desk have the charger, so when it needs to be charged, you'll have to give it to them. You can only have it during the daytime. You'll have to hand it over after dinner every night. This is a big privilege, Cam. The commissioner had to jump through hoops to get this approved."

"Yea, so try not to hit anyone over the head with it." When Levine added the jab, Hunter shook his head at him.

"There's another surprise," Hunter continued, scowling at Levine. "You can call me whenever you like. Just ask the guards. You can only call me—they will dial the phone for you, and it has to be related to the case. If you have questions or, hopefully, a breakthrough, you can get in touch with me. Just don't abuse it or the commissioner will find out and you'll lose everything. Cam, do you understand?"

She nodded as she slid her hand across the laptop's cool metal case, just to make sure it was real. She wanted to kiss it, but could wait until they were gone. It represented the outside world. It was beautiful and just so...normal.

"I think we're done here for today." Levine stood and stretched his back. "Let's go, Hunter. Goodbye, Cameron." Levine signaled to the guards on the other side of the cameras that they were done.

Hunter gathered his papers and files and placed them back into the black leather messenger bag he had brought the laptop in. Once Levine had turned and begun to walk toward the door, Hunter held out his hand to Cam, and when she took it, he leaned down and kissed the back, giving it a little squeeze. He looked up at her with the boyish grin she loved so much and said, "See you soon, Cameron Cooper."

Cameron hugged her new laptop as John Mercedes walked her to the cafeteria. Things were definitely looking up.

CHAPTER 7

Max

NASH WAS IN A pissy mood, and we were in the thick of a heated argument. He'd just declared that without him, I had no one. We'd been living together for months, and I was used to his occasional outbursts, but he had just taken it to a personal level.

"I have people who love me, you know," I'd shot back. This was his game and lying was part of that game.

"Do you? Like who? Who loves poor, misunderstood Max? Hmmm?"

"Plenty of people—my grandmother, and my mother and stepfather. I call them once a week just to say hi, and you know, let them know I'm okay."

"Really? That's fascinating that you're able to call them and speak to them, given that your grandmother died—suspiciously, I might add. And your mother and stepfather were murdered several months ago—axed to death. Nice touch, by the way, throwing the ax in the fireplace and burning the handle to ashes, no fingerprints, and barely a weapon left."

Crap! How did this son of a bitch know that?

"I don't know what you're talking about," I said, as a rush of panic spread throughout my body. "MeeMaw, Momma, and my loving stepfather aren't dead."

"Relax Max. I won't turn you in. I get it. Your mother was a drunk who didn't give a hill of beans about you. She didn't feed you, clothe you, make sure you had the things you needed for school. Didn't protect you from her jackass husband, who preyed on you. And when your grandmother died, the one person who cared about you, you snapped, lost it, took an ax to it."

Nash took a long drag from a cigarette, releasing a plume of smoke casually into the air above his head, where it hung like a dark cloud until it slowly dissipated.

"And you know, I think your suspicions were correct. I think mommy and stepdaddy did granny in... smothered her with her own pillow and then cried at her funeral. Talk about depraved—killing a helpless old lady for insurance money. Those two were lazy and selfish; they deserved to die. I think you were justified in your actions. You did it for MeeMaw, right? To avenge her?"

I didn't know where he'd gotten this information, but I did it, and I did it for MeeMaw. The memory of my grandmother made me feel sad. MeeMaw was wonderful and the only person I felt had ever truly loved me. And those two miscreants took her away from me, first, by putting her in a nursing home, which was unnecessary—they just wanted her out of the house because she could see what immoral jerks they were, and then by killing her. I knew they did it.

My mother, if you could call her that, Clara, and stepfather Wayne, had come home that night, gotten drunk, laughed, and talked about collecting insurance money. Laughed! They'd murdered that sweet little old lady, and they were laughing about it. I didn't want to believe it, but when the nursing home called the next day and said a nurse found her deceased that morning in bed and that she must have died in her sleep, I knew it was true.

They weren't just drunk and stupid. They were drunk, stupid murderers.

The roaring fire in Nash's living room reminded me of the fireplace of my childhood home and the night that I'd claimed my independence from two people I'd grown to hate. I could have turned my mother and stepfather in, gone to the police, and told them everything I'd heard, but they deserved worse, and I needed time to work out a plan. I needed money and some idea where I was going to go. So, I waited for the insurance money to come in and for those two to cash the check.

First, I'd needed an alibi, so I stole a piece of my mother's jewelry, sold it a few towns over, and bought a bus ticket for the next morning. Then I texted my friend, Katie Smyth, and told her thanks for always being so nice to me, but I was leaving home and never coming back. It was time to say goodbye.

Sometimes I missed Katie and her family. Maybe I should have taken them up on their offer, and then I wouldn't be here fighting with Nash. Katie and I had grown up together; we'd been best friends since kindergarten. She was the only one who never made fun of me to my face or, as far as I knew, behind my back. Katie had protected me when other kids bullied me about my clothes, my crappy house, or my crappy, drunk parents, or whatever else they felt like harassing me for. But not Katie.

She always had sympathy for me and told me they didn't understand and that I was always welcome to stay at her house, which

I did. But when I would go home again, my mother would be pissed-off and attack me, sometimes with her hands, sometimes with whatever was nearby—she especially liked the broom handle. She would scream at me about being ungrateful and telling lies to Katie's family about her, embarrassing and shaming her.

I never told them anything about my mother. I pretended Clara and Wayne didn't exist when I was at Katie's.

Images of Mr. and Mrs. Smyth flashed through my mind like photos I'd mentally stored. They were the opposite of Clara and Wayne. The Smyths were loving, supportive, kind. They were both bankers and were tall, trim, attractive, and beautifully dressed. Their home and family reminded me of a TV family and something that couldn't be real. They were an escape for me. I could go there and pretend I was normal for twenty-four hours, and that I belonged to a typically normal family, with the beautiful Mr. and Mrs. Smyth as my parents. I did it as often as I could, even though it meant I would pay for that escape when I got home.

Katie had an older sister and twin brothers, and the Smyths gave me some hand-me-downs that were so much nicer than my own clothes, including the jeans I currently wore. They fed me and they even asked if I wanted to live with them. They offered to fix up the basement for me...there was already a bathroom down there, and they said they would create a bedroom just for me. I guess they knew more about my parents than I'd imagined, but I had turned them down.

At the time, I had MeeMaw to look out for. If I wasn't there, Wayne and Clara would forget to feed her and would leave her cooped up in her room all day. But then they shoved MeeMaw into the nursing home.

Of course, when I had texted Katie and told her I was leaving, she told me to come to her house instead, that I didn't need to go. I could stay with her and be a part of the family, another sibling in a house with four kids already. It was tempting, but I needed to punish Wayne and Clara, so I told her thanks, but no. I'd said that I was going to go see my father and hoped to stay with him for a while. It was a lie—he wasn't as bad as Clara and Wayne, but he was an asshole nonetheless and would have slammed the door in my face.

I'd disappeared that night. I didn't go far, just next door to the neighbor's shed. They were away, on vacation at the Jersey Shore, and it was at least a roof over my head.

It had taken Clara three days to realize something might be wrong, and she'd finally called Mrs. Smyth to see if I was hiding at their house. Katie had texted me to warn me. She also said that when her mother had asked if she knew where I was, she confessed to her mother that I had run away and was headed to my father's place in Arizona. Mrs. Smyth called Clara back and gave her the new information. Alibi set.

I had watched Clara and Wayne through the living room window at night, just waiting for the right time to do it. I couldn't have gotten luckier—the right time happened to be two days later when they cashed MeeMaw's life insurance check. Twenty-five thousand dollars! The amount shocked me. I thought maybe five or six thousand at best, just enough, I figured, to cover MeeMaw's funeral expenses, but twenty-five grand! It was unreal.

And there was no way I was going to let her killers enjoy one dollar of it.

Clara and Wayne had gone to the bank, cashed the check, and brought home twenty-five thousand in cash, all hundred-dollar bills.

God, what a couple of idiots. They had gotten drunk, tossed it up in the air and danced around on it in the living room, not knowing I was watching, growing angrier and crazier by the second.

They were blasting music, drinking heavily, laughing, and so wasted they were nearly falling down. The expressions on their faces when I walked in through the kitchen door carrying an ax were first of surprise, and then they'd pointed and laughed. I could see it unfold in my mind as if it were a horror movie on a screen in front of me.

Clara sputtered, "I thought you were running away to your precious daddy. What happened, baby? Did he tell you to fuck off? Cause I know he don't want you. Never did." She gave me a sad face with an exaggerated pouty lip and then laughed again.

Wayne pointed a short, stubby finger at the door. "Now, we don't want you neither. You left here, and there ain't no coming back, so go on, get outa here." He'd fallen back into an armchair near the fireplace, nearly missing it with his fat ass. He sat there, his eyes glassy, his round face red from the heat of the fire and from dancing around, sweat staining his cotton T-shirt under his man boobs and his underarms. He was nothing more than a fat pig dressed in men's clothing.

I had let him have it first.

I'd walked right up to him, raised the ax high over my head. He'd looked up at me and furrowed his brows, too drunk to understand what I was doing, and I gave that ax a full swing, landing it right in the middle of his chest. Blood squirted out from both sides of the ax as if I had just smashed a ketchup packet with my fist. His eyes bulged, and he gasped for air as he tried to grab the ax head protruding from his chest. I yanked it out and took another swing, this time at his crotch. He may have been dead already at that point, but I preferred to think he knew what had happened.

Then I turned to Clara, who stood with her mouth hanging open, a crystal stream of snot running from her bulbous nose.

"What's wrong, Mom? You don't think that was funny? Do you know Wayne thought I was better in bed than you? He said you repulsed him with your fat thighs and droopy boobs. That's why he needed to visit me in the middle of the night after you passed out because you couldn't satisfy him the way raping me satisfied him."

I raised the ax again, this time in Clara's direction. She backed up, her hands out in front of her, as if they could shield her from me and my ax.

"Max, please, I'm sorry. I didn't know that was happening." She was shaking now and pale, terrified by what she had just witnessed. "Please, sweetie, you did what you had to do. I understand. He hurt you. Now put the ax down before you know, you...uh...hurt yourself..."

At that moment, I had almost felt sorry for that simpering, selfish excuse of a woman, but then I remembered MeeMaw.

"Is it true? Did you kill MeeMaw? For this money?"

Clara had looked around at the money strewn all over the floor and sobbed, "Yes. It's true. But there's plenty here. We can split it. You can leave here and start over. I'll never tell. I swear."

"That's a good idea. I'll leave here for good with the money, but I won't be splitting it with you."

And with that, I let loose, whacking at Clara until she was nothing more than a broken mass of blood, meat, and bones lying at Wayne's feet. I really thought I had some kind of mental break that day, snapped, except I was never sorry I did it. Maybe I was always mentally broken, and it all had just come rushing out in a violent torrent.

I'd gathered up the money and put the bills that had blood on them in the sink, rinsed them off, and threw them in the clothes dryer. Then I ransacked the house so it looked like a burglary gone wrong, taking anything valuable that I could sell at some point. I'd pulled out some drawers and tossed stuff on the floor. There wasn't much—Wayne had a decent watch, and Clara had a few more pieces of gold jewelry.

And then there was MeeMaw's wedding band. I'd examined it under the lamp on Clara's dresser. The inscription inside the thin gold read *H.W. + A.W. 5/3/53*. MeeMaw and Pop's anniversary date. I slipped it onto my finger—MeeMaw had told me it was the only thing she had that she valued, and she was leaving it to me when she died. It gave me a sense of peace that I finally had it. Wearing the ring made me feel like MeeMaw was always with me.

When the money dried, I'd stacked the bills, tied them with rubber bands, and put them in an old make-up bag of Clara's. I grabbed my backpack and stuffed the money bag into the bottom. Then I took some warm clothes and any edible food I could find in the kitchen, which was just a couple of apples and a muffin. Clara and Wayne survived on daily takeout, so there wasn't much there.

The fire was dying in the living room, so I'd thrown another log on it and poked it with the ax to get it going again, and then I'd wiped off the ax head with a cardigan draped over the sofa arm and shoved the ax and the sweater into the flames. I'd kneeled in front of the fire and watched the sweater melt into it, the wooden ax handle eventually catching fire and burning.

Then I'd stood and looked around the room. It looked like a scene from a bad Halloween movie. None of it looked real to me. Even now, thinking back on that night, it didn't seem real...but I suppose it was.

I had no one left after that night. The one person who cared about me, MeeMaw, was dead. And the two jerks I was forced to rely on for basic needs were also dead. I had only myself to depend on from then on. Until Nash.

Nash took another drag of his cigarette before snuffing it out in a dish on the table next to him. He stood and walked over to me, placing a hand on each of my shoulders, rousing me from my thoughts of that horrible night.

"You know who does care about you? I do. That's why I offered you a place in my home. That's why I feed you. Make sure you have good shoes and warm clothes. I care about you, Max, very much."

He rubbed my cheek with the back of his index finger and smiled. Every day that I lived with him, we grew closer. And I grew more attracted to the mysterious southern gentleman with a rabid temper. His touch sent an electric charge through me, and my pulse picked up.

Then he turned and sat on the couch, patting the seat next to him. I obeyed and sat down on the Victorian-style sofa—an odd choice for a man, I thought, but Nash was an odd man. I didn't sit right next to him, but left a foot of space between us. I was still mad at him and wasn't ready to give in quite so easily. We'd been fighting because he said without him, I had no one. No friends. No family. No one who loved me.

It pissed me off not because it was true, but because I didn't want it to be true. It was pathetic to not have anyone to love me or for me to love back. And I didn't want him to know that I was beginning to love him—it gave him too much power.

"By the way," he said with a soft drawl, "I love you."

What? I leapt over to him, wrapped my arms around his neck, and kissed him on the cheek.

"I love you, too." I was so happy he had said it outright that I let my own words slip out, unfiltered. But I still had to clear up one thing.

When our fight first started, I had stated that I was going to take Sammy Cat and go home to the people who really loved me. That was when Nash had thrown out the tidbit about Wayne and Clara being axed to death.

I needed to address the comment with, if not shock, at least innocence. I snuggled up next to him.

"It's not true about Wayne and Clara, right? They aren't really dead—you just said that to upset me, right?"

He glanced down at me and then pulled back to look straight at me. He smiled and took my hand.

"Please don't insult me, Max. I know you did it, and I told you already I don't blame you. You know, we aren't so different. Tell me one thing, Max—were you sorry when it was over? Or did you feel...good?"

I had to admit, I was a little shocked by how nonchalantly he reacted to the knowledge that I had killed my own mother and stepfather. I stared back at him, not sure what the right answer was.

"It's okay, you can tell me," he said, as he stroked the back of my head like I stroked Sammy Cat. My mother had only touched me to beat me. This was so much better. I could feel the love in his touch. I knew I could confide in Nash—he was my only friend. He loved me and would never betray me.

"I wasn't sorry. I felt nothing. They killed my grandmother for money, so I did the same. That's all. In fact, I kind of felt satisfied when it was all over. So, I guess, yeah, it felt good."

He smiled at me and nodded his head as if he understood. Then he leaned down and kissed me softly on the mouth. It was brief but sensuous and just enough to make me nervous in a happy way.

"Is it okay that I did that?"

"Yes," I whispered. I realized I was breathing faster, but this time it wasn't because I was terrified like when he'd thrown a knife at me. I wasn't afraid or appalled like with Wayne. I was curious and wanted to do it again. I leaned in for another, but instead, Nash kissed me on the cheek.

"I'm going to bed. See you in the morning, Max."

Nash left me sitting there alone on the dainty, flower-covered sofa, my heart beating a little faster, and I realized as I watched him walk up the stairs that I could trust him—he'd taken me off the streets and given me a safe place to stay, a warm bed, nice clothes, food. I realized he was turning into more than a friend. I wanted him. I needed him. I loved him.

We continued to grow closer...like a real family. We cooked and ate meals together, we talked about movies, and he taught me about the appraisal business. Then one night, he asked if I had ever gone hunting.

"Yeah, with my father, Jackson, when he still lived at home with us. He told Mom there was something wrong with me because it didn't faze me one bit when he killed a deer and dragged its carcass into the back of his pickup. She asked him what did he expect? After all, I was his kid. He told her to shut the fuck up. Lovely people."

"I like to hunt too," Nash had said casually. "Maybe someday we'll hunt together."

I'd soon discover Nash's idea of hunting differed entirely from my father's.

CHAPTER 8

Cameron

Cameron Cooper's days at St. Christina's State Hospital for the Criminally Insane were criminally boring and routine. She surmised that if she weren't crazy already, the monotony at St. C's would certainly have driven her there.

Her days began with the sunrise over the city and the park outside her window. The sun shining through the crisscrossed bars exaggerated their existence by painting a diamond-striped effect across the floor and up the adjacent wall. As the sun rose, the shadowy bars grew shorter until they disappeared, and only a soft glow of sunlight filled the room. It was in those early mornings when the shadows decorated her room in modern jail cell bars that Cam felt the most hopeful and the most defeated. She couldn't help but be reminded of where she was living her life as the shadows of the bars stretched across her blanket.

All the patients had the same routine. Those who didn't need assistance with hygiene and dressing showered in a large locker room-style chamber with open stalls. Female guards stood watch to maintain civility. The women changed into fresh clothes every morning after showering—the majority wore light-blue, pull-over cotton shirts—no buttons to swallow, or belts to hurt themselves or someone else with, and matching pull-on pants that featured stylish elastic waistbands. Patients who required special attention wore pink, and the more violent wore orange to stand out more easily in the population.

They were permitted to wear non-hospital-issued items, like cardigans with buttons removed, over the uniform. For a period of time Cameron had worn the orange, but with good behavior and the progress of the last several months, Dr. Heisser had assigned her the light blue clothing. The guards still kept an eye on her, afraid she could flip a switch and turn into the murderer who had attacked and nearly killed Myra Gordon, the orderly. White Velcro closure sneakers completed the ensemble.

Staff ushered patients who could feed themselves into the cafeteria for breakfast. Cam despised being in the caf with all the other patients, so she would take her time showering, dressing and making her way to breakfast. When most of the patients had finished, she would grab a tray and whatever was left. Most of the time, the kitchen staff, who she had the good sense to befriend, put food aside for her.

After breakfast, the group shuffled along the corridor to the common room. A large, open space with televisions, card tables, games, books, security cameras, guards, and more bars on the windows.

Cameron would sometimes sit in a corner alone, observing the other patients, silently diagnosing them. When she was really bored, which was most of the time, she would engage some of the milder patients in conversation. Talk about what acts they had committed to be incarcerated at St. Christina's. She was sure the guards laughed at her and her "pretend" therapy sessions, but she thought: *Let them laugh. The state may have stripped my license from me, but I'll always have the training, and maybe I can help them.*

The common room wasn't all fun and games. It was also a dangerous place filled with dangerous criminals who mostly remained calm only because of the medications that were forced on them daily. And now and then, Cameron received a violent reminder that she was not just a patient, but a prisoner who was incarcerated with some very threatening people.

One of the more interesting patients was "Broadway Joan" Namath. When Cameron was first made aware of Broadway Joan, she thought the walleyed woman had received the moniker because her name was so similar to the famous football player, Joe Namath. She'd actually received the nickname because she had killed thirteen homeless people all along Broadway.

Broadway Joan, who was also homeless, was a serial killer. She was quite large and intimidating at five-eleven, and two hundred pounds. She liked her wild red hair cut short and always wore her shoes on the wrong feet. Cameron recognized she was intellectually disabled, a paranoid schizophrenic with a low IQ, which was probably why she'd ended up at St. C's and not at a max prison. Joan had wandered up and down Broadway having animated conversations with herself during the day and at night she had killed.

Police determined that if another homeless person harassed her or looked at her, or just got too close to her, she would kill them. She would react immediately and homicidally by way of an aluminum bat she kept among her prized possessions. It had been a very scary time for the homeless community in the Broadway area.

As Cameron sat on the worn couch in the corner observing the activity around her, she spotted Joan clutching the TV remote control to her chest as she watched her favorite television show. It reminded Cam of an outbreak that had happened a few months after she'd arrived at St. C's.

Broadway Joan had been watching television peacefully one day when another patient, Leslie Hawkins, or as she preferred, Hawk, had turned the channel. It wasn't the first time Hawk had antagonized Joan, and she had had enough. As Hawk turned around to laugh at Joan, the larger woman lunged at her. The two had punched, kicked, bitten and pulled the hair on the other. Joan had gripped Hawk around the neck and was squeezing tightly when the guards rushed her.

A guard named Merck had given Joan a hard whack across her back, but Joan didn't loosen her grip as Hawk choked and gasped for air. Petey Johnson had had to taser Joan to get her to let go, which she did. Joan had fallen to the floor, where she convulsed from the shock and, once she was down, Merck let her have it, striking her over and over with the club. The other patients had backed away. They knew Merck was not to be messed with and feared being next.

Officers Rosalie Diaz and D'Shana Abrams rushed into the common room as a siren blared. The guard in the control room would have seen the fight erupt and hit the alarm. They barked orders at the other patients to back away. Once they'd corralled everyone to one side of the room, Abrams turned her attention to Merck. "That's enough, Merck," she yelled. When he struck Broadway Joan again, she commanded him to stop. "I said, that's enough. Now back off, Merck, or I'll make sure you're put on shit duty on the men's floor."

Merck stopped attacking Joan and glared over a shoulder at Abrams. He was twice her size, but her power was in her authority at the hospital, and she was his supervisor. She never made idle threats. If she said it, she meant it.

"Call for two gurneys, Merck," she'd said. "And I want a full report on my desk by the end of the day on what just happened here. I'll review the video feed, so make sure there's no BS in your report. And Merck, I'll be writing my own report on what I saw here today."

In a far corner of the room, the timid Audrey Lloyd cowered, whispering over and over, *Merck the jerk. Merck the jerk. Merck the jerk.*

Cameron had stood by, stunned at what she had just witnessed. She'd spotted Audrey sitting on the floor, rocking back and forth, chanting, and approached her to see if she could help the petite, older woman. She'd heard Audrey had been in St. Christina's for the past twelve years for killing her elderly parents, but didn't know how Audrey'd landed in the hospital instead of jail. Cam squatted down a few feet from the woman, well aware that just because she was smaller didn't mean she wasn't stronger or capable of hurting her.

"Hi," she whispered to Audrey. "You okay?"

The gray-haired lady with milky, cataract-filmed eyes had stopped chanting and rocking, looked at Cameron, popped up onto her feet and kicked Cam in the face. She'd shrieked, "Leave me alone, bitch," before running from the room.

Cameron had lain splayed out flat on her back on the cold linoleum floor, holding a hand to her mouth where Audrey's sneaker had made contact, blinking the tears from her eyes. Diaz leaned over her. "I guess she wasn't in the mood for a pretend therapy session today, huh?" Diaz had chuckled and moved on, admonishing the other patients to behave or they'd get taken away next.

Cam had eventually sat up and wiped a slight trickle of blood from her split lip, which was already swelling. She'd looked around. The commotion was over, the alarm silenced, and the patients returned to their daily monotony of cards and television. The drugs in their systems never really allowed them to overreact, anyway. She'd slowly risen to her feet, the room shifting beneath her, and made her way to the cafeteria.

"Hi." She'd waved to the cook preparing lunch. "Can I have some ice, please?" She'd pointed to her swollen lip. But he'd shaken his head. *Of course not*, she'd thought.

"Enfermeria." He'd pointed back out the door.

She'd waved over her shoulder and headed for the infirmary. Just another day in St. Christina's. It was typical that someone ended up in the sickroom almost daily. That day had been her day. And Broadway Joan's. And Hawk's.

Remembering the kick to her face, Cam unconsciously ran her finger over the small scar on her bottom lip, a remnant of that day and a visual reminder to always keep her distance from the other patients.

She was wasting time analyzing the activity around her until her appointment later that afternoon. On Mondays she'd meet Dr. Heisser for her weekly one-on-one therapy session. On Thursdays, she attended group therapy. On Fridays, art therapy, which Cam had enjoyed until Joan had attempted to stab another patient with a paint brush. Now they painted with their fingers. On Sunday, Tuesday, and Wednesday she attended yoga and meditation therapy. Every day was a different type of therapy. On Saturday they all rested—the patients, the staff, the guards. Everyone was on their best behavior because it was visiting day. If you misbehaved on visiting day, you'd lose your privileges for a month.

The rest of the time that wasn't filled with mandatory therapy sessions or meals was filled with a restlessness brought on by the stale, vapid, tediousness of confinement. It was during these lows that Cam struggled the most. She wrote in a journal, exercised and visualized a better life—one where she was free not just from St. Christina's but from her own mind. Free from her alters and made whole. Sometimes she dared imagine a life with Hunter in a little cottage by the sea, where they could live out their lives together. Happy.

The day that Hunter and Levine visited her and left her with a brand-new laptop, a pile of case files, and a reason to get out of bed each morning had changed her existence at St. C's permanently. She replaced the boredom with research, and the puzzle that was The Chelsea Choker. The question, *Who is The Chelsea Choker?* consumed her, humming in her brain and in her thoughts day and night. It was thrilling to stretch her deducing muscles, have work, genuine work, and something to think about other than the whitewashed hell she was living in.

Alone in the cafeteria, she carefully unfolded the paper map Hunter had provided and smoothed it out with her hands. Next, she opened the brand-new package of colored markers and took the red, blue, and green ones out, laying them on top of the map. She felt like a kid on her first day of school, excited to examine her new supplies.

From the folder Hunter had given her, she extracted the sheets that provided photos of the victims and the pertinent information as to where they lived, worked, and died. Lives summed up on one page. It broke her heart to think how a chance meeting with a psychopath had robbed the women of their futures.

Her mind flashed to the women whose lives were ended by her alter, Jason Jonette, and how they'd been robbed as well. The freedom to live and love stolen from them by her splintered mind. Would she ever recover? Could she be whole again? Could she ever make up for the damage done?

Not to the women whom The Stealth Stalker had hunted and murdered. Not to their families. Never.

She shook her head to clear the thoughts, as if her mind were an Etch A Sketch, and a mere shake was all it would take to start fresh, a clean slate. If only it were that easy. If she could shake her head like a toy and erase all the events from the memories, suppressed or otherwise, that had caused her mind to fracture, would she be whole again?

It certainly wouldn't bring the dead back to life.

Cameron laid each sheet across the top edge of the map, distracting herself from her thoughts. She pressed her finger to the number one she'd written on the map on Pier 59, ran it across to number two on Pier 61 and then to number three on Pier 63. Perfectly straight. It bothered her just how in line the kill spots were.

The next one wasn't on a pier, but crossed the avenue at a slightly downward, sloping angle. The one after that continued the inland trajectory. There was nothing random about the kill sites at all. All the murders lined up neatly. And the pattern of days between kills was also way too obvious. Cameron could practically predict exactly where and when The Choker would strike next. Was he taunting them, or did he want to get caught?

No, serial killers never want to get caught. They think they're too clever to end up arrested. Too smart for the police to zero in on. Eluding the police—leaving them frustrated and angry—was as much a part of the game as selecting the next victim and killing them just before the cops swooped in. But this killer was practically drawing a line to...*where?*

Cam looked closely at the map. The killings had started at the far south side of the piers and moved conspicuously north until they turned inland. She traced the red numbers with her finger. The next killing would happen...she had no idea. It was too broad of an area.

Shifting her attention to the photographs of the women, something gnawed at her. They were part of the puzzle, and it was just beyond her reach how they fit in. What was it about these four women that tied all the pieces of the puzzle together? Was it the piers that linked these women in some way?

It was driving her crazy.

CHAPTER 9

Max

"MAX, I WANT TO show you something in the cellar. Follow me, please."

Nash had never allowed me down into the creepy underbelly of the house. He called it his workshop and explained that he had precious possessions down there that he didn't want me messing with. The secrecy got me curious, so one day, when Nash was out, I had tried the door, but he had it locked tight. I'd looked around for a key, under the plant in a nearby bookshelf, over the molding of the door, but had found nothing. I should have known Nash would never be careless enough to leave a key to his most "precious possessions" in such obvious hiding places.

As I'd followed him down the open wooden staircase that creaked with every step, I was a little excited. It was like Christmas, and I was finally going to see what it was he kept hidden and wrapped up.

The cool, musty cellar looked like the perfect place for a vampire to hide out. It had stone walls, a poured-cement floor, and a large center area. The far wall to the right featured crypt-like stone archways that led into spaces too dark to reveal their contents—like maybe a coffin. Hung on the stone walls flanking the archways were various medieval weapons, all of which would not bring a quick, humane death but a slow, painful, torturous demise. I'd wished I had put on my hoodie so I could pull it up—I was sure there were some enormous spiders with hairy legs and sharp pinchers watching and waiting to shimmy down a web onto my head.

As I'd looked around, I noticed the obvious—it was neat and clean for a cellar, or for any room, really. Definitely cleaner than the mess of a shack I'd grown up in. In the center of the open space stood a modern desk, with four straight legs and no drawers. A closed laptop sat on top with a mouse and pad next to it. Behind it was a black plastic chair. Against the stone wall where the stairs ascended stood a huge, black safe, six feet tall and probably three feet wide. Down the center of the room, four bare light bulbs hung from electrical cords. Nash had turned them on with a switch at the top of the stairs.

There were two things that had struck me as strange, even for Nash; a container of Lysol wipes and a box of surgical gloves sitting to the left of the laptop.

He'd grabbed a stool that was in front of the safe and placed it next to the chair by the desk.

"Have a seat, Max," he'd said, motioning to the stool. When I sat, my back was to the dark spaces beyond the archways and I had a creepy feeling of getting jumped or drained of my blood.

Nash plucked two vinyl gloves out of the box, handed them to me, and then two more for himself. "Put those on." He'd walked over to the safe as he put his gloves on and tapped a code into an electric keypad. Then he turned the three-spoke handle and pulled the heavy door open. I'd waited with expectation for the incredible prize he would drag out.

It was a scrapbook.

As he'd walked toward me with the oversized album, I could see some more of the contents of the safe, most notably a spool of blue ribbon and several vials containing clear fluid.

"Did you know I'm famous, Max?"

"Ha! You? Famous? For what?" I had never heard of him or seen him before that night in the alley. "Don't tell me I've been living with a famous actor all this time and didn't know it."

He'd had that look on his face again. He was amusing himself at my expense.

"No. I'm not an actor. But I am quite famous in certain circles. I have many, many followers. People who would literally kill to be where you are right now." Nash had brushed his hand over the cover of the book, as if it were a luxurious fur. "People who love me, worship me, want to be just like me. Strangers propose marriage daily. They beg to meet me. To learn at my feet. They would give anything to have a relationship with me, like the one you and I enjoy. There's even a fan club. I'm invited to speak daily, but I have yet to accept."

He was standing next to me, and as he glanced down at me, I could see devilish Nash in his eyes. He'd opened the cover of the album to the first page, revealing a yellowing newspaper clipping, dated July 1, 1998. A bold headline read:

MISSING MISS GEORGIA PEACH FOUND DEAD

Beneath it was a black-and-white photograph of a pretty young woman in a tiara. The caption under her photo read:

Amber Clarke, 23, the current Miss Georgia Peach,
had been missing for five days before workers at

Fowler's Peach Orchard found her body. The Macon-Bibb County Sheriff's Department offers a reward for any information. All tips are anonymous.

I'd turned the page to find more newspaper clippings. More dead women. Page after page.

"What's up with the scrapbook of dead people?" I'd asked, hoping he was revealing a strange obsession he possessed and not that he was actually a bounty hunter, and these were all cases he'd closed—he'd caught the killer, brought justice for these poor women and was about to do the same for Clara and Wayne.

"Max, for someone who has proven to be deadly, you can still be quite naïve at times, can't you?"

As I skimmed the articles, Nash opened the laptop and turned it on. He opened the browser and typed in a web address.

"Why? I don't get it. Did you know these women? Why do you keep these articles?" *And why do you keep them in a safe like they're valuable or something?* A chill had danced its way down my back—not a good sign.

Nash turned the laptop toward me so I could clearly read the page he opened. It was a message board, and all the messages were addressed to Nash@AngelsOfDeath. As I read through the messages, dread turned to shock and concern. One message was more disturbing than the next.

> *I would kill for you. Tell me who you want to die. I'll make sure they know it's your desire.*

> *I am your disciple. Your wish is my command. Teach me how to kill like you.*

> *Will you marry me? We can bring death to life together. Forever.*

> *Make me your instrument of death. Please…*

> *What's the best way to kill my husband?*

Some included photos of people who appeared to be dead. Maybe they were all actors. Maybe it was some freaky Halloween thing, like the walking dead parties that some people liked to attend. *Maybe not.*

The page count at the bottom read one thousand plus. There must have been tens of thousands of messages. I'd read one message out loud.

"I can't wait to meet you and learn your ways. Teach me to be the perfect killer." I'd looked up at Nash as his lips formed a soft smile, like a proud parent listening to someone extol the virtues of his child. "What the hell is this?"

"These are my followers. My inner circle. A fan club devoted entirely to me."

"And they want you to teach them to be the perfect killer? Is this for real?" I'd asked, rolling my eyes, certain I was being punked.

"No eye-rolling, Max." Nash looked down at me, his face flushing in displeasure. He hated it when I rolled my eyes. "To answer your question, yes, this is real. It is a real message board, devoted to me, by real people who…admire my work."

"They sound like a bunch of psychos. *'Let's paint the town red — with blood.'* Jeez, what the hell? Are you telling me you're some kind of killer? And these people want to be just like you? And what? These newspaper pictures are of people you've killed? Seriously?"

"I told you we weren't so different," he'd whispered, stroking my hair and smiling down at me. "None of them"—he nodded at the laptop—"are as special as you, Max. I chose you over all those people to be here, with me, my special student and confidante."

"Your student? You want to teach me to kill? Don't you think I've already mastered that one? Besides, I'm not into killing strangers. Clara and Wayne got what was coming to them. I don't want to turn into some kind of psycho."

Nash had moved closer to me and pulled me to a standing position. He'd put his arms around me and pulled me toward him so that our bodies pressed together. With his left hand, he'd held me to him at the small of my back and with his right hand, he smoothed my hair, running his fingers over the back of my head. He'd leaned in and kissed me. It was slow, deep, and sensuous. My body instantly reacted—his mouth sent a flame through me, touching every nerve, rippling over my skin as I arched into him. A sound I wasn't aware I was capable of making escaped my throat—a deep moan betraying me.

"I love you, Max," he'd breathed out in a soft southern drawl. "Do you love me? Really love me? Because if you don't, I can have any one of those people here tomorrow to replace you. They love me. They would do anything for me. Would you do anything for me?"

I'd felt so lightheaded, I thought I was going to pass out. "Yes, Nash, I love you. More than any of them possibly could. They don't know you like I do. But I don't need to hurt anyone to love you. I'll go anywhere with you…live off the grid, away from all the crazies in the world. Just you and me. Can we do that?"

He'd kissed me again, pressing himself to me even harder. The anger and passion startled me before the kiss turned tender and consuming. I'd wanted him more than anything. I would do anything not to lose him or his love. No one would take him from me.

I had grabbed the hem of my shirt to peel it from my body, but he stopped me.

"No. Not yet. Not here."

"What? What do you mean?" I was breathing heavily. His touch and his kiss had temporarily erased the disturbing images and words from the forefront of my mind. "I want to be with you. I want to show you how much I love you."

"And you will, dear, sweet Max. You will. You will prove it to me over and over until I say I believe you."

Confused and frustrated, I'd taken a step back from Nash. "How can I prove it to you? By killing innocent people? Is that really what you want? You want a lover who's a killer? Does that turn you on?"

"You're looking at it all wrong, Max. We aren't going to kill anyone. We'll set them free."

"I'm not following."

"Your mother and stepfather weren't very religious, were they? You didn't go to church every Sunday? Or celebrate any religious holidays?"

I'd shaken my head. "MeeMaw would mention Jesus every once in a while, but my mother always said religion was just a bunch of mumbo jumbo meant to control us and keep us in line."

"Some people believe that life on earth is a test. That our souls are here to determine our heart's true intent. Are we good or are we evil? Will we fall to temptation or will we rise above and earn redemption? If we're good, we earn our reward and go to heaven or paradise, the spirit world, or whatever name an individual's religion or beliefs label it.

"Some people believe in reincarnation; some believe this is it—there is nothing after we die. For those who believe in heaven, they think that if we possess and act on evil intentions, we go to hell. Follow me so far? I believe our life here on earth is a prison sentence. This is hell. Our souls end up here to fulfill a sentence for a sin we've committed, and once we've paid our debt, we return to paradise. You and I are simply speeding up the process. Setting deserving souls free to return to the other side sooner than later."

I'd stood staring at him, not sure what to say. Even my father, who, in my opinion, was a lot smarter than my mother, said this was it. We live. We die. The end.

"This is your test. I want to know how far you will go to prove your love to me. This"—he'd nodded to the computer screen and the thousands of messages addressed to him—"is about loyalty. I need to know you're loyal to me. The people in this chat room? They're loyal to me. They state emphatically what they would do for me. If you aren't willing to do the same, then say so. I'll find someone else."

As I'd reflected on what Nash had just told me, it started to make sense, sort of. I'd always wondered how someone as decent and kind as my grandmother was forced to share the same space as those evil bastards, Clara and Wayne. It'd never seemed right to me. And I liked the idea of MeeMaw and Pops together again, in paradise. Yet, my mother had ingrained in me that religion was for nut jobs and I still couldn't help but think that Nash simply enjoyed watching me kill another human being because he was a little nutty too.

He was my nut, though, and I loved him and no one was going to replace me.

"How can I prove my love and loyalty to you? Tell me what to do and I will do it now, right this second. I wish you would just tell me what to do so we can get on with our lives."

What's that expression? Careful what you wish for?

A week later I was on a super-yacht moored at the Chelsea Piers. There was a girl, Chef Britt something, who didn't look much older than me, making dinner for some ritzy party. I'd snuck on board and when she went to the bathroom, I poured a clear liquid from a vial Nash had given me into her wine glass. Nash hadn't told me what was in the vial, but he said it would make her pass out, and that was when I was to take the blue ribbon he'd given me and strangle her with it. I'd asked him, why her? Had she done something to him? "No," he'd said. "She is the first piece in the game we are playing."

I'd watched her through a window in the galley as she began her food prep. Another chef had arrived, but luckily was carrying supplies in from the dock when Chef Britt began to look woozy.

She'd staggered from the galley down a hallway, shaking her head as if trying to clear it as I'd stalked her from outside, peering through the portholes. Britt nearly fell down a flight of stairs and I almost lost her by the time I found my way down. She'd gone into a stateroom and left the door open behind her, or else I probably wouldn't have found her. There she was, passed out on a bed with a hand thrown over the top of her head, her silky brown hair splayed out like a crown.

I'd quickly unraveled the ribbon and slipped it around her neck. I'd hesitated. Did I really want to do this? Was Nash worth it? The sound of people arriving startled me and, panicking, I'd decided it was best to get it over with quickly, so I did it. She was so drugged up, she didn't even flinch. The voices were getting louder. When I was sure she was no longer breathing, I quickly tied the ribbon in a bow with trembling fingers, placed her hands folded over her stomach just as Nash had instructed, and slipped out of the stateroom and off the yacht before anyone discovered me.

When I'd thought about what I'd just done, it disturbed me in a way I didn't feel with Clara and Wayne. I'd felt a pinch in my stomach as I nervously looked around myself. No one was paying attention to the stranger in the gray hoodie, hurrying along the pier. It must be guilt, I thought, this feeling pricking at me. Chef Britt had done nothing to me. Why did she have to die? I'd felt terrible. Not so bad that it compelled me to turn myself in, but bad enough that my stomach hurt, just a little.

When I'd arrived home, Nash was waiting and...glowing. He couldn't wait to hear every detail. *Every* detail. He wanted step-by-step, minute-by-minute details. He wanted to know what she was wearing (a white jacket), what she was cooking (I had no idea), what did she smell like (garlic), and where did I finally free her soul (in a dark cabin on the bed). After I'd given him all the details down to the tiniest, most obscure fact I could think of—there was a giant stove on a boat (who knew?), he smiled a full smile. I mean lips parted, toothy, "I'm so happy" smile, something I'd never witnessed before that night. He was practically giddy. Then he turned on some slow music.

Nash had reached out his hand. "May I have this dance?"

I'd taken his hand. He pulled me close, pressed his cheek to mine, still grinning, albeit not as widely but just as happily. He'd turned his head, so his mouth was right next to my ear, and whispered, "I'm so proud of you, Max. You really love me, don't you?"

His breath tickled and traveled from my ear down my body, awakening my senses with tiny vibrations.

He released my hand and pulled me even closer, wrapping his arms around me as we swayed to the music. "I'm so happy," he whispered again, his lips brushing my skin. "Because I really love you, too."

I had rested my head on his shoulder, enjoying the warmth of his embrace, the gift of his love. I was afraid to speak. Afraid I would break the spell of this perfect moment when I'd made Nash so happy, so appreciative, so...proud. I didn't think I'd ever made anyone proud of me and no one had ever held me like this, made me feel like this—tingling from my scalp, down my spine and all the way to my toes.

I wanted to undress him, make love to him, but I held myself back. I knew well enough at this point that when it happened, when Nash and I were finally together, it would be on his terms and when the time was right for him. We would become one in our hearts and minds and desires first, and only then could we join and be one physically. I needed to prove myself to him. I would have given anything to see that wide-ass smile one more time. I would have given even more for our naked bodies to be entwined. And I did.

The next morning, Nash had expectantly turned on the news to see if there were any reports on Chef Britt's mysterious death. He'd flipped out when the anchor reported that the woman had died from strangulation by a ribbon left tied in a bow around her neck. I didn't get the big deal.

"What the hell were you thinking? Did I tell you to tie it in a bow?" Nash had screamed, grabbing a vase and smashing it in the fireplace, which caused me to flinch.

"What's the big deal?" I'd shrugged. "It looked pretty. What was I supposed to do with the ribbon?"

"I told you...wrap it around her hands...just once. Remember? We only went over it about a dozen times," he'd said, pacing back and forth like a tiger I'd seen in a cage at the zoo once.

Oh yeah, I remembered. "Sorry, Nash. I got scared and wanted to get out of there, so I quickly tied it, you know, out of habit, I guess. I promise, next time, I'll get it right."

He'd shook his head and closed his eyes as his face glowed devil red. "No, you won't."

"I will, I swear. Give me another chance, please?"

"No, you don't understand. Next time, you will do it exactly the way you did it this time. Bow and all. So, I hope for your sake, you remember what you did and what it looked like. Exactly."

Oh, crap, do I? "I...I will. I do," I'd stammered. "Exactly. I promise. Are you still mad?"

Nash had sat himself in a wingback chair, cleaned his glasses with a satin cloth he'd pulled from his pants pocket, put them back on, perched perfectly at the bridge, and scanned me from head to toe.

"Don't you have anything else to wear?"

"Um...I don't have a lot of clothes," I'd said, embarrassed.

"Well, you can't walk around dressed in the same clothes as last night. Understand?"

"I think so." I'd shrugged. I hadn't given it any thought.

"We need to buy some new clothes for you. The hoodie, jeans, and sneakers will be your uniform when you are working, but other than that, you will not wear those clothes. Ever. Got it?"

"Okay." I wasn't following why it was so important to Nash and why he was making such a big deal about it, but if it was going to make him happy, then I would do it.

"Good. We'll go shopping as soon as you change."

I'd stood still, not sure what to do.

"Max. Go change your clothes. Now."

"Right." I'd flown up the stairs and into my room and found a pair of navy chinos and a white shirt, some hand-me-downs from the Smyths, and put them on, hoping Nash would approve. When I reappeared, he smiled, took me by the hand and we went shopping. He bought me a whole new wardrobe, including new shoes. No one had ever done that for me before.

After Chef Britt, there was a drunk lady I pushed down a flight of stairs, and two others that I drugged with what Nash finally admitted was ketamine. The first time I'd heard of the drug was when I was living in a box on the street. The homeless surrounding me called it Special K. I thought they were talking about cereal. Nash was right—I had been naïve.

Ketamine is painless and so none of the souls freed felt anything, except the lady on the stairs. She screamed and made so much noise tumbling down the steps; I thought for sure someone would run over, but no one did. It's the state of our society. No one cares.

CHAPTER 10

The Chief

CHIEF OF DETECTIVES MICHAEL Dwyer was in his glory. He stood at a podium erected just for him, before a crowd of reporters who had gathered, just for him. Television cameras zoomed in, camera shutters clicked off in rapid succession, and reporters with microphones, notepads, and recorders waited for him to bestow his words of wisdom and authority on them. That was how he saw it, anyway.

"Good morning, everyone," Dwyer said, stone-faced and serious, his booming baritone voice amplified by a microphone. He really didn't need mechanical help, as he could project his deep voice like a stage actor. He was looking sharp in his full uniform, replete with numerous commendation bars collected over his career, first as a patrol officer, then a detective, and so on up the ranks. Every detail of how he looked, what he would say and how he presented himself, he'd carefully orchestrated as part of his act to impress and command.

"Thank you for coming this morning. I'm here today with an update on The Chelsea Choker serial killer case. To date, there have been four murders in the Chelsea Piers vicinity and all the victims are female. The cause of death is strangulation with a blue satin ribbon. Toxicology reports found high levels of ketamine, a powerful anesthetic, in three of the victims. The medical examiner has concluded that the killer incapacitated his victims with ketamine and then strangled them to death with the ribbon. Jessica Ericsson, the second woman to die, was incapacitated by a fall down a flight of concrete steps first and then strangled."

He paused for effect, meeting as many of the eyes staring up at him as he could. His thick hands gripped the sides of the podium, as if he were the captain of a massive warship and the podium was his helm. He *was* steering, after all. Steering the reporters into providing news stories that would paint him in a favorable light. Chief Dwyer, the hard-working, heroic savior of the city. The man who brought down The Stealth Stalker and who would soon capture The Chelsea Choker.

The next police commissioner, if things went his way. And then who knew from there? Mayor? Governor? President? He did like the sound of President Dwyer.

"The attacks happened before ten o'clock at night," Dwyer continued. "I have mandated that the precincts in the Chelsea Piers vicinity work together to put a stop to the person behind these horrendous deaths. At this time, we are looking for a young Caucasian male, twenty to twenty-five, wearing a gray hoodie and blue jeans as a possible witness. We are only interested in questioning him and do not consider him a prime suspect." A transparent lie.

"I can assure the public that *my* people are working on this twenty-four seven. The Piers are safe to visit for work and play. Tourists and residents alike should not panic but should remain vigilant of their surroundings. If you see anyone who appears to be suspicious, call nine one one. Do not be a hero. That is why we have the highly trained men and women of the New York City Police Department."

The Deputy Commissioner of Public Information had insisted he add the bit about the piers being safe. That's what they were good for—putting the proper spin on the worst news so it didn't sound half bad.

Dwyer placed his right hand on his chest, over his heart. "I make my solemn vow to the City of New York that I will not rest until we apprehend this person and send him to prison. I am actively working with detectives and uniformed police officers daily to put an end to The Chelsea Choker."

Dwyer stopped meeting the eyes of the reporters and looked directly into the cameras pointed in his direction. He made sure he held his gaze at each one for several seconds before moving on to the next, so that each news station and newspaper would have a clear shot, and a clear image of the city's savior, as he spoke.

"It is our priority to catch this criminal before he can strike again. And we need the public's help. We need your help," he said, as he nodded at a television camera. "If you're visiting the piers, stay alert. Watch out for each other. Try not to walk alone late at night. And if you see something, say something. I have doubled police presence on the piers and the surrounding area to ensure the safety of the public. We are confident that the information we have already gathered, about which I cannot go into detail, is leading us to an arrest forthwith."

He gripped the podium again, narrowed his eyes, pursed his lips, and slowly bobbed his head up and down. "We are closing in on this murderer. This Chelsea Choker. A crazed killer will not hold New York City hostage. When I have more information, and I will before long, I will disseminate it to our citizens immediately. And when we catch the suspect, I will announce it to the world. Thank you. I am not taking questions today."

Dwyer abruptly turned his back on the reporters and went up the steps to the station house, shaking hands with random officers along the way, and back inside. He hated taking questions, hated how the reporters didn't seem to pay attention to the previous question before they got their precious chance to speak. He would answer a question just to have the next reporter ask the same one differently. Or sometimes the questions were so inane it was all he could do not to lose his famous temper. How the hell should he know if someone was killing as a statement on current affairs? If they were out there killing, it's because they had a screw loose and needed to be locked up. *Current affairs.*

Dwyer went back to his office, closed the door behind him, unbuttoned his uniform jacket, took it off carefully, and hung it on the wooden hanger dangling from a hook on the wall. He sat down at his large mahogany desk, positioned in front of a tall window overlooking the part of the city where the buildings didn't scrape the sky but were older and with a lower profile. Just beyond them, a slice of the Hudson River shined in the sunlight.

He swiveled the black leather chair around so he could look down on the reporters below. Some were standing in front of cameras, giving their account of his briefing. Some gathered in small groups, chatting. He despised them and he needed them. As long as they were on his side and they believed he was on theirs, they would carry him wherever he wanted to go.

Dwyer knew they hated when he walked away, leaving their questions hanging in limbo. But it was good for them, he thought, to leave them unsatisfied from time to time. That way, when he took the time to stay and take questions, they appreciated it more. They knew what a busy and important man he was and how precious his time was, so when he stopped for them, it made them feel important, he thought. Everyone likes to feel important, the center of someone's attention, the only star in the sky.

Besides, what if one of them had gotten wind of Hunter and Commissioner Tate's deal to read Cameron Cooper, convicted psychopath, in on the case? He would not field those questions. That was Tate's bonfire. She would have to address that quagmire. Unless, of course, things went south, and Cameron's involvement somehow made things worse. Then he would happily address her involvement and mention how Tate had gone over his head and ignored his pleas not to include her. The press would devour it, and they would see him as the wisest in the land and the obvious choice to replace Tate.

When he leaned back, his chair creaked under his weight. He imagined the day he would be rid of Cameron Cooper, Hunter Finnegan, and Olivia Tate for good, and smiled. A deep sigh of happiness wheezed from his large frame just as his stomach gurgled, reminding him it was lunch time. He had a lunch appointment with the mayor; maybe he would take the opportunity to alert the old guy to Hunter and Tate's deal with a serial killer. He'd feel him out first, see what kind of mood he was in, and then act accordingly. Mayor Wallace might be a liberal, but he was an old-fashioned liberal. A Kennedy-era liberal. He and Tate had butted heads before, and the mayor might not agree with the approach that the commissioner and Hunter had taken.

Dwyer's assistant interrupted his thoughts. "Time for lunch with the mayor," she said as she retrieved his jacket, admiring the many bars decorating the left breast. "I love it when you wear your dress blues. Nothing like a man in uniform," she commented, as she helped him slip back into it. She stood back and admired him for a moment. "You look perfect. Enjoy lunch."

Dwyer checked himself in the mirror hanging over his credenza. *You are a good-looking son of a bitch, and this is turning out to be a great day. The press is eating out of your hands,* he told himself. *The Choker hasn't been heard from in days and Hunter Finnegan and company are about to be sidelined. Time to charm Mayor Wallace and pave your way into the commissioner's seat.*

CHAPTER 11

Cameron

Therapy with Dr. Reid Heisser was something Cameron looked forward to every week. She felt that their combined efforts to make her mind whole were working, and she had made excellent progress. She had been in denial for far too long as to how much the traumas in her life had affected her mentally and emotionally. Now she was beginning to understand the why and how of it all.

Dr. Heisser had decided he wanted to approach Cameron's alters one at a time and in the order that they had manifested.

During hypnosis, Dr. Heisser kept Cameron firmly planted in the present and aware of Angel as he spoke to the alter who was a child. He also assured Angel that the man she referred to as Kurt Monster could no longer hurt anyone, and explained that Cameron was an adult now, a former federal agent, and capable of protecting herself.

When he asked Angel to talk about the last night she'd seen Kurt Duprée, Cameron was aware of what was happening as a childlike voice streamed from her own mouth. She couldn't control what the child was saying, but she could hear Angel's voice for the first time outside of her own head and not on a videotape recorded during therapy.

It had all begun when she was a child, and her mother had married an older man. Kurt Duprée had started out kind and gentle, seemingly in love with Madeline Chadwick, Cameron's mother, but things changed rapidly once they were married. Kurt was a weak man with a penchant for the bottle and the more he drank, the angrier and more abusive he became.

He would arrive home after work already drunk, with a half-empty bottle of whiskey in tow. A cloud of rage and resentment hung over him before he stepped through the front door. After he crossed the threshold, he would spiral even further until the rage had turned into violence.

Cameron had few memories of Kurt and none that were happy. Through hypnosis, Dr. Heisser had discovered that Cameron's alter, known as Angel, held most of the memories of Kurt Duprée or Kurt Monster, as Angel preferred to call him. She told him stories of Kurt Monster and his abuse, pulling her by her hair, hitting her and screaming at her.

Angel described him as a tall, skinny man whose face turned red when he'd scream at her. His hair was wild black-and-white curls that could never touch his collar.

"Mommy had to shave his neck clean, and buzz the hair going up the back, every week. He didn't let her touch the top. He liked it just the way it was...floppy, messy curls. He smelled like cigarettes and the brown drink he brought home every night. Sometimes he poured it in a glass and sometimes he drank it straight from the bottle," Angel told Heisser. "Mommy begged him to stop drinking that stuff, but Kurt Monster would scream at her that she should mind her own business 'cause she wasn't his mother and couldn't tell him what to do."

Angel became quiet as Cameron's lip involuntarily pouted.

"What's wrong, Angel?" Heisser asked.

"He was mean. After he yelled, that's when he would start hitting her with his hands. Sometimes he would take off his belt and..." Her voice trailed off as she looked down at her intertwined, wiggling fingers. She continued without looking up. "But the next day he'd be different. He would say sorry and cry like a baby to Mommy. He'd promise never to do it again and he would put ice on her bruises and kiss them. But I knew he was lying. He broke his promises every day."

Cameron could only remember the last time Kurt had attacked her and her mother, up to a certain point. He'd beaten Madeline Chadwick momentarily into unconsciousness and then turned his attention to his stepdaughter, who was hiding in her usual place, the coat closet.

He'd flung the flimsy door open hard. It struck the wall and bounced back, hitting Kurt, setting off a string of slurred curse words. Cameron had pressed herself into the corner of the dark closet and covered her face with her trembling hands, silently reciting the Guardian Angel prayer her mother had taught her. Kurt swept the hangers and the clothing on them to one side with a rough, calloused hand, exposing Cameron as she squeezed her eyes closed even tighter.

She could never remember what had happened from that moment on. When she'd awakened, she was in the hospital, her right arm firmly pinned against her body with a sling. Apparently, she'd dislocated her shoulder. She couldn't remember how she'd done it, but her mother assured her it would heal in a few weeks, and she'd be as good as new. Welts covered Cameron's small arms and legs as pain shot throughout her body. Her mother had a fat lip and the skin on her face looked puffy and yellow and green. Her right eyelid had swollen under purple bruises.

Madeline Chadwick also explained to her young daughter that they would move away without Kurt. Then her mother asked Cameron if she had questions about Kurt and what she'd seen her do to him. Young Cameron thought it was a funny question—she hadn't seen her mother do anything to Kurt, but she had seen Kurt yelling at her mother and hurting her, and that was when she'd run to the closet and hidden.

Cameron knew the story of Kurt Duprée's demise; she'd read the newspaper articles to the point of memorization. She knew her mother had shot him to death, but try as she might, she could never recall that night.

As Angel spoke, the memories flooded her consciousness like a dam finally breached from years of erosion. It was overwhelming and terrifying for Cameron as the six-year-old Angel spoke to her, and for the first time, she could envision what had happened that night.

Angel told Dr. Heisser how she'd been hiding in the closet when Kurt Monster had found her and dragged her by an arm into the open.

"He grabbed me and yanked me hard," she said. "My shoulder made a popping noise, and it really hurt and made me cry. His face was red and scary like a monster, and he kicked me and was screaming at me. He raised his hand to hit me again when Mommy yelled from behind him. Kurt Monster turned around to look at Mommy. When I opened my eyes and looked for her...Mommy was kneeling on the floor, shaking and crying, and pointing Kurt's gun at him. I knew it was his gun because Mommy had told me what it was and that I should never, *ever* touch it. I saw the gun go BOOM! The noise hurt my ears. I squeezed my eyes shut and pressed my hands as hard as I could to the sides of my head 'cause it was so loud.

"Then I heard four more loud bangs and Mommy was screaming. Kurt Monster fell on the floor right next to me. His shirt was turning red. I was crying, so Mommy picked me up and hugged me. Then she stood and ran outside. She was holding me and covering my eyes. We sat on the front lawn and Mommy rocked me and sang to me until policemen came and an ambulance, too. They put me and Mommy in the ambulance and drove us to the hospital with sirens and everything," Angel exclaimed, her eyes wide. "That was where the doctor tied my arm to my body so I couldn't move it. I was so-o-o tired after all that, so I closed my eyes and went to sleep."

Tears streamed down Cameron's face. She could finally see it unfold, just as Angel had described. The whole terrible scene had always been in her head, in a dark corner locked in a box where Angel stored it, protecting her always.

Angel described other terrifying encounters with Kurt that Cameron had no idea had happened. Angel detailed his screaming fits, the beatings, the rage. She said he would always say sorry the next day, but then he would do it again.

"Angel," Dr. Heisser said gently, "I think you know the reason you never saw Kurt again after that night is because he died that night. Is that correct?"

"Yes." Her voice was a quiet whisper.

"And Cameron is a grown woman now. She's not a child who needs protecting."

"I don't protect her. I just whisper to her and warn her when she might be in danger. Kurt Monster wasn't the only bad man in the world, you know."

"Yes, I know," Heisser replied. "Cameron is like a police officer. She works to put bad men like Kurt Duprée in jail so they can't hurt anyone anymore. Sometimes that means she has to put herself into a dangerous situation, but she's the one who is in control now, not the bad guy. She went to school and learned how to protect herself and she's had special training."

"She's not *always* in control," Angel protested in a singsong voice. "Sometimes Jason is, and Cammie doesn't know. That's why she still needs me."

The alter known as Angel may have been a child, but she had a point.

Dr. Heisser brought Cameron out of the hypnotic state she was in. "Your alter Angel is quite clever, isn't she?" he asked, handing Cameron a box of tissues.

Cameron blew her nose and dried her face, gaining control of her emotions. "Yes, she is." Cameron nodded. "All these years, I've tried to remember that night and I never could and now, it's like it was always there behind a veil, just out of reach...and I can remember it perfectly. It was just as she said. Kurt's rage, my mother's screams, the gun exploding. I can see him lying there...wheezing his last breaths...the blood seeping onto the floor...my mother's terrified face as she carried me from the house."

Heisser closely watched Cameron trembling as she spoke. "You're safe, Cameron. Your mother was a hero for what she did. She saved both of your lives that night."

"I know…I know." Her voice shook. "I read and re-read the newspaper accounts so many times, always in awe of how brave she'd been. She did what she had to do to protect us both."

"Cameron, Angel's last comment about how you still need her has made me realize we're going about this the wrong way. As long as Jason Jonette exists as one of your alters, Angel is going to think you need her and I'm afraid we won't be able to purge her. I think we might have better luck purging the alters if we work backwards. Purge Jonette, then Charlotte, and finally the protector, Angel. And hopefully, not discover anyone else along the way."

Cameron knew what this meant. It meant facing Jonette in the same way she'd just faced Angel. And being aware of what the alter known as Jason Jonette would have to say—the sins he would confess. It would mean Cameron would have to face the grisly crimes Jonette had committed in his effort to be the dominant personality. In his effort to destroy Cameron.

"I…I don't know if I'm ready," she said. "What if hearing what he did and how he did it is too much and it breaks me even more?"

"I'll never let it go that far. If I see you are in too much distress, I'll bring you out of hypnosis. You've already watched the video footage of Jason from other sessions. You've heard him speak. You know his madness…what he did and how. There's nothing he can say that will shock you."

"It's not hearing him speak about it in a fully aware state that I'm worried about. Just now, when Angel was describing the night my mother shot and killed Kurt Duprée, for the first time, I could see it unfold. The memories were unlocked, and I could *see* it. If we go this same route with Jonette, I will see the victims as he stalks them, drives a knife into them. I'll know everything. The expressions on their faces, their last words, the way Jonette felt as he did it. It's bad enough to know what happened, but to live it, to see it unfold from his perspective. To see my hands take someone else's life. Do I really want that living inside me?"

Cameron stood. She needed to move, expend some of the energy building in her. She paced between the couch and the window on the far side of Heisser's office as he watched.

"We'll do it together," Heisser said gently. "You have to face this if you hope to become whole again. You have to confront Jonette if you want to purge him for good. I know it won't be easy, but we can take it slowly. And I strongly feel that if you want to purge the others, you need to start with him. That's my opinion. If you like, we can get another opinion. Hell, we can get ten more opinions. I want to do what is best for you, but you have to be comfortable with however we progress. What do you think, Cameron?"

"I think I need time first to process everything I've just learned from Angel, and while I'm doing that, I'll consider Jonette."

"I know you're scared," Heisser said, standing and facing Cameron. "But he can't hurt you or anyone else now. The crimes he committed are not yours to bear the weight of—it was not your hands, but his. They were not your thoughts, they were his. Those were not your crimes, they were his. I agree that seeing the murders as he committed them will be difficult, but we can change our approach so that it's like you're watching a movie instead of living through it. Which is really what happened. You were an outsider to his crimes, a witness, not a participant. I'll always have control over the conversation, and you will always feel safe. His killing spree will not be something you will have to live with—it will be a different perspective on events that you are already fully aware of and you know you didn't commit."

Heisser walked to his desk, placing his notepad on it, and sat on the edge, waiting for Cameron's response.

She stood still, arms crossed, hugging herself tightly. It had already been a very revealing session. She needed to process Angel's insights before she could even think about Jonette. So much had just changed in the last hour. Memories of her childhood were converging in her mind, as if Angel had opened a cage of birds and let them fly out freely, one after another.

Cameron turned to look at Heisser. "My mind is being assaulted by my childhood. Memory after memory is springing up and not one of them is good." Her body shook as a fresh tear spilled over and trailed down her cheek. She brushed it away with her hand. "I can't decide about Jonette while all of this is going on in my head," she said, tapping her temple.

"I understand, and you're right. I jumped the gun, bringing up Jonette before we finished discussing Angel. Let's sit back down and you can describe to me what's happening, what you're recalling."

"I...I don't know. I'm exhausted. I feel awful. It seems like my childhood was fraught with abuse and unhappiness, even though I know it wasn't. I can't find the happy memories right this minute because I'm being so overwhelmed by the scary ones."

"Sit down, Cameron. I can use hypnosis to keep you from getting lost in the terrible memories. To give you a way to balance the good and the bad in a healthy way, so you can process them and come to terms with what happened when you were a child and the adults in your life failed you. I want to remind you, none of it was your fault.

You *were* a child." Heisser nodded to the couch for Cameron to sit again.

Reluctantly, she sat back down on the deep, cushy couch. Heisser sat in the adjacent navy club chair and began the repetitive relaxation techniques involved in hypnosis. Cameron could feel the heaviness that Angel's words had left slowly lift. Dr. Heisser asked Cameron about her mother. What did Madeline Chadwick look like? What was her earliest memory of her mother? What did she love most about her mother?

It was working. Cameron could recall her mother and the way she looked and sounded when Cam was just a child. Her dark, shiny brunette hair brushing the tops of her shoulders, her eyes the color of washed-out blue jeans, and around her neck, a small heart charm that hung from a gold chain.

Memories of laughing and snuggling, smiling and holding hands, wonderful times with her mother flashed in Cameron's mind. Madeline always smelled like flowers to Cameron. Just as the happy memories flowed so freely, they suddenly withered. Behind the joy-filled memories was something sorrowful, sinister, cruel. Cameron had flashes of her and her mother, hungry, cold, and sometimes afraid.

They lived in a tiny apartment with sparse furnishings and shared a bed. Her mother tried her hardest to make the best of their situation. She took Cameron to the library, where they would take out a stack of books and then read together, cuddled in the bed. An elderly neighbor would give them food in exchange for odd jobs that she was no longer capable of doing herself. They had no one to turn to for help.

Cameron shook as tears once again freely spilled. There was as much sadness in her childhood as there was happiness and somehow, she was the reason for it all.

"Cameron, you're safe," Heisser said in a soothing, calm tone. "I want you to go back to the happy memories. Tell me about a time when you had a wonderful afternoon with your mother."

"Mom had finally found a job. It was babysitting and she could bring me with her. She had to prepare dinner for the little girl and her parents always had enough food for all of us. It was the first time since we'd left Kurt that we had some stability in our lives. I loved playing with the little girl, and Mom was a superb cook. The girl was a couple of years younger than me and still napped, so when she slept, Mom and I would play together.

"We would pretend the big house the family lived in was our own, and one day we had a tea party in the toy room. Just the two of us. We wrapped feathery boas around our shoulders, stuck our pinkies out when we sipped our juice from tiny teacups, and ate cookies she'd just baked. We were fancy!" The tears had stopped, and Cameron was smiling. "It was one of the best afternoons of my life."

At that moment, Dr. Heisser changed his tone and slowly woke Cam from the hypnotic state. He wanted her to feel the love and peacefulness of that moment when she became fully aware again.

"That was a beautiful memory you just shared, Cameron. How do you feel?"

"I can feel my mother's love. We had a hard life when I was a kid. She had a hard life, but she always protected me. Everything she did, she did for me."

"I think this is a good place to stop today. Hold on to the feeling of your mother's love and the happy memories you have of her. We'll continue tomorrow, after you've processed today's session and had a good night's sleep."

Heisser stood and went back to his desk. As he sat, he said, "Cameron, it sounds like you had a wonderful mother who loved you very much. That's a blessing, something to be thankful for. Tonight, when you're lying in bed, I want you to count your blessings and be thankful for all the good things in your life."

Cameron nodded. "Okay, see you tomorrow."

She walked down the hall, still feeling the euphoria of the tea party with her mother. Yet, scratching at the back of her mind was the thought that all the misery, all the hard times, were all her fault.

CHAPTER 12

Max

Nash patted the couch next to him with one hand, brandy snifter in the other, as a signal for me to sit. I happily plopped down as close as I dared next to this quirky southern gentleman. We'd been living together for the better part of ten months and, except for proving my love and loyalty to Nash, and our occasional fights, it had been incredible! I loved living in this huge townhouse with Nash and Sammy, having a belly full of good food, a warm bed and a brand-new wardrobe, but what I really loved? I loved Nash. And Nash loved me—he'd proven that by letting Sammy stay.

I was finally part of a real family.

"It's time for the news," he said. He pointed the television remote at the modest flat-screen hanging above the fireplace and pressed the power button. The television picture came into focus just in time for Diane Dowling to introduce the news at seven.

"The news?" I moaned. "I hate the news. It's boring. Let's watch a movie. *Skyfall* is on Prime."

Nash shot me a side glance. He hit pause and Diane's image froze in mid-sentence. "We are watching the news. It's part of your education. We watch the news to see if they mention the work we're doing—saving people from themselves and this wretched life on earth. We watch to learn what the police think they know and have divulged to the media."

"Saving them? Cut the crap, Nash," I sighed and rolled my eyes. "I know we aren't *saving* anyone. I get it—watching me with those women turns you on. It's a little freaky, but I don't judge. Obviously, you know I'd do anything for you. I already have." He made it sound like we were doing the work of saints. I'm not an idiot. I knew we were killing people because he got off on it. As of now, I had proven my love with the release of four souls while Nash watched.

Listening to me describe Chef Britt's release was not satisfying for Nash. He'd wanted to watch in real-time. So, whenever I left to save a soul and release it, I wore my phone in a special case and harness Nash had designed that held it in place right in the middle of my chest. Our phones were connected for live video, so when I'd crept up on the woman at the top of the stairs on Pier 61 and shoved her, Nash witnessed every tumble, every scream, every bone-cracking thud as I did. And when I'd slipped the blue satin ribbon around her neck and pulled tight, I could hear him coaching me through the phone—*That's it, Max, a little tighter...just a few more seconds. You did it.*

"Sometimes, Max, you are such a child. But you are a child, aren't you? Sometimes I forget how young you really are." Nash studied my face. He brushed his fingers against my cheek and then ran a finger along my jawline to the tip of my chin. He tipped my face up to his as he looked into my eyes.

I could feel my skin tingling as a million goose bumps sprang up along my arms and thighs and down my back. *Is he going to kiss me? Please, do it...kiss me.* I leaned into him as I examined his lips. I licked my lips and prepared for contact.

"What are you doing?" he said, scrutinizing my puckered face.

It startled me. My eyes popped open, and I could feel a warmth envelope my face as the flush of embarrassment spread. I pulled back from Nash, releasing my chin from his fingertip.

"Nothing. What are *you* doing? You should probably keep your hands to yourself." I shifted in place, widening the gap between myself and Nash on the sofa.

Nash chuckled softly, shaking his head as he watched me. He looked entertained, which annoyed me.

"Something funny?" I asked.

"No, not at all. I want you to understand something very important, Max." He spoke in a hushed tone. "It doesn't 'turn me on' watching you work. Our work is important. It makes an impact far greater than I think you seem to realize. Your single act has a trickle-down effect.

"First, it affects the person or persons who find your work. Then it affects the responders—police, EMTs and so on. Then, of course, there are the family and friends of the soul you have released. But it keeps on spreading. Do you see? Your single act becomes news.

"You've heard of morbid curiosity? People want to hear about death. The more gruesome, the better. They become interested in you—fascinated by the mystery person behind the scenes. The person, creature, *savior*, who dares to take another's life. They wonder themselves, what would that be like...to kill another? What would it feel like to own that power? And then you become part of history. Someone to be remembered. You caused a ripple in time where there shouldn't be one, and, in that moment, you change all of those lives. You own that power."

I stared at Nash as he spoke. His drawl and soft tone made every word he said seem so charming and sensible, even when they were the words of a deranged madman. There were two Nashes, as far as I was concerned. Nash, the southern gentleman, who was concerned about me, fed me, clothed me, loved me. And there was Devil Nash, the man who had a basement full of medieval torture devices, who had a following of crazed disciples, and who took pleasure in hurting others.

The two sides of him were unmistakable. I lived with the southern gentleman but occasionally, it was necessary to feed the desires of the devil if I wanted to continue living with the man I'd fallen in love with. He'd promised me over and over that it wouldn't be this way forever. That we were almost to the endgame and then he would never ask me to prove my love and loyalty to him again. It would satisfy him that I was true to him, devoted, and that he loved me just as much as I loved him.

"Um, okay Nash, but releasing souls is not exactly a great thing to be remembered for. I'd rather people remember me for doing something good. And they can only remember me if they know who I am, which won't happen. And I think this might be a good time to tell you…I don't want to do this anymore. It makes me feel bad. I lo…I like you a lot, but this game we're playing…well, I'm over it. I just want to be with you. Haven't I proven myself to you yet? Haven't I done enough to show you how far I would go for you?" I took his hand in mine and held it. "Let's leave here before it's too late. Before something goes wrong and I get caught."

I thought Nash had a pleasant look on his face, like I was saying everything he wanted to hear. I fidgeted nervously, waiting for him to respond. I thought I had gotten through to him, and we could go to Georgia and start a new life together. A normal life, like MeeMaw and Pops had shared. It was what I'd wanted more than anything...to have a normal life with someone who loved me, in a home...with a cat. I knew I could make him happy without someone paying the price with their life.

"No."

No? I was too stunned to respond.

"Listen Max—we still have work to do. The big prize is still out there. The one we're really after is almost within our reach. And when we get her, then we can move on with our lives. You can make all the plans you want. And you won't ever have to do anything again that you don't want to."

"When will that be, and who is the big one? You never mentioned a big one before."

"You're right. I've been holding out on you. There is a bigger picture here. The ripples I was talking about? They're meant to get the attention of someone. Someone very important to me. She hurt me badly a long time ago. I thought maybe you would help me hurt her back. It would mean so much to me, Max, if you could hurt her the way she hurt me. I don't think I could ever say no to you for anything if you were to accomplish such a thing. Do you think you could do it, Max? Do you think you could avenge me?"

I thought I saw the glint of... what? A tear? In Nash's right eye. Was he about to cry? *My poor Nash. Some bitch hurt him.* "Yes, of course. I'll get that bitch and make her regret hurting you. Just tell me what to do." I hoped the sooner I got the bitch, the sooner we would start our new life together.

He patted my hand and then rubbed it. I loved it whenever he touched me. I ached for more. "With each release, we lead her down a trail. She's following that trail right now. Digging, deciphering, analyzing. She can't learn enough about you," he said, tapping me gently on my chin. "She wants to know you...and she will."

"Who is she? What did she do to you?"

"Do you remember how it felt to be made fun of at school? To be bullied in front of all your classmates? How small and embarrassed you felt because of your tormentors?" I nodded silently, not wanting to think about how mean the other kids were to me. "She mocked me in front of the entire world."

From what I could fathom, he was serious. "I think so." I imagined someone mocking him would make Devil Nash go ballistic.

"It made me...angry," he said with a heavy sigh. "I need my revenge and I will have it."

"Why'd she do it? Does she know you? Is she one of your disciples?" Now I was serious. I never would've imagined I'd ask someone that question in my life, unless I was speaking directly to Jesus. MeeMaw had told me all about him and his disciples. Different men. Different disciples.

"No," he said dreamily, staring off into the fire. "She was one of two that got away."

A knot tugged at my stomach. I'd seen Nash at his worst. I could only imagine what he'd be like if things didn't go his way. Off-the-charts batshit crazy.

"She's within my reach, and you're going to be my weapon."

He glanced at me with a small, proud smile. The reflection of the flames danced across his pupils. "I don't know Nash—"

"Oh, don't worry so much, Max. You're not going to kill her. You're going to lead her to me, so I can," he said with a shrug.

That was a relief, and yet, I still felt sort of scared. "If she's a, uh, like you, isn't there a good chance she'll try to kill me?"

"Like me, hmm? You mean like me and...you. Don't you?" His shiny eyes stared me down. "We're the same, remember? I didn't set four souls free in the past three weeks. You did." He patted my leg and gave it a squeeze. "While we're on the subject, let's talk about what I want you to do if you should get caught."

I didn't like where this was going. "Why are we just talking about that now? Shouldn't that have been a discussion since day one?"

"The police didn't know there was about to be a killer on the loose. They weren't expecting you. Now, they are. They're looking for you and so is the public. People are paying attention, I suppose, at least a little more than they were before four bodies turned up strangled to death with a blue ribbon. They're looking for you now, setting traps, installing more cameras, roaming the docks undercover. Don't worry, Max. I have a plan if, by some slight chance, they apprehend you."

"Yeah? What is it?" I said, exhausted from listening to him. I would not get caught, but this was the game, and I had to play by Nash's rules and listen.

"We'll talk about it after we've watched Diane Dowling. Now, Max, pay attention. You're about to learn everything they don't know."

CHAPTER 13

Max

After our little chat, Nash announced it was time to set another soul free. It'd been more than a couple of weeks since the last one and I'd hoped I'd proven my loyalty to his satisfaction, even though our conversation indicated I hadn't.

Nash helped me strap the custom harness around me and secured my phone in it. I wore it under my sweatshirt and while I worked, I would unzip the sweatshirt halfway down so Nash could see the play-by-play.

Tonight, he had me wear different clothes to throw off any undercover cops looking for someone in a gray hoodie and blue jeans. I wore a plain black T-shirt and black jeans. Over the shirt, I had a light black jacket that zipped and was perfect for a cool autumn night and for concealing the phone strapped to my chest. It also had the convenience of a hood.

He also had something else new up his sleeve—an earpiece. I obediently placed it in my left ear as Nash went into the kitchen and tested it. I could hear him as clearly as when he was in the room with me. He instructed me to go to a bar on an old barge on Pier 66 and wait for further instructions via the earpiece.

The bar was packed when I'd arrived, and I had to squeeze my way through the crowd. I checked my surroundings for anyone who looked out of place, like an undercover cop just waiting to pounce on an unsuspecting stalker.

Nash's revelation that there was a possibility I could get caught weighed heavily on my mind. I couldn't help but think it was part of his plan—for me to get caught. Loud music played as some patrons danced in the middle of the floor. I ordered a soda and sat at the end of the bar, trying to act like I belonged, although I was painfully aware that I did not, and waited for Nash to pipe up in my ear. It didn't take long.

"Hello, Max. Scratch your nose if you can hear me," he whispered, in his sweet southern drawl.

I scratched my nose, realizing that Nash must be in the bar as well, watching me.

"Excellent," he said. "Don't look over yet, but to your right is a group of five women laughing, drinking and dancing. Their drinks are in their hands mostly, unless they move onto the dance floor, and then they leave them on the high top they've gathered around. One of the women is a petite blonde, early forties, wearing a black, low-cut, knit dress. She's your soul. I'm so pleased to watch you in action personally tonight."

Casually, I scanned the bar until I spied the group of women Nash described. I nodded to let Nash know I spotted his intended. From where I sat, I could watch them and follow their movements.

They already had several empty glasses on the table in front of them and were laughing and getting loud. They must've been drinking for a while already. The place was so packed, and the women so drunk, that they didn't seem to care as other patrons bumped into them or put their hands on them as they shouldered their way around the bar. My girl had the bad habit of holding her drink down at her side, out of view, as she swayed to the music. As I watched, she spun and walked directly toward me.

"Tonya!" One of her friends called out, and she turned to look back. "Get me another," the friend shouted, holding up her nearly empty glass. Tonya gave her a thumbs-up and continued in my direction.

She sidled up to the bar, just on the other side of the guy sitting next to me. I could see her features clearly now. Blue eyes lined with black eyeliner and lightly accented with smile lines; a slight bump in what would otherwise be a perfect nose; and thin lips that seemed incapable of corralling liquid as she drained her glass and dribbled the contents onto her chest. She giggled to herself, wiped her chin with the back of her hand, and blotted her left boob with a cocktail napkin snatched from a stack on the bar.

She was obviously so drunk that I didn't think I even needed to use the ketamine Nash had provided. Her blonde hair had telltale dark roots—time for a touch-up lady—and was a mess from dancing on the crowded dance floor.

The guy sitting next to me spotted someone interesting on the other side of the bar and left. Tonya planted herself in his chair, waiting for the bartender to take her order. She was so close to me now that I could smell her. It was the distinct, perfumy aroma of dryer sheet. Strong, like she had rubbed it on. Not a bad thing, but not a good thing either. She caught the bartender's eye, and he nodded at her.

"Another vodka soda?" he asked. Not a good sign when the bartender handling such a sizeable crowd remembered your drink.

"Yes, please," she said, smiling at the much younger man. "And an old-fashioned for my friend."

He slid her drink in front of her and she took a long sip through the straw, then held the glass down at her side, as if her arm were too tired to hold it up as she swayed hazily in her seat, waiting for the other drink. I twisted in my seat and moved my leg around the outside of her hand so it would block what I was about to do, and dumped the contents of the vial into her glass. It was too easy. The move would impress Nash. The bartender placed the old-fashioned on the bar in front of her.

"Put it on your tab?" he asked.

"You got it," she said, as she turned toward me to get up.

I didn't look up. No eye contact with anyone, ever. That's what Nash had taught me. Stay invisible.

I waited for the drug to kick in and for Tonya to react. She mimed to her friends that she was going outside to have a smoke, and started staggering toward the exit, with me close behind. She made it to the sidewalk without falling, but was getting dangerously close to collapsing. Just when she was about to go down, I swooped in.

"Whoa...are you okay?" I asked, grabbing her arm to keep her upright.

"Huh? Oh, yeah. I just need to sit down for a minute." She started laughing and grabbed on for support, and I laughed too.

"Let me help you."

I pulled her arm around the back of my neck and held onto it with one hand as I grabbed her around the waist with the other. We crossed the street, giggling as we went. I kept my hood up and head down to obscure my face from any cameras as we walked past where

I'd set my last soul free. We passed the soccer field, but now she was getting harder to keep up on her feet and moving.

But I only needed to make it to the basketball court. That was where Nash had said to let her soul go.

"Thas nice. Whas your name?"

"Max."

"You a sweetie...I need a lay dow, Max." Her words slurred as she crumbled beneath me.

I led her into the empty basketball court, helped her sit gently on a bench, and laid her on her back, brushing long blonde strands from her face. In the moonlight, I could see a slight scar under her bottom lip I hadn't noticed in the bar. A remnant from her childhood, no doubt.

"You rest. I'll make sure no one bothers you." She slightly nodded her head and then nothing.

I sat down next to her, held her hand, and talked to her, laughing out loud occasionally in case a passer-by noticed us on the court. We needed to look natural, like we were just a couple hanging out on a starry night, looking up at the moon.

She had a beautiful ring on her left hand ring finger, with a large, blue stone surrounded by two rows of smaller ones that I assumed were diamonds. For a moment, I considered taking it. The ring looked like it was worth a lot of money, and I could hock it for some cash to hide away, but Nash had told me that under no circumstances was I to steal from the souls. So I resisted the urge, but only because I couldn't be sure Nash hadn't seen the ring on her hand and would know I took it.

I squeezed onto the bench to lie next to her and put my hand on her belly. I could feel the air moving in and out of her, see her full breasts that peeked from the top of her dress rising and falling, hear her heart beating. When I was sure she was out cold, I sat up and straddled her, moving my hands up over her breasts, feeling their heaviness, leaning down over her as if I were telling her a secret or about to kiss her. But I was actually slipping a blue satin ribbon around her neck, crossing it at the back, and wishing her a pleasant journey home.

I pulled on the ends of the ribbon as tightly as I could, the excitement building inside of me. Her eyes sprang open, deep blue, pupils dilated, round and wide in fear as the ribbon choked her. She tried to hit me, but it was a weak and futile attempt. Her mouth gaped open, and I took the opportunity to kiss her, our tongues brushing together. She gagged a little and then her eyes rolled up, her hands fell limp to her sides, and her body lay still. I pulled a little harder on the ribbon, my biceps burning as I ground my body against hers, panting, excited to be so close to another person, but this chick did nothing for me. They never did.

When she'd stopped struggling, her jaw slack and mouth agape, eyes half-closed and unmoving, I collapsed on top of her, my head on those soft, full breasts, and I listened again for a heartbeat, but there was none.

Tying the ribbon into a bow around her neck, I kissed her on her lips, putting on a show as if we were a couple for any passersby, and placed her hands on top of one another on her belly exactly as I had done the four previous times. A wristlet with some cash peeking out flopped onto her when I moved her arms. Temptation to steal grew once more, but Nash was watching, so I resisted.

I snapped a picture of Tonya on my phone, a trophy for Nash. I took a quick look around to make sure no one was watching and then loudly announced, "I'm going to get a bottle of water...be right back, love."

Tonya was the fifth soul Nash and I had set free.

In my ear he cooed, "Well done, Max. I'm so proud of you. I knew I chose perfectly when I chose you. The others are wannabes. You, Max, are the real thing. Hurry home, Max, darling. I'll be waiting for you."

I walked out of the court and hurried home. I'd hoped that night would be the night Nash would show me how much he loved me.

CHAPTER 14

Cameron

CAMERON FOLLOWED JOHN MERCEDES to the nurse's station, where he said she could pick up a call from Hunter. She knew it had to be something important for him to be calling her. "Hello? Hunter?" Cameron said, smiling into the phone.

"Morning, Cam. How are you today?" he answered.

"If I could start every day hearing your voice, life would be almost perfect, so right now, I'm good. Very good. How're you?"

"I'm happy to hear your voice as well. However, the reason I'm calling is not so happy. We have another victim."

"I was worried you might say that. It was day sixteen. Tell me what happened."

"Her name is Tonya Nathan. She was found in the basketball court on the piers, lying on a bench, hands folded, blue ribbon tied around her neck. Just like the others." Hunter sighed. "A group of guys who had an early game found her. They thought she'd gotten drunk and passed out. One of them tried to wake her and realized she was dead. He called nine one one. We've gone over the scene, collected everything, including the actual bench they found her on, but I don't expect to find anything. The Choker never leaves any evidence behind." Hunter sounded defeated.

"Do you have any clue as to what she was doing on the piers last night?" Cam said.

"Yeah, she was at Hudson's Bar on a barge on Pier 66. One of her friends—uh—Tracy Lynch, contacted us this morning when the news broke. She was afraid it was Tonya, and she called, frantic. Said her friend disappeared last night and hadn't answered her phone since she last saw her. She texted Levine a picture, and the coroner confirmed it was her. Tracy said they were celebrating another friend's promotion—drinking, dancing, having fun, but apparently, they were regulars.

"Tonya went to get a couple of drinks. When she came back to the group, she seemed disoriented. Said she was going outside to have a cigarette, and they never saw her again. She left her sweater at the bar. She had her phone tucked into a wristlet still attached to her arm when the guys found her. Money, a credit card and I.D. were inside. We found a trampled, half-empty pack of cigarettes at the entrance of the bar. We're running tests on that as well."

"How old? Physical description?"

"She was forty-two. Five-five. Thin. Shoulder-length blonde hair. She was a marketing executive for Chavelle Jewelers. She had on a diamond and sapphire ring that Levine said was worth a small fortune."

"Wow, Chavelle! That's expensive stuff." Cameron said, as she formed a visual of the woman in her mind. "It appears he didn't steal anything, so it's not about theft of material things. Theft of life is all this guy can think about."

"We've had some credible tips come in already. Witnesses said they saw her swaying as she walked down the pier, but that someone in a black-hooded jacket came to her aid, helping her walk, and that they were laughing as they went along the sidewalk and appeared to be friends. Barone accessed the cameras in the area showing them crossing Twelfth Avenue at Twenty-Fourth Street, walking right past where we found Michelle Roberts. We couldn't make out the face of who Tonya was with, but one witness said it appeared to be another woman, but he couldn't be positive. Another witness said it was a young guy. Barone still has more footage to go through."

"What time did that happen?"

"It was approximately nine-thirty. The piers would have been hopping at that hour. Especially on a Friday night. This guy has no fear. And he's not stupid. Or she. Whichever knew we'd be out looking for someone in a gray hoodie, jeans, and sneakers. That's what he's worn the last four times, but last night, he changed it up. Black jacket and black jeans and boots. We had undercover cops all over the place, but at that exact moment, we had no one on Pier 66. When you look at the video, they look completely natural. She has her arm around him or her. They look like any other couple out on a Friday night. It's so damn frustrating."

"Can you send me her picture and the video footage? I'd like to view it for myself. And any other footage Barone comes up with. We know more than we think we do. And we knew it was going to happen last night—right on schedule. Sixteen days since the last kill. You're right, this person is brazen, walking around at such a busy time of night, but I'm confident that there is no way they could avoid every camera out there, especially the ones just installed."

"I can do better than that. I'm on my way there...should be there in about twenty minutes, depending on traffic. I have my laptop and a folder of information for you. See you soon, okay?"

When Hunter said he was on the way, Cameron forgot for a moment that someone was dead. The thought of him walking through the door to see her was exhilarating. She caught herself, though, remembering the tragic circumstances that were bringing him to her. He wasn't just coming to see her. He was coming to St. C's because of a murdered woman. It dampened her elation, but it still thrilled her Hunter would be there soon.

"Yes, see you soon!"

She hurried back to her room, where she brushed her teeth minty fresh, then brushed her hair and secured the blonde ends into a neat bun behind her head, making the inches of grown-out brown roots less conspicuous. She coated her plump lips with ChapStick and pinched her cheeks for a glowing pink effect.

In the small mirror over the sink in her room, Cam noticed that new dark circles shadowed her eyes, and her face was thinner than before she'd been incarcerated at St. C's. She tried to think positively. *I'm lucky I have good skin, no wrinkles, no scars.*

She smoothed the light blue hospital uniform top, tucking it into her pants, so it hugged her body a little more, and with more than a little disappointment, gave up. *Maybe someday Hunter will see me in something other than this horrible uniform.* Sighing, she convinced herself not to give it another thought and slipped on the beautiful, cream-colored cashmere open cardigan Hunter had given her for her birthday. Every time she wore it, it was like getting a hug from Hunter.

Cam stepped out into the brightly lit, light-blue-and-white hallway and headed for the security booth and John Mercedes.

John spotted her coming his way and nodded in her direction. Before she could say a word, he spoke. "Hunter called back. Told me he was on the way. I suppose you want the laptop and for me to walk you to the conference room?"

"Yes, please," Cam answered with a broad smile.

"You know, he's coming because someone was just killed, right? Maybe you could subdue your excitement just a teensy bit," he said, holding his thumb and index finger close together.

"Sorry, you're right. I can't help myself. Whenever Hunter is on his way, I get so excited. He's the only visitor I have, you know. He's the only friend I have."

"Yes, I've noticed. Don't you have any family, Cameron?" John asked, as he handed her a pencil case with colored markers and the fully charged laptop.

She hugged it to her body. "No. Growing up, it was just me and my mother. I never knew my father. And my mother and her parents were not close." It wasn't necessary to go into the story of her stepfather and how he'd died. "My mother died when I was in college." Another tragic story she didn't want to talk about.

"That's rough. Sorry, Cameron," John said.

"My work and the friends I made through work were always my family," she said, her thoughts turning to Jeff Alexander, who was also a friend but had never visited her at St. C's. "I guess if I ever get out of here, that's something I'll need to work on. Making friends and perhaps creating a family of loved ones to surround myself with. I'm sure I'll need them." She smiled weakly up at the large man.

"I'm sure you have more friends than you're aware of," he offered. John unlocked and opened the door to the conference room, where she would wait for Hunter's arrival. "*When* you get out of here, you can count me as a friend." He nodded sincerely with a wink.

Cameron squeezed his arm. "Thanks, John. I appreciate that and everything you do for me. You know, *I know* you're the only guard who's not somewhat spooked by me. You're not afraid I'm going to snap and then snap your neck."

"That's only because you can't reach my neck," he said with a deep laugh. "And even if you could, you couldn't get your hands around it. It's so big and muscle-y. You see that?" he asked, pointing at himself. "Sheer muscle...like a granite column." He shook his head as he exited the room, locking the door behind him. "Snap my neck, *as if*!"

Cameron sat down, still amused by John, and opened the laptop she'd named Sylvie for its silver case. "Let's see what's happening today, Sylvie."

She typed Chelsea Choker into the search bar, hoping to find an update on the latest killing. An article from the *New York Post* topped the page.

CHELSEA CHOKER STRIKES AGAIN - CHAVELLE EXECUTIVE FOUND MURDERED

Cameron clicked the link, and the page opened, featuring a photograph of Tonya Nathan. She looked a few years younger than Cam, and had thick, dark brows that framed expressive topaz-blue eyes, a heart-shaped face, and a complexion as fair as her own. She also had the telltale dark roots, which miraculously transformed to blonde locks about two inches down.

Cam self-consciously ran a hand over her hair...*what I'd give for a couple of hours at a decent salon.* She skimmed the attached article, which revealed nothing new. The newspapers had the same information she did.

She returned to the original search and scrolled down, opening other articles from *The Daily News* and *The New York Times*, but they reported the same information as the *Post*.

Voices in the hallway alerted her, and elation spread through her like fire at the sound of Hunter's voice. Grey Turner and Hunter were talking about the previous weekend's Giants football game like two little boys as Grey opened the conference room door.

"Ms. Cooper," Grey said sarcastically, "your ten o'clock is here. Shall I show him in?"

Cameron nodded, ignoring Grey, her heart beating a little faster at the anticipation of seeing Hunter in person.

"Good seeing you, man. We'll be keeping an eye on you." Grey shook Hunter's hand. "Give me the signal when you're ready to leave." He glanced up at the camera mounted over the door.

After Grey locked the door behind him, Hunter turned to Cam. "Ms. Cooper," he said, imitating Grey. "I'm glad you could take the time to see me today."

"I always have time for you, Detective," Cameron said, smiling coyly.

Hunter placed his messenger bag on the table while he peeled off his wool peacoat and hung it on the back of a chair, revealing the typical button-down shirt he wore to work daily in a crisp white. He sat across from Cam, his eyes scanning her as a tight smile tugged at his lips.

"No Levine today?" Cam asked, hoping the irritable detective wasn't merely lagging and would open the door at any moment.

"No Levine. I got the impression he didn't think this visit today was necessary. A phone call would have sufficed."

"I'm glad he's not here. I understand Levine is always going to have a problem with me, but he doesn't have to throw it in my face every chance he gets. I'm trying to help...to make amends."

"I'll have another chat with him. Tell him to take it down a notch. If nothing else, keep it professional. Okay?"

Cameron nodded with a sigh. She didn't want to talk about Levine. There was no point. He'd do whatever he wanted to do, anyway.

Hunter opened the black leather messenger bag he lugged with him everywhere, took his laptop out and opened it. "Reading anything good there?" He nodded at Cam's laptop.

"Nothing you didn't already tell me."

"Well, the newspapers can only report what we tell them, and of course, we wouldn't provide them with any pertinent information unless it served us in some way." He turned the computer around so Cam could see the screen. "This is a view of the sidewalk that runs from Hudson's Bar on Pier 66. You can see it was a pretty busy night. Lots of people wandering around, nothing unusual."

Hunter tapped the play button. "Watch right along here," he said, pointing at the screen with his finger. "That's Tonya, and right behind her, there, is the person who helps her."

Cameron watched as a drunken Tonya staggered along the sidewalk and the person behind her swooped in and helped her just as she was about to fall. The person was a few inches taller than Tonya, a slim build, black pants, and a black jacket with a hood pulled over their head.

"I can't really see anything. It's too far and dark to make out any details. Do you have any other views?"

"Yep." Hunter tapped at the keyboard, once again turned the screen to Cam and tapped the play button on the video.

Cameron watched intently as Tonya and the helper passed the enclave where Michelle Roberts, the soccer player, was discovered dead under some bushes. The camera was on their backs.

"This is no good. The camera is behind them. Do you have any views with them walking toward the camera?"

"Not yet. Barone is working on it. Now that we know the time frame, it'll make searching video footage easier and faster. Saintil and Murphy were helping him today. Hopefully, we'll have more useful footage by the end of the day."

Cameron hit replay and watched the video once more. Tonya's tight knit dress showed off her curvy figure and, comparatively, the person helping her had no shape. A boxy jacket hid the form beneath, and the black jeans were loose-fitting enough not to reveal anything about the wearer's legs. The video stymied her.

"I'm still on the fence about whether this is a young guy or a young woman. The ribbon, the bow, screams female to me, but strangulation, as a means to kill, is a masculine method. Rarely do you find a female serial killer who implements strangulation, guns, or knives, although, historically, it has happened.

"Women serial killers rarely troll for victims. That's a male trait. Women do it more for monetary gain, like someone who marries wealthy men and kills them, or for sympathy. This killer is obviously not in it for the money, or he would have taken Tonya's expensive ring and other jewelry. And I don't see how there could be a sympathy connection. None of the victims had been recently hospitalized or under someone's care.

"That would be typical of a female serial killer…a nurse who kills elderly patients, or a caregiver who moves from patient to patient, losing them to sudden death along the way and receiving sympathy for having lost another person so special and dear to them. They move on to a new patient and kill again, garnering more sympathy and attention. Those kinds of killers typically employ poison or smothering to kill."

Hunter nodded as Cam spoke. He offered his own theory. "Maybe it's a young guy with a mother fixation. These women remind him of his mother. Maybe each victim represents a different aspect of his mother."

"Not a bad hunch. They're definitely connected…like a puzzle, but how do they fit together?" She flipped open the manila folder Hunter had given her the last time he visited and took out the fact sheets on each victim, lining them up in order. "They're getting progressively older."

"Levine pointed that out this morning as he was charting the victims' stats. Do you think it means something?"

"Maybe. Maybe not. Most of the time, what seems logical to a serial killer is completely illogical to everyone else." Cameron watched the video once more. "It's hard to tell The Choker's gait because they're holding up Tonya, kind of walking together, but they appear strong enough to hold her up even as the drug is debilitating her. I'm going to go with my experience and say The Chelsea Choker is a male, eighteen to twenty-five, white, and has a penchant for older women."

Then she opened the paper map Hunter had given her. "Can you mark exactly where they found Tonya?" She handed Hunter a red marker.

He stood up and leaned over the map as Cameron bent in to watch. She drew in his scent. Hunter had a unique essence that was a combination of the starch in his shirt, the Speed Stick deodorant he used, and the light scent of his shaving cream. It all mixed with his body chemistry to create an irresistible fragrance. She leaned a little closer, closed her eyes for just a moment, and inhaled deeply, creating a memory.

"Right here," Hunter said, marking a red X on the map. "In the basketball court...if you're done smelling me, that is."

Cameron sat up straight, her face warming, pulled her eyes from him to study the map, and ignored his mortifying comment. With a finger, she traced the series of X's that were drawn on the map, starting at Pier 59 and Chef Brit, to the basketball court and Tonya.

"It's a straight line until here," she said, tapping the map, "where the killer left Michelle Roberts's body at the corner of Twelfth and Twenty-Fourth. The line turns in and continues to the basketball court. The killer has never left the boundaries of the Chelsea Piers or Water Park, but he's running out of real estate. Look...it's almost the end of the line. The only place left is the dog park. If he strikes again, this will be the spot."

"Isn't that a little obvious?"

"He's playing with you—the police. Taunting you...showing you that even when he leads you right to him, you still can't catch him. This is what I think you should do: ask around, see if any cops have dogs. Have them hang around there with their pets, like any other dog owner, and keep an eye out for a young male who seems to study the park and its exits.

"He won't be wearing the black jacket and jeans—that's his work uniform. He'll be wearing what every other young guy wears these days, casual athletic pants, sneakers, and most likely a loose jacket like snowboarders wear. He'll be hanging around watching, not talking to anyone. You should have cops wandering in and out of there all day and night with the dogs. And you need cameras—everywhere. In the trees, in the bushes...anywhere you can place a camera, especially along the areas that lead to the dog park. Think wireless cameras you can connect to your phones. Everyone on your team has a different section of the park that they monitor twenty-four seven."

She stopped and smiled at Hunter. "We're going to catch this guy. He thinks he's smarter, but he's getting arrogant, and over-confidence always kills the cat."

"He could lead us to nowhere. Maybe he'll double back. Maybe he'll strike again tomorrow. These guys are nuts. You can't predict what they'll actually do."

"No, we can't predict, but we can deduce. He's taunting you. Evading the police is as much a thrill as killing. He's combined the two into a game of cat and mouse with you, and by making it more dangerous for himself, it becomes more thrilling. If I'm wrong, you can fire me."

Hunter sat back down and leaned back in his chair. He had a serene look on his face as he stared across at Cameron, as if he was seeing something very pleasant.

"Okay, boss, I'll get right on it. Cameras, dogs, surveillance. We are going to catch this son of a bitch or I'm the one who's going to get fired." He passed another folder to Cameron. "That's the updated information we have on The Choker and the fact sheet on Tonya."

"You could have emailed this to me."

"I could have, but you know me...I like to do things old school." He leaned onto the table again, clasping his hands in front of him within Cameron's reach. "How are you doing?"

"Good as I can be, considering where I am. Truthfully, St. C's isn't as bad as I imagined. Except for Myra the Bitch, I haven't experienced any abusive behavior by the staff, and they haven't experimented on me. I keep to myself, mind the rules, and I've made friends with many of the staff—at least the ones who aren't afraid of me. Sometimes I hear questionable sounds, but I guess considering the patient profile here, it's expected.

"And... my sessions with Dr. Heisser are going really well. He thinks I've made a lot of progress in the last six months. The alter Jason hasn't emerged in months. Dr. Heisser believes it's because we're managing my stress and headaches. And I'm working through the traumas of my life. I feel good—better than I have in a long time."

Cameron wanted to tell Hunter about her last session with Dr. Heisser. She wanted to explain how she could envision the night her mother had killed her stepfather as Angel described it, but she wasn't ready to discuss what it would mean for facing the alter known as Jason Jonette. And the repercussions of facing what he had done.

"I'm glad to hear you're doing well. If your contribution to The Choker case results in us catching the bastard, I know the commissioner will be open to you working on other cases. How would you feel about that?"

"I don't want to get ahead of myself and get excited about something that can easily disappear, but I feel hopeful. It's hard to investigate a case fully from behind bars, but it just means I have to find a new way to work. I think I'm doing okay. I just have to approach the case differently, and I'm figuring out what that means. And you know how much I love computers....Yuck! But since it's what I have, I love it." Cam stopped, and then whispered, "I kiss it goodnight, you know."

"Lucky laptop."

Cameron examined Hunter's handsome face. He was her best friend. She loved him so much. She was in love with him. She was thankful for his support, for never giving up on her, and for giving her purpose again. Cameron reached across the table and gently squeezed his arm. "Hunter, thank you."

"For what?" He smiled softly at her.

"For being my friend."

CHAPTER 15

Max

LAST NIGHT, I LEARNED a lot about Nash and what it means to live in his world. The first thing I learned was that Nash was even more unpredictable than I had initially gauged. Even after all these months we'd been together, he still shocked me. I discovered there was yet another side to this eccentric southern gentleman, who was a mastermind of death, and had a following that, if discovered and revealed to the public, would cause an uptick in home security and gun sales.

This new-to me-version of Nash delightfully combined charming Nash and devil Nash...he was devilishly charming.

On my way home last night, after my date in the basketball court with Tonya, I had a very explicit fantasy running through my mind: As I walked through the front doors of Nash's gorgeous townhouse; he was waiting for me, smiling, with just a hint of devilish Nash in his eyes. Just enough to be sexy, not scary. He was holding filled crystal champagne flutes, sparkling in the light as tiny bubbles fizzed and danced on the surface of the wine. Soft music played in the background. He passed me a flute.

"Cheers to you, Max, for an exquisite execution of our plan tonight." We clinked our glasses and sipped the expensive champagne, the finest bottle he had in his collection, the one he'd been saving for the most special of occasions.

As we drank, our eyes locked over the rims of the fine-cut crystal, the excitement between us palpable, building, a magnet drawing us together. He took my glass from my hand, placed it on the dainty coffee table, and reached out to me to dance. He pulled me close to him.

Imagining this glorious fantasy, even out in the cold dark of night, awoke my senses and I could smell his minty breath, the aftershave clinging to his skin, and the lavender he used in his laundry. I felt the warmth of him, and my body warmed in reaction.

Then, in my fantasy, he held me even closer, our bodies pressed together. I imagined his excitement.

I hurried home faster, my thoughts building my anticipation. I was practically jogging.

I envisioned him whispering in my ear, "I'm so proud of you Max. You've made all my dreams come true and now I'm going to make yours come true. What do you wish for, Max? How can I please you?"

He'd then lay a trail of soft kisses down my neck before stripping me of the black jacket and the shirt beneath. He'd move to my pants, silently undoing the button and zipper while staring into my eyes. I'd undo the buttons on his shirt, and it would drift to the ground like in a commercial for a romance novel. We would collapse onto the soft carpet in front of the roaring fire, wet our lips and sweeten our mouths with sips from the champagne before taking each other into our arms and kissing passionately. He'd kiss me like no one had kissed me before, like in the soap operas MeeMaw used to watch.

I'd slip my hands down his back and around to the front of his pants, undoing them and slowly sliding them off him as I kissed his thighs along the way.

It would be beautiful. We'd finally be together. Nash and I making love in front of the fire. Celebrating our love together. Afterward, we'd lie in each other's arms, sipping champagne and planning our future. We'd discuss where we'd go next. Georgia? Florida? Who cared as long as it was warm and sunny?

I hurried up the front steps, my fantasy fueling my need to get laid, to be loved, to have some kind of human touch. No, not some kind...to have Nash's touch. To be with the man I'd fallen in love with.

I flung open the front door, expecting Nash to be waiting, the champagne flowing, the fire crackling, music playing. There was nothing. The house was quiet.

"Hello? Nash?"

"In here, Max."

I followed his voice. He was sitting on the dainty flowered sofa, reading. *Some welcome home.* I stood in the doorway, disappointed to the point of grief. This was how he welcomed me?

"I see you made it home safely."

"That's it?" I asked, my mouth open, eyes wide, brows lifted as far as I could get them up my forehead, exaggerating every feature. He glanced at me from his book and then did a double take.

"Something wrong, Max?"

"Yes, there's something wrong! I thought you'd be a little more...enthusiastic when I came in."

"Enthusiastic? What do you mean?"

"Did you watch? Were you there? This was supposed to be our big night, you know, our first time working together...out there." I nodded my head toward the front of the house.

"Of course, I watched. You were perfect, as always. Come, sit." He patted the prim fabric of the couch.

I started to go over to him, but then stopped. "I'm tired. I think I'll go to bed." I turned around and trudged up the stairs, defeated and exhausted from getting myself all worked up without a release.

I closed the bedroom door behind me and stripped naked. A cold shower waited, but I hated cold showers, so it would be as hot and steamy as my skin could stand. I turned on the shower and as I waited for the water to warm up, I examined my face in the mirror over the large, white, ceramic pedestal sink.

Maybe he doesn't find me attractive. My mother had always made a point of saying I resembled my father and his side of the family. Then she'd say they were a bunch of naked mole rats. We'd visited the zoo once where we saw a colony of the wrinkly, buck-toothed rodents, the ugliest thing I'd ever seen, and ever since then, anytime she wanted to insult someone, she'd call them a naked mole rat, like she was some great beauty and had room to criticize.

My mother's pudgy red face and bulbous nose popped up in my memory. Then my father's sagging, wrinkled and spotted face, with his nasty beady eyes, popped up next to it. *Jeez, I never had much of a shot at being good-looking, but I'm no naked mole rat either.*

I wasn't bad looking, I didn't think. Somehow, I seemed to look more like Pops. And Pops was handsome, in a plain sort of way. MeeMaw always said he was the most handsome man in the world to her. How did two such wonderful people, MeeMaw and Pops, spawn that woman who was my mother? Maybe ugly skips a generation.

I stepped into the shower, hoping to wash off my self-loathing, cleanse myself of what I'd just done, and think about what I'd do next. I was tired of this game with Nash. Me doing his bidding. Him doing...what? He wasn't fulfilling his promise to make us a family and take me away from here.

Yet, I loved him.

Was I so starved for love and affection growing up that it had somehow turned me into a monster? I wasn't like Nash. Not really. He was cold and malicious. I wasn't cold, not exactly warm, but not cold in the way he was. Killing things never bothered me, but it wasn't something I lived to do. He seemed driven by death. And revenge. That's what this was all about, wasn't it? Revenge. His revenge, not mine. I'd already gotten mine.

I squirted some shampoo into my hand and rubbed it into a lather. I washed my hair as the hot water ran over my body, rinsing away the sins of the day. I grabbed the body wash that Nash had provided. He was very particular about scents. The label touted organic coconut and shea butter. I had no idea what shea butter was or what it smelled like, but this stuff smelled pretty good.

I soaped myself up to the point where bubbles and foam covered me from head to toe. Over the sound of the rushing water, I heard a light rap on the door.

Nash slowly opened the bathroom door and entered. I could just make him out through the haze that had built up in the small bathroom. He closed the door behind him and leaned against the pedestal sink, watching me through the misty, glass-enclosed shower.

What the hell? I didn't say a word. He'd come to me. He'd have to speak first, but I thought this was an opportunity to see what made him tick. With my soapy hand, I wiped away the fog that clouded the shower's glass so that he could see me better and so that I could see him as well, and I made a show out of it.

I squeezed some more body wash into my hand and swirled it onto my naked body, running my hands all over myself, never taking my eyes from his. He watched, unflinching, his hands pressed deep into his pants pockets.

He wore dark-gray, wool flannel pants that had been custom fit to his lean physique, and a black, fitted turtleneck. Damn, those pants looked good as they skimmed his perfect ass.

I turned around so he could get a full view of me from behind, and I thought, why not? I bent over—naked ass alert—and pretended to wash my ankles. I almost laughed at that point. The move was something I'd seen on MeeMaw's soap opera, and I felt ridiculous, and perhaps a little desperate. I had nothing to lose, except my dignity, which I'd lost so many times that I wasn't sure I had any left.

I straightened myself up and turned to see what he thought of my full moon, ready to invite him into the shower with me...but he was gone. *Son of a bitch!*

I actually looked around the small bathroom for him, like, *where'd he go? Is he hiding behind the toilet?* Idiot!

I rinsed off, more frustrated than ever, stepped out of the shower and grabbed one of the oversized and super-fluffy towels hanging on a stand just next to me. I couldn't understand why he'd done that—why come in here and watch me, just to leave? He was even more twisted than I realized. But then it occurred to me...maybe there was something wrong with him physically. An injury or some kind of deformity? Or maybe *he* thought I was ugly. Maybe he was just a jerk, and I was a fool in love...with a jerk.

I dried off, towel-dried my hair, and pulled my flannel pants and T-shirt on. As I brushed my teeth, I examined myself some more in the mirror. I needed to give myself more credit. I was a lot better looking than my mother had ever said.

I didn't need to live like this anymore—beholden to Nash and his murderous ways. I'd probably never live this well again, but at least I'd prove to myself that I was better than Clara and Wayne. They killed for money. I killed for love. Love that just never seemed to fully materialize.

I opened the bathroom door expecting to get in bed and watch some television with Sammy, but when I opened the door, I was gobsmacked, as MeeMaw would say.

Only the bedside lamp was lit, and it had a red scarf thrown over it, casting a pinkish hue throughout the room. On the nightstand was a bottle of champagne, two glasses, and a small plate with a bunch of chocolates. And in my bed, stroking the cat he hated so much at first sight that he'd nearly killed her, was Nash, propped up on an elbow. What's more, as far as I could see, he was naked. He flipped back the comforter on my side and patted the bed. "Care to join me?"

I took tiny steps toward the bed, afraid that if I moved too fast, I'd spook him, and he'd bolt. I climbed into the queen-sized bed, the sheets cool and silky to my touch, and cautiously lay down next to him. Sammy scurried away, as if she didn't want to see what was about to happen.

I was on my back, angled up on two fat pillows. Nash leaned over me, his naked chest grazing mine as he reached for the champagne glasses. He handed me one with a steady gaze.

"To you, Max. You've proven your dedication to me."

Nash lightly tapped my glass and sipped, and I did the same. He placed his glass on the bedside table on his side and, again, I followed his lead.

He brushed the side of my face with his hand and let his fingers trail down my neck to my shoulder, where he slowly rubbed my upper arm with his thumb.

What in holy hell is happening?

I didn't know what to do. Everything I knew about sex between consenting adults, I'd learned from General Hospital. So again, I mimicked him. I gently traced his arm with my fingertips. I could feel my heart pounding and my breath became shallow. What would happen next?

He leaned in for a kiss, and my entire body tensed like I was about to be murdered. *Hmm, not a good comparison with Nash. New thought.*

"Relax, Max," Nash cooed as he kissed my neck, his goatee tickling and scratching me, and feeling amazing. "You're so tense." He sat back and looked at me. "Is this your first time?" His eyes narrowed slightly as he watched my face with an intensity that made me blush.

I wasn't in the mood for games. Not now. "You know it's not," I whispered, ashamed. My stepfather didn't count under the umbrella of consensual, but thanks to him, I was no virgin. I wanted to have an honest relationship with Nash and that meant owning all the ugly.

"That bastard. I wish I could bring him back to life just so I could kill him again. Slowly. Don't worry, Max. If you want to stop, we stop." His drawl soothed my nerves. "I want to show you how to make love the proper way. A toast, Max," he said, as he leaned back and took the champagne glass in hand, "to your real first time."

I clumsily grabbed my glass, spilling a little on myself and then knocking it against Nash's glass too hard. He didn't react to what was obviously nerves. We sipped, or rather he sipped. I downed the contents of my glass, resisting the urge to let loose a burp. It was the carbonation of the wine, just like soda. It got me every time.

We placed our glasses back on the nightstands and turned to one another. He pulled me closer to him, our mouths coming together, his hands exploring my body, slipping beneath my clothes, and leaving a trail of goosebumps in their wake. It was abundantly clear that there was nothing wrong with him physically. This was it. I was finally getting my wish.

I've mentioned before...careful what you wish for.

CHAPTER 16

Hunter

"Hey, Hunter! Check this out." Detective Vince Barone placed a laptop on Hunter's desk in front of him. "I've spent the last week checking the cameras along the esplanade between the bar where Tonya Nathan was with her friends and where we saw the other video of her crossing the street. I've gone through hundreds of hours of footage, and it's finally paid off. I just found this—it's a little grainy, but I think we may have our first lead." Moving the cursor over a figure in the video, he said, "This is Tonya after she left the bar. It looks like she's about to fall when someone comes to her aid, right here." Barone pressed Pause and pointed to the figure on the screen.

"Now, watch what happens next." Barone started the video again. Hunter leaned closer and watched as the figure, someone in a black jacket and jeans, looked right at the camera.

"Whoa! Did you see that?" Hunter asked. "He looked right into the camera. Was it on purpose? Like he was taunting us? Or was it an accident? Is the camera obscure, and he didn't see it there?"

"Not sure. It might be The Choker. It's definitely the same person we saw helping her cross the street. Anyway, this is most likely the last person to see Tonya alive." He zoomed in. "It's hard to tell if it's a man or a woman, but if you examine the hands and the feet, they seem to be smaller, like a woman's. What do you think, Boss?"

Hunter sat back in his chair. One long finger pressed his lips as he scrutinized the paused video. His head told him it was a man killing the women, but his gut told him a different story. Cameron was sure it was a male.

"Let's get the image out to the media and ask the public for help. We are looking for the person in the video as a potential witness, not a suspect in a crime. Make sure they include our tip hotline number and mention there's a $10,000 reward for any information that leads to an arrest."

"Got it, Boss. I feel good about this, like we've gotten a solid break."

"Yeah, I agree. Forward that video to me, too." Hunter watched Barone walk away with his laptop, a bounce in his step. There was so much about this case that reminded him of The Stealth Stalker... of Cameron. He didn't mean to think of her that way, but the two were inseparable. It also reminded him of The J-Bird, aka Jason Julian Jonette.

Jonette strangled his victims. The Chelsea Choker also used strangulation. Jonette left a calling card, a blue feather tucked into his victim's hands. The Choker tied a blue ribbon around his victim's throats. To Hunter, it felt similar, not enough that he thought it was the same person, but enough that he thought the criminals were associated.

He wanted to bounce his ideas off Cam and called her.

"St. Christina's State Hospital," the operator answered. "How can I direct your call?"

"Grey Turner, please." As head guard on Cameron's floor, Turner had been appointed the arbitrator for Hunter and Cameron.

"Ninth floor, Turner speaking."

"Hi Grey, it's Hunter Finnegan. How's it going?"

"Hey, Hunter, man, we're having a quiet day here at St. C's. How're things on the Lower West Side?"

"Could be better. We're still chasing The Chelsea Choker. That's why I'm calling. Any chance I can talk to Cameron?"

"Yeah, I can get her. She just finished her therapy session with Dr. H. Hold on a sec."

A minute later, Hunter heard Cameron's familiar voice on the other end.

"Hunter?"

"Hi, Cam." He smiled at the sound of her voice. "How are you?"

"I'm having a good day, but it just got a lot better. I'm so happy to hear from you. Is everything okay? You're not calling because there's been another murder, are you?"

"No, but we had a break in the case. Barone was reviewing the video of the night Tonya Nathan died, and he caught something. The person who helped Tonya when she was having trouble walking looked right at the camera. The picture's not great. Barone pointed out that the person's hands and feet are smaller, like a...woman's," he said, cringing at the words. "Uh, and we were discussing the possibility that The Choker is female."

"Could be. As we already discussed—there's no rule saying a serial killer has to be male. You need to be really strong to strangle someone to death. That may be why The Choker drugs the victims first," Cameron said.

"I know. And I know that we've already discussed this, and you said it's a guy, but I have this knot in my gut...and I don't want you to think we're making assumptions based on... your case." Hunter stood and paced as the conversation took a turn he hadn't expected. "That's what I wanted to talk to you about. The Choker reminds me of The J-Bird, even though the calling cards are different. I can't shake the thought that they're connected. Maybe Jonette is back, and The Choker is a protégé or a copycat."

"I doubt Jonette would work with anyone, but it could be a copycat with a flair for the dramatic that would explain the blue ribbon. Remember, women serial killers working alone lean more toward poison as a weapon."

"You didn't," Hunter faltered, "I mean, your alter didn't." He wasn't sure what he meant. Sometimes Cameron's case still confused him.

"*You* didn't? Seriously Hunter? The alter known as Jason is a male, and it wasn't me." Her voice quivered.

"I'm sorry, Cam. That was just a slip of the tongue. Obviously, you didn't hurt anyone. Can you forgive me?" She didn't answer, but Hunter heard her breathing as he paced, waiting for her reply.

Cameron cleared her throat. "It's fine," she finally conceded, her voice was still shaky. "I was just going to say, sometimes serial killers have groupies. People who follow them, usually female, who become captivated by the killer. If you really think The Choker is a woman, then that might be an answer. She incapacitates them, the way Jonette did with a sedative, and then strangles them. But she puts her own spin on it with a pretty ribbon, differentiating herself from Jonette while still paying homage to him."

"The sedatives aren't the same. The Choker uses ketamine—"

"Doesn't matter. It doesn't have to be exact."

"It's kind of a coincidence, isn't it? You had an alter calling himself Jason Jonette, and now it appears there is someone out there copying him?"

"Which is another reason it sounds more like a groupie. Someone who saw the news about me and the alternate personality, Jason Jonette, got curious about the real Jonette, did a little digging, and became intrigued. That would explain why it's a younger person. Someone in their twenties would have been a child when Jonette was active—too young to know about his crimes. She could be in contact with him, but most likely, she's trying to get his attention. Groupies sometimes become enamored by or fall in love with their serial killer of choice. If Jason Jonette is still alive, and I didn't get his attention, this will."

"People fall in love with serial killers?"

"It's called hybristophilia or Bonnie and Clyde syndrome. They're attracted to someone who commits crimes—doesn't have to be murder—but you know, the good girl falling for the bad boy."

"Great. And what do you suppose would happen if either case got Jonette's attention?"

"That's hard to predict. It might flatter and intrigue him enough to come to New York and meet his fan. It might make him angry enough to put an end to The Choker himself. Or he may not care. The Choker might have nothing to do with Jonette at all. There are plenty of serial killers throughout history who used strangulation as their instrument in death."

"So? Yea or nay, The Choker is female?"

"I'm still leaning toward no. The blue ribbon tied in a bow is a feminine touch, but I'm sticking with strangulation typically being a masculine method of killing. I would say someone abused him growing up, and he has a lot of anger... and a vendetta. He didn't just wake up one day and decide to kill. Something happened, and he snapped. You should look into unsolved murders that occurred within six months to a year of the first killing." Cameron paused. "He could also be a vagrant. If he did impulsively kill someone, his being on the run and hiding among the homeless is a safe bet."

"Wouldn't a homeless person be an easier target than the women he chose?"

"Yes, but he or she doesn't have a problem with the homeless. He has a problem with successful women, who are also active. The killings happened during social events—a soccer game, a fancy dinner on a yacht, a celebration in a bar. You get the idea? The Choker is targeting busy women. They aren't sitting home at night, taking care of the family, and watching TV. Which would leave me to assume his own mother didn't make time for him. She was too busy with her own social life to care for or pay attention to a child. And if she wasn't paying attention, that child was easy prey for someone to abuse."

Hunter felt good about the professional exchange with Cameron. Anything that came from Cameron's insight and experience would prove to Commissioner Tate they had done the right thing by reading Cam in on the case, or at least it would prove it wasn't the worst thing.

"There's one problem with that theory, Cam," Hunter said. "None of the victims were mothers or married. It seems like if it were a vendetta against women who reminded him of his mother, then the vics would have children. No?"

"That's a good point. No children to neglect?" Cameron blew out a heavy sigh. "Well, I still think the perp is a white male, in his early twenties, and comes from an abusive home. The women have a connection. We just can't see it. Yet." She paused for a moment. "Can you check into the women's education and also see if they served on any boards together or on the same board at different times?"

"Sure, no problem. Where are you going with that?" Hunter asked.

"I'm not sure. The victim's occupations don't link them, and so far, there were no overlaps in salons, churches, ex-boyfriends... hmm, what about girlfriends?"

"All the women were heterosexual. And no, none of them dated the same guy. There's also a thirteen-year age difference between the oldest and the youngest, making it unlikely the women traveled in the same social circles."

"We have to dig deeper. I tried to research forums dedicated to serial killers but I keep hitting blocked websites. Apparently, somebody doesn't want me, of all people, researching the dark web, so you'll have to do it. If you've never done it before, brace yourself. There's some grim stuff there. But you'll want to check for references to The J-Bird, New York City murders, blue ribbons—anything connected to The Choker."

Hunter jotted down the request on his note pad. "Okay, I'll have Levine check the dark web and get back to you. Anything else?"

"Yes...see if any of the women gave up a child for adoption."

"Interesting angle." Hunter jotted again.

"If I come up with anything else, you'll be the only person I call," Cam said with a chuckle.

Hunter laughed too. "I suppose if it were an emergency, they would put you through to Levine, but I know you would have to be desperate for that to happen."

"Agreed. And knowing Glen, he may not take the call."

"How are you managing with all this, Cam? Is there anything I can do for you?" Hunter wanted to get some personal conversation in before he had to disconnect.

"Good. I...I've had a bit of a breakthrough with Dr. Heisser. I've been meaning to talk to you about it, but I..." Hunter heard her blow out a breath. "I wasn't ready. Next time you visit, perhaps you can leave a little extra time so we can talk?"

"Of course. This sounds important. I can make time later today."

"It's not pressing, but it is important. I don't want to put you out or interfere with your work on the case. The Choker is more important."

"Okay, I'll check my schedule and visit as soon as I can. Good?"

"Yes, good. How are you? Has Dwyer been on your back since you set all this in motion?"

Hunter laughed. "Good old Chief Dwyer. No, he stays away from me. He's giving me enough rope to hang myself. I think he figures when this blows up in my and Commissioner Tate's faces, he'll be rid of me, and he'll get her job. It's all the motivation I need to make sure this doesn't go sideways and make the commissioner come out of it looking like a national hero. That will surely make the vein in Dwyer's temple blow."

"It is the Mount Vesuvius of bulging veins." Cam half-laughed again. "I hope the outcome is favorable for you. I'd hate to be the reason you get into more trouble."

"I'm not in any trouble, and don't worry about me. I know what I'm doing. I've got to get going. Levine is waiting for me—we're going to stake out the piers tonight. This was good. We're on to a lead here, right?"

"Right. I'm going to work on my favorite laptop right now and see what I can discover about the victims. You know, there really *are* a lot of blocked websites on here. I'm beginning to feel like someone doesn't trust me," Cam said slyly. "Talk to you soon?"

"Yes—talk soon."

Hunter ended the call and sat back, wondering what Cameron wanted to discuss that was so important. He considered calling Dr. Heisser for an update but thought better of it; she would feel betrayed by both of them. So he would have to wait until tomorrow when he had the time to make the trip out to St. C's.

The staff wouldn't appreciate him showing up late in the evening anyway, unless it was a dire emergency. The hospital was very strict about late visitors, and for good reason. It was an unpredictable group they managed there and messing with schedules, stirring things up after hours could set off a chain reaction ending in violence.

Cameron had had a breakthrough, she'd said, but wasn't ready to talk about it. What did that mean? A breakthrough should mean good news. So why did it sound so ominous to him?

CHAPTER 17

Cameron

"Morning, Grey," Hunter said, as he placed his revolver in the gun safe on the ninth floor of St. Christina's Hospital.

"Hunter, how's it going?" Grey asked, as he routinely patted Hunter down. "Here to visit our resident doctor again?"

"Yes, sir. Anything new around here?"

"Same shit, new day. You know how it goes...which patient attacked who first, who dumped all their food on the floor, who's moaning and shrieking.... Sometimes it's like a bizarro world circus in here and all the clowns are deranged. You know what I mean?"

Hunter nodded, even though he could only imagine what St. C's was really like on a daily basis. "I guess you get used to it?"

"Yeah, some of it, but sometimes they spook me a little, especially the ones who hallucinate. That shit freaks me out." Grey nodded to Petey Johnson, who was watching the camera feeds. "Hey, Pete, open her up." Petey pressed a button and a loud buzzer sounded, indicating the door had unlocked. Grey led the way down the too-bright corridor to where Cameron waited in a conference room.

Hunter looked up at the endless rows of bright lighting fixtures embedded in the ceiling. "Are those fluorescents?"

"Huh?" Grey's eyes followed Hunter's. "I don't know, man. That's maintenance's job, not mine." Grey unlocked the dark brown door to the conference room and stepped to the side, giving Hunter room to pass. "Give me the signal when you're done and Petey'll come down and let you out." He closed the door firmly and locked it again.

Hunter smiled at Cameron. "He's a little testy today. Things not good here at St. Christina's?"

"Ah, ignore him. A couple of patients got into it yesterday and when he intervened, he got clobbered. He'll get over it, eventually. Come, sit." Cameron patted the mahogany table in front of her and smiled happily.

Hunter slipped off his navy peacoat, threw it on the chair next to him, and sat across from Cam.

"No Levine again?" she asked.

"Nope."

"I think he doesn't enjoy coming here and visiting me," she said with a grin.

"I'm sure it doesn't bother you, right?"

"Well, I suppose it might hurt my feelings, but it doesn't." She smiled. "I have Sylvie all warmed up and ready for action. What's on the agenda today?"

"I wanted to catch you up on our plans for The Choker. Day thirty-two is fast approaching, and we have the piers covered from top to bottom. We set up a series of new cameras along each pier, along the sidewalks, inside the soccer field, the basketball court, on The Great Lawn, which was a challenge, and throughout the dog park. They're state-of-the-art CCTV with high-resolution night vision. You can see what color eyes a mouse has with these things.

They're high, they're low, they're at eye level. The tech guys did an amazing job planting these things. Some look like rocks, and they actually embedded others into trees. No wires—they run on rechargeable batteries. They're all connected to our phones, so we can pull up live feed anytime, anyplace. Look..."

Hunter turned his cell phone on and tapped on the screen. A series of thumbnail videos opened. He tapped the top one and handed the phone to Cameron. She watched the live video of the dog run as he watched her.

"If you tap the icon on the top left, it'll go back to the thumbnails and you can open a different feed someplace else on the water."

Cameron followed his instructions, tapped a different thumbnail video, and The Great Lawn appeared on his phone. It was a beautiful day as the sun reflected off the Hudson River. With winter on the horizon, the trees were bare and there were only a few people out for an afternoon walk. "So that's the outside world? I'd almost forgotten." She handed the phone back to him and he noted a sadness that hadn't been there a moment ago. "How long can you keep the surveillance up?"

"Commissioner Tate gave us forty-eight hours after day thirty-two just in case The Choker doesn't own a calendar or is trying to throw us off."

"Sounds like a lot of activity. The Choker could have been watching for that kind of movement. It might be a problem."

"That's why we dressed the tech guys as everything from sanitation to ConEd to just people hanging out as couples. They did a lot of the work in the middle of the night, with a close watch on the surrounding area. If The Choker saw any activity, it would be minimal and expected. He knows we're watching, waiting, and he'd expect amped up security. He'll have scoped out his next kill zone, looked for cameras and maybe even spotted some, but there's no way he'd find them all without us finding him. I did as you suggested—had cops and their dogs walking through that area day and night. We would have spotted someone looking a little too closely at a tree...or a rock."

"Good, good. What else?"

Hunter scoffed. "That's not enough? You want more? Okay, we've also tripled police presence on the piers, in the park, and the surrounding areas. Uniformed and undercover. Every cop has been told what to look for, who to look for, and what to do. The mounted unit will patrol for the next five days or until we catch this son of a bitch. Also, K-9 will patrol twenty-four seven, so even if this guy can outrun one of us, he will not outrun one of those dogs. This is a high-alert operation; all hands on deck. It's costing the city a fortune, but if The Choker strikes again, he will not get away."

"I'm impressed. Seems like you've thought of everything. Make sure no one does anything to violate his rights that would give him a loophole to go free, right? Everything has to be by the book and everyone has to be strictly professional. No excessive force; we want him alive."

Hunter felt pride as Cam's words evoked the FBI agent within. He considered her words, *we want him alive*, and wondered at that moment, *do we?* He shook the question out of his head. Of course he wanted him alive. He wanted the asshole to pay for every life he took, and he wanted him to pay for it daily in a maximum-security prison that offered its own brand of justice. Envisioning The Choker—a small, weak man who had to sedate his victims before he killed them—in a max facility, facing off with guys two to three times his size, gave Hunter a feeling of satisfaction.

He eyed Cameron, and the memory of The Stealth Stalker popped up. He'd never wish that on her, and now he felt conflicted. How could he work so hard for her freedom and wish the worst for someone else? Both had committed murder. Multiple murders.

It wasn't her, Hunter reminded himself. He always had to remind himself that the woman he loved and the monster who inhabited the same body weren't the same person.

"Right. Of course. We all want the same thing…for this bastard to rot in prison for the rest of his life, however long that may be."

Cameron sighed. "Let's just focus on catching him first. You can entertain yourself with the various ways he'll die in prison later."

"You know me so well," Hunter replied with a smirk. "I can't help myself. It's a cop thing."

"Is there any way I can tap into that live feed? I'm sure I can move some things in my schedule to sit and watch at least—I don't know—twenty-four hours a day."

"Ah, sarcasm. Grey isn't the only one who's a little testy today." He sat back, his boyish grin taunting Cameron.

She stared at him for a beat before leaning onto the table and clasping her hands in front of her. "Hunter, there's something I'd like to talk to you about."

"Is this about the breakthrough you mentioned on the phone?" Their phone conversation was the real reason he'd visited. It had bothered him overnight after she'd mentioned that she needed to discuss something important with him, but hadn't been ready.

"It is."

Reading the serious expression on her face, Hunter sat up straight and leaned into her as close as the table allowed him to get, which, with his size, was pretty darn close. "What's up, Cam?"

She cleared her throat and began. "So, you're aware I work closely with Dr. Heisser to address the many reasons that I'm a resident here." She spread her arms out in a sweeping motion and looked around the room. "And you know that the alter known as Angel results from childhood trauma. My stepfather was not a good man, and my mother shot him to death, in self-defense, in front of me. Right?"

"Right." Hunter tensed, not knowing where the conversation was heading, but his gut told him it would not be a pleasant journey.

"Dr. Heisser has been using hypnosis to communicate with the alters. He can hypnotize me and bring them out, one at a time, and talk with them. Hypnosis isn't always successful, but it's worked enough that he's been able to ascertain certain things about each alter. I know how it sounds, but please, keep an open mind."

"Of course, I will." He grasped her hand and gave it a quick squeeze. "I want to help you in any way I can."

She continued. "A couple of weeks ago, he hypnotized me so that I was aware of the conversation as he was talking to Angel. It was her voice coming from my mouth. I experienced her emotions...whether she was happy or terrified. She recounted the night my mother killed my stepfather. And for the first time. I saw it unfold in front of me. I could smell the meatloaf that my mother had made for dinner that night, I could hear her screaming in pain as he beat her, and I felt Angel's paralyzing fear as I hid in the closet and tried to camouflage myself with coats and boots." Cam stopped for a moment and took a swig from her water bottle.

"You okay?" Hunter asked softly.

Cam nodded. "I need to tell you this. If it's too much, I'll stop."

"No, it's not too much for me, but is it too much for you? Do you want me to talk to Dr. Heisser instead?"

"No...I need to tell you myself." She closed her eyes for a moment, took a deep breath, and blinked away welling tears from her eyes. "I could never remember how I hurt my shoulder that night. One moment it was fine, and the next, I was in the hospital with my shoulder immobilized. Kurt had dislocated it when he yanked me by my arm out of the closet. I felt the pain streak through my body as Angel described it. And then she talked about the gun and the noise it made. I heard the explosions of each bullet and the grunting sound Kurt made as each one ripped into his body, spraying blood out of him, some of it landing on me. I remembered the loud thud of his body hitting the floor next to me. I saw him...his white cotton T-shirt absorbing the blood, quickly staining it crimson. I heard him...the wheezes of a man who was just shot multiple times and was dying.

"After all these years, I could see it all unfold like a movie. As Angel spoke, the dam holding my memories back broke and flooded my mind, and with it, all of my senses. I could hear, feel, and smell that night as if I were reliving it, not just remembering it."

Hunter stood and retrieved a box of tissues that sat on a table in the corner. He pulled one free and handed it to Cam. "I'm so sorry you had to go through that. Are you certain it helps, or is it doing more harm?" Hunter was concerned that the trip down memory lane was going to cause damage, sending her further away from reality and him, and not heal Cameron at all.

"Yes, I'm positive it's helpful." She wiped her nose and took another sip of water. "Dr. Heisser said it's important for me to witness and comprehend what each alter has to say so that I can face what caused them to manifest in the first place. I...I never realized how traumatic my childhood was or how other events in my life impacted me. I need to face those traumas so we can purge the alters and I can be whole again."

An alarm sounded in Hunter's head. *Witness what each alter has to say? What would that mean for the killer who called himself Jason Jonette?* "Do you think that's a good idea? Isn't there another way to purge them without you having to relive...everything from each one's perspective?"

"I know what you're not saying. That's why I wanted to speak to you. I'm going to need your help...when I face Jason Jonette and all that he did. We had no idea what it was going to be like to listen to an alter and have the floodgates opened, but the session with Dr. Heisser and Angel showed me. *Everything.* Afterward, my first concern was what was going to happen when we confronted the alter known as Jason Jonette. I wasn't aware that as the alter spoke and recalled an incident, I would too. I experienced everything that Angel experienced, which means I'll experience everything that Jason experienced."

"Are you sure you want to do that?" Hunter didn't want to imagine what the impact of living through Jason killing another person would have on Cameron. He was worried she'd have a mental breakdown that would rip her from him forever. "I don't want you to rush into anything. And maybe a second opinion isn't such a bad idea. I can find a specialist...fly one in, if I have to. I want to do what will help you heal, not something that may permanently scar you."

Cameron wrapped her hands around his. "Warm hands *and* a warm heart," she said as she studied his anxious expression. "Thanks, but I'm certain this is the way it has to be done if I want to heal. We tried to purge Angel first, but Dr. Heisser realized she's not going anywhere as long as Jason is around, and she perceives a need to protect me. So next session, he's going to hypnotize me, keeping me grounded and in the present, and speak to Jason. And...I know this is a lot to ask, but I was hoping you could be there for moral support. Dr. Heisser said it would be good for me to have someone there who cares about me, and you're it. You're the only person I have who truly cares about me. I want to assure you that it's okay to say no. I completely understand."

Hunter turned his hands over and gripped Cam's, squeezing them gently. "Whatever you need me to do, I will do. If you need me there, I'm there. We will do this together because there is nothing more important to me than your health. Do you know why?"

She slowly shook her head.

"Because I love you. That's all. I love you and I want you free of this place...forever." He pulled her hands up and kissed them, his own eyes moist.

"Thank you, Hunter. I love you too, and your support means everything to me. I could never do this without you." She pushed her seat back, walked around the table as Hunter stood, and they embraced one another as Cameron inhaled deeply, making another memory.

They were breaking the rules, but Hunter didn't care. He leaned down to kiss Cameron, and their lips came together passionately. It only took a moment before the door unlocked behind him and Grey's massive body filled its frame.

"Ahem! That's enough. You two are lucky I was the only one who noticed this nonsense happening, or else I'd have to report it and fill out a shitload of paperwork. Now step apart. *Farther.*"

Hunter smiled at Cameron before glancing over at the angry Grey Turner. "Where's Petey? I thought he was watching us."

"Oh, so that makes it okay to break the rules? You assumed Petey was asleep on the job, so you'd slip in a little play time? No such luck. I forgot—this one scares Petey shitless," Grey said, motioning to Cameron. "He'd rather escort Broadway Joan to the infirmary than deal with Cameron." He shook his head at them, like a bug-eyed bobblehead that was about to blow its top. "Let's go, Hunter. You've had enough visiting today."

Hunter grinned at Grey, enjoying how obviously annoyed he was. "Okay, okay, Grey, don't freak out. We were done anyway." He turned back to Cameron. "Tell me when and I'll be here." He snuck in one last kiss to her forehead and grabbed his coat and messenger bag before Grey could say another word.

"See you soon, Hunter," Cameron called out.

"See you soon, Cameron," he called back as Grey poked him in the back to hurry him along. Hunter was still smiling—until he remembered what was probably going to happen the next time he saw her. They'd both face her alter named Jason Jonette.

CHAPTER 18

Max

WAITING IN THE DOG park, I fidgeted with my grandmother's delicate gold band on my pinky finger. The sensation that something was not quite right was making me anxious. Nash had told me this hunt would differ from the others. He'd take part this time. I'd thought we were finished, since it'd been a month since the last kill. It didn't matter to me. It pleased him, and that's all I cared about.

Nash told me he would slip the sedative into the woman's drink tonight, and he would wait near the giant bird statue that I was now leaning against, and together we would set her free. He insisted she had to be freed and left at the base of the statue. *Her name is Angela, and tonight she becomes an actual angel, right, Max?*

Our days had become routine, and I was getting bored. I loved Nash and wanted to please him, but his obsession with revenge was exhausting. I was ready to move on, for us to become a family, and to get out of here before we were caught.

It was nearly eleven o'clock, and the woman I was waiting for walked by the park every Wednesday night at the same time. Nash said she was a doctor, had a weekly tennis game on the piers, and offered some other random information about her. I hadn't paid close attention when he was speaking, not caring who the woman was or where she was coming from. He always had a photograph of the "soul" I would set free. The good person who deserved to go to paradise sooner rather than later.

I would have had an easier time if they were horrible people like Clara and Wayne, but over the last several months, coached by Nash, I'd become desensitized by what I was doing for him. It was the endgame that mattered: Nash and I leaving this city and being a family somewhere where the weather was warm, and the police wouldn't be looking for me.

A figure appeared heading my way along the sidewalk and I looked around for the telltale signs of police. I figured it'd been so long since the last kill that the police probably thought we were done. Her features came into focus the closer she came to me. It was my soul, Doctor Angela. Satisfied no one was around, I pulled my hood over the back of my head and covered my hair.

I was hard to see in the dark, unmoving in my uniform—black jacket and hoodie, black jeans, boots. The soul I was about to free was oblivious as she approached the dog park. I scanned the area again and saw no one. As Doctor Angela passed the entrance, I attacked from behind a large tree. I grabbed her by the arm. She struggled more than I'd expected her to as I dragged her into the dimly lit park, over to the giant steel bird. She was fighting me when she should have been falling over from the drugs. I gave her a violent shove that should have thrown her on her ass and examined her face as she landed hard against the sculpture. It was the right woman. The drug must not have hit her fully yet.

Where was Nash? He'd said we'd free her together.

There was no time to wait. I yanked the ribbon from my pocket. Stretching it out between my hands, and lunged at her.

It'll be over quickly and tonight Nash will love me enough to end his work and take me away.

As I hurled myself toward the prey, the woman recoiled her arm and smashed a fist into my face. I stumbled backward, wincing at the unexpected strike. Tears blurred my vision as pain imploded in my head. I put my hand to my face, shocked by what had just happened and dizzy from the blunt force that struck me. I felt the warmth of my blood oozing from what I was pretty sure was my broken nose. When I looked at my palm, it was slick with blood.

What the hell? I thought, as I tried my best to remain standing. *This bitch should be falling over from the drugs.* Regaining my composure, I went in for a second strike, but this time the woman's foot met the back of my knee, knocking me off balance, followed by an elbow to the side of my head. Sounds muffled in my ears as I fell to the ground, my head bouncing off the pavement. I was barely conscious as I tried to keep from passing out. I heard Angela's voice. *Is there someone else here?*

"My name is Angela James. I was just attacked in the dog park at the entrance of the Chelsea Piers. Yes... uh, huh... I'm not sure...I think it's a guy. The person has on a black jacket with a hood pulled up. They're face down. I can't see and I don't want to get too close. He dragged me into the park, and I knocked him on his ass. I need police now... no, he's on the ground. It looks like I knocked him out, but he won't be down for long... yes, okay. I hear the sirens. No...I won't touch him. Thank you."

I held my palms to the sides of my skull, struggling to clear my head. Then I understood what people meant when they said they were seeing stars. Hurried footsteps approached like people running and they were getting louder...closer.

A pissed-off German Shepherd appeared out of the darkness, growling and snarling. It grabbed me by the ankle and sunk its teeth into me. I screamed out in pain as I struggled to get away, kicking at it with my free foot. Two men appeared right behind it and seized me by the arms, twisting them behind me roughly and heaving me to my feet. They were shouting at me, but I couldn't focus. The world was blurry, its sounds muted by the ringing in my head. Another man grabbed the dog by the collar and gave it a treat and a pat on the head.

A man about my height, with dark, deep-set eyes and black curly hair, pulled out handcuffs and waved them in front of me before he grabbed my arm. The cold steel clamped down on my wrists. At the waist of the other man, I saw a gold shield and a revolver.

Shit! They're cops.

An angry-looking woman in uniform bent down and, with a gloved hand, picked up the blue ribbon I'd dropped, dangling it in my face. As the effects of the pounding I had just taken wore off, I realized the severity of my situation. I searched the area, frantic for Nash to swoop in and save me. He said he would be close by. He said he'd be watching. Why was he not helping me?

The detectives shoved me along the concrete toward blue and red lights dancing wildly in the night as one of them read me my rights. A spotlight mounted on a police car blinded me, and I tripped, nearly falling on my face. The officer next to me grabbed my elbow, and I winced in pain as he jerked me back upright. The pain was an afterthought as I searched the shadows frantically for Nash.

Where was he? Panic was building. If they got me into a police car, I was doomed. There'd be no rescuing me at that point. And then it hit me—the number of cops and weapons surrounding me, the police dogs sniffing in the bushes, search lights, a helicopter hovered overhead...I was already doomed.

"Murphy, put 'im in that one," a voice called out.

The officer yanking me around by my arm shoved me toward a patrol car, his face a deep red, as a trickle of sweat ran down its side. A brawny cop with a mustache standing next to the car opened the back door and stepped aside, one hand on his gun. As they forced me into the back seat, pressing down on my head, I could see Angela acting out the attack for a group of cops surrounding her.

Angela pointed in my direction, shaking her head, a look of disbelief on her face. I overheard her say, "That's The Chelsea Choker?"

Between the flashing lights and my throbbing face, nausea had taken a grip on me. I surveyed the scene, looking for Nash. A large group of people had gathered to see what had happened, and in that group stood Nash—the collar of his black coat pulled up around his ears and in front of his face, a black baseball cap pulled down to shade his eyes, and his hands clad in black leather gloves. He blended in with the curious bystanders.

I was terrified and wanted to call out to him to rescue me, but I knew he wouldn't help me. He had said getting caught was a possibility. Even though he took extreme measures of caution when sending me out, we'd still prepared for my capture. I just didn't know tonight was the night.

We had practiced it repeatedly and I knew this was the ultimate test for him. He had never said it outright, but it was always there, the implication, just beneath the surface. This would prove my faithfulness and love to him, and he would reward me.

Amidst the surrounding chaos, I sat locked in the back of the cruiser, patiently waiting to catch Nash's eye. Officers shouted to one another as they cordoned the area off, sirens blared occasionally, and onlookers snapped photos and videos with their cellphones. People seemed to run in different directions.

Except for me and Nash. We remained frozen, me staring intently at Nash, and Nash ignoring me, staring at a tall, handsome man with sandy hair who I thought might be Hunter Finnegan. I followed Nash's gaze to where the guy stood with the paramedics treating the hand of Dr. Angela James.

Ha! Good. Maybe my nose broke her hand. But then I had to wonder, w*hy weren't they helping me? I was the one covered in blood.* And then it hit me. Angela should have been unconscious at this point. Nash had never drugged her. He'd set me up.

I didn't know whether I should be pissed or hurt. It felt like both.

I regained my focus on Hunter Finnegan. Nash was sending me a message with his unyielding stare. I knew the vital role Finnegan played. He was the lead detective on the case and he was connected to Nash's "big prize". Nash had shown me his picture and drilled it into me. If I were to get caught and had the opportunity, I would get bonus points for killing him.

Judging by his height and size, it wouldn't be easy for me to get the jump on him, but nothing was impossible.

CHAPTER 19

Max

"Let's start with your name. Okay?" Detective Glen Levine sat across from Max in Interrogation Room Three, his bald head shiny under the fluorescent lights.

"I...I don't remember. I hit my head on the ground really hard when that woman attacked me. Have you arrested her? I didn't see her anywhere when the policeman brought me here."

Hunter entered the room carrying a manila folder. "Got it." He put it in front of Levine and opened it.

"Maxine Jane Hoyt," Levine read out loud. He moved the top page to the side, revealing a Missing Persons bulletin with Max's photo front and center.

"People are looking for you, Maxine," Hunter said. "Apparently, it's feared that you were the victim of a home invasion."

"A home invasion? I... I don't think so... I don't remember," she said, wiping a tear from her cheek. "I need some water. Can I have some water, please?"

Levine tapped his pen on the table and nodded. "Sure, Maxine, we'll get you some water, and we're going to get to know each other very well. Even if it takes all night."

"Aren't you going to take me to the hospital? I think that woman broke my nose," Max said, barely touching the newly protruding lump on her nose.

Hunter stood to get her water. "Yep, it looks broken to me, but no, you're not going to the hospital. When you get to prison, the doctor there will examine it."

Levine added, "The sooner you answer our questions, the sooner a doctor can check it. I imagine it must be painful. The doctor can give you something for the pain, too. We're not even authorized to give you aspirin."

Nash had warned Max the police would try every trick to get her to slip up. They had practiced multiple scenarios, including this one, where they attempted to piss her off.

Hunter came back with a bottle of water. He handed the warm bottle to Max, who gulped a few mouthfuls and wiped her lips with her sleeve.

"Let me start with the list of charges against you," Levine said. "First-degree murder in the deaths of five women, assault and battery, stalking, illicit use of a controlled substance. I'm sure the D.A. will come up with a few more. You're looking at several lifetimes in jail. Too bad—someone as young as you. And those are just the charges here. I think the police in your hometown may have a different take on your parents' deaths when they hear what we charged you with."

"Wait. What? I haven't hurt anyone. And what did you just say? My parents are dead? Nooo... I don't remember them. Please, officers, I need help." Max gasped, tears springing to her eyes. She was an expert at crying on cue. "I...I don't know why you're saying these things."

Hunter and Levine exchanged looks.

"Maxine, we caught you red-handed tonight. Your calling card, the blue ribbon, was on the ground next to you. You grabbed Angela James and dragged her into the dog park. She's already given a full statement to the sergeant."

"That wasn't my ribbon. The woman who broke my nose, she dropped it. She dragged me, not the other way around. She forced me into the dog park, and then she beat me. Then she took a ribbon out of her pocket and unrolled it, told me I was about to die. What the hell?"

Hunter dragged his fingers through his hair, shaking his head. "Maxine, lying to the police is a felony and will only hurt you in the end. If you admit to what you've done, the D.A. may go easier on you."

"But I haven't done anything," she sobbed. "I was just walking to the bus stop when that crazy lady jumped me. And now I have a broken nose. I'm covered in blood and you're accusing me of hurting her? And you said something about five women being murdered?"

"That's right," Levine said, calmly. "We have pictures, video, and eyewitnesses to prove that you are The Chelsea Choker."

"The what?" Max laughed out loud. The nickname had always cracked her up.

Detective Bobby Murphy opened the door, laptop in hand. Max recognized him as the sweaty cop who had shoved her into the back of the police car. "We have the camera footage from tonight." He placed the open laptop on the table where everyone could see the screen and pressed the enter button. Two videos played side-by-side. One showed a woman walking down the sidewalk toward the dog park. On the other, Maxine stood unraveling a blue ribbon.

"Wow, these videos are really clear," Hunter said.

"Yeah, we installed state-of-art, high-definition cameras with night vision all around the entrance to the piers. The pattern of the killings suggested that was where the next murder would take place. We were staked out in that area. I was only about fifty yards away when Dr. James called nine one one."

The pattern of the killings. There was a pattern? It was news to Max.

Hunter, Levine, Murphy, and Max watched the screen as Max clearly grabbed Angela James and shoved her into the dog park. Max cringed at the moment Angela broke her nose and then elbowed her in the head with enough force to knock her down, the ribbon released from her hand, floating to the ground next to her. Reflexively, she touched the fractured bone of her nose with her finger.

Crap. That video was clear, Max thought. *The cops were waiting. They knew where I'd strike next. But how?*

Max realized it was time to change strategies and bring on the crazy. Nash had gone over the tactic of innocence by insanity.

"Should the police out-maneuver us, which they won't, but if they do, and you're caught, this is how I want you to proceed—act crazy."

"Act crazy? What does that even mean?"

"When you're taken to the police station, you'll lie at first, of course, proclaim your innocence. Loud and clear. If you can't convince them, you'll have to change your approach. Be careful what you say, though. They'll try their best to entrap you. When things get serious, I want you to pretend to be insane. Just go for it. Act out. Act up. Tell them an evil cat made you do it. Do whatever you have to do to make them think you're crazy."

Max looked at the empty chair next to her and said, "Wow, that is clear. Did you see that? Who would've thought you could get such a good video at night?" She nodded her head as if agreeing with something. "I know, right? Cameras today are so much more advanced." And then she let out a raucous laugh, slammed her palm on the table and doubled over. "Stop, please stop. You're killing me. Oh, my nose. It hurts...it hurts."

She looked at the officers, who stared at her, unmoved. "You don't think that's funny? Come on...he's hilarious."

"Who's hilarious?" Levine asked.

"Nash. Duh?" She looked at the chair, shaking her head. "They don't think you're funny, babe."

Hunter asked, "Who's Nash?"

Max motioned to the empty chair. "This is Nash."

"You named the chair Nash?" Hunter said, squinting at the chair.

"What?" Max tilted her head to one side. "Why would I name a chair? I'm talking about the handsome devil in the chair, my boyfriend, Nash. Geez, he's a little slow, huh?" she asked, eyes darting between Levine and Murphy.

"We're not playing this game, Maxine," Hunter said, staring her down. "You're going to prison based just on this video, whether you confess or not. But I'm warning you, if you don't cooperate with us, things will be much worse for you in court."

"Game? What game?" She looked at the empty space next to her again. "What's he talking about?" She shrugged, nodded her head and added, "Ohhhh, he thinks we're playing a game?" Max looked back to Hunter. "No games, officer. We'll cooperate."

"How many women have you killed?" Levine said.

"Killed?" Max looked again to the vacant chair, shaking her head, and back to Levine. "We didn't kill anyone. No, no, no."

Hunter leaned in toward Max. "I thought you were going to cooperate? Detective Levine asked a question. How many women have you killed? Now answer him before I tire of this crap."

"We didn't kill anyone. We freed them. Freed from these decaying bodies that hold us prisoner on Earth. Right, Nash?" Max glanced to her side again. "Yeah, that's what life is, you know, a prison sentence. Whatever we have done wrong in the other world determines how many years we get here on Earth, trapped in these bodies that hold us here. And if our crimes were especially bad, then we suffer here; disease, broken bodies, heartache. Those beautiful women we set free, they've gone home, they're back in paradise because of us."

"How many women have you set free?" Hunter asked.

"Five beautiful souls are in paradise, thanks to us." She paused and looked at the emptiness next to her. "Oh, that's true."

"What's true?" Levine said.

"What Nash just said." Max studied the scowl on the bald man's face. His complexion had reddened since he'd first sat across from her, a telltale sign she was aggravating him.

Hunter slammed a large hand on the table, startling Max. "What did Nash say?"

"Aren't you paying attention? He said it would have been six, except Dr. James, *Angela,*"—Max giggled—"wasn't lucky tonight." She was enjoying tormenting the detectives more than she had expected.

Hunter asked, "Where did you get the ketamine?"

"Ask Nash—he gets it and gives it to me."

Levine asked, "Why these women?"

Max shrugged. "Nash picks them, but then he likes to watch…"

"What does Nash look like?" Levine said.

"He looks like this," Max said, pointing a thumb at the empty seat next to her.

"I'd like to hear how you'd describe him, so I'm sure we see him in the same way."

"He's very handsome." She paused and again looked to her right and the invisible man. "Yes, you are babe! You're *very* handsome with your wavy, chocolate-brown hair that begs me to play with it; and gorgeous eyes that bore into my soul; that chiseled face and the most sophisticated salt and pepper goatee. And you're lean, not skinny. *Sexy*." She giggled again.

Murphy shook his head. "This is bullshit."

Hunter added, "Look Maxine, based on the video surveillance we have of you, you're going to jail. This imaginary friend of yours won't help your case." He stood and leaned down on the table, his long body crossing over it so his face was only about a foot from hers. "You start talking or I'll make sure you suffer the same way Clara and Wayne Meyers did."

Max realized it was time to really pour on the crazy and she also saw an opportunity she likely wouldn't get again.

She stared up at Hunter, a vacant expression on her face. "Clara," she whispered, and her left eye twitched. She eyed his Adam's apple, ripe for the plucking.

She whispered again, in a trance-like state, "Clara." Her eye twitched again.

"Clara." Twitch.

Max suddenly lunged at Hunter's throat, grabbing onto it, squeezing, and digging her nails in and around his trachea as she pressed her other hand against the back of his neck, pulling him toward her. She had him in a vice-like grip as she put her face to his. "Nash says hello." Hunter yanked himself free, gagging and falling to his knees.

Murphy tackled her with pleasure, landed on top of her and slammed her in the face with a fist, breaking her nose again. Blood streamed down her cheeks. She cackled and howled as she sang, "I picked an apple. I picked an apple. But it wasn't Adam's...It was a Hunter's. I picked an apple. I picked an apple..."

Hunter gasped for air as he wrapped his hands around his neck.

Chief Dwyer and Barone, who were watching from the next room, ran in and helped Murphy restrain Max. Levine hauled Hunter to his feet as he choked and rushed him, gasping for air, from the room and down the hallway.

Levine shouted, "Rhonda. I need help—Hunter's hurt. We need to get him to the hospital."

She ran to them, grabbed Hunter's arm, and wrapped it around her shoulder. Another officer at a nearby desk also ran to help. The three of them assisted a towering and now weak-kneed Hunter down the stairs as he wheezed, unable to get air past his swelling larynx. They dragged him to an SUV, putting him in the back with Rhonda. Levine jumped behind the wheel, the truck's tires screeching as he pulled away, rushing for the hospital.

CHAPTER 20

Levine

BY THE TIME THEY arrived at the hospital, Hunter was barely conscious, and his breathing became shallow as the tissues in his throat swelled, blocking his airway. Emergency room doctors and nurses converged on him. Levine had called ahead to expect them as Rhonda Saintil tried to comfort Hunter. He was turning blue, a sign that the injury was severe.

"What happened?" A middle-aged female doctor in green scrubs demanded from Levine.

"A prisoner attacked him—she grabbed his throat and yanked it."

The doctor palpated Hunter's throat. Fine lines of blood marred his neck where Max's nails had dug in, breaking the skin. Horizontal scratch marks showed the direction her nails pulled out. She put a stethoscope to his chest and listened for breath sounds.

"We need to trach him." A nurse was way ahead of her and had the kit ready. "He needs a CT." The nurse nodded. "Officers, please clear the room...we need to work here," the doctor said, as she administered a sedative to Hunter.

"Okay, but keep us posted. We'll wait right outside," a worried Levine said. "You're going to be okay, Hunter. You hold tight."

Levine and Saintil retreated to a spot near the nurse's station, where they could monitor the activity surrounding Hunter.

"What the hell happened?" Saintil said, looking in the direction of Hunter's room.

"We were interrogating Maxine Hoyt. Hunter leaned over the table when he was talking to her. She was acting crazy, talking to an invisible boyfriend. Hunter mentioned her mother's name, and she got even weirder. She kept whispering her name, and she had this tic," Levine said, pointing to his eye.

"Yeah, and then?"

"And then she lunged at him, grabbed him by the throat, and he dropped to the floor. I could tell right away he was in trouble. He was... gurgling...trying to get air in," Levine said, rubbing his bald head. "Jesus...did you see him? He was blue."

"Yeah, I noticed. He'll be okay. Right?"

"I hope so. I've never seen Hunter like that... so weak and..." Levine shook his head.

"Do you think Maxine was faking it, or is she really a nut job?"

"I thought she was putting on an act, right until she started repeating her mother's name and the facial tic kicked in. It was eerie. She looked all spaced out. I thought Hunter hit a nerve when he mentioned Clara and Wayne Meyers, but the way she reacted... and then, after she attacked Hunter, Murphy tackled her and gave her another shot to the face. Maxine was lying on the floor. Blood was running out of her nose, and she was laughing. But not a normal laugh—a deranged cackle. And then she started singing."

"Singing? What the hell do you mean? What was she singing?"

"I don't know—something about picking apples. It happened so fast, and all I could think about was Hunter not being able to breathe. I ignored her and rushed him out of there."

"Dwyer is here." Saintil nodded in the chief's direction.

"You keep an eye on Hunter's room while I talk to Dwyer."

Levine walked over to the chief, who was on his cell phone. He stood nearby, waiting for him to finish the call.

When Dwyer ended the call a few minutes later, he made eye contact with Levine. "How's Hunter doing? Everything okay?"

"No, everything's not okay. The doctor said they would have to trach him. He was blue when we got him here and barely breathing. I'm not sure what's happening in there. People are flying in and out. Saintil and I have been waiting for an update."

Dwyer said, "I'll see what I can find out." He patted Levine on the shoulder and walked towards ER 21, where a team of medical professionals worked frantically on Hunter Finnegan. Levine followed.

Dwyer stuck his head in the room, not wanting to get in anyone's way. "I'm Chief Dwyer. You have one of our best detectives there, Hunter Finnegan. Can you tell me what's happening?"

A petite woman in scrubs with short salt and pepper curls stood next to Hunter and replied, "I'm Dr. Katz. I'll be with you after we've stabilized Detective Finnegan."

"Yeah, okay," Dwyer said, backing up a step or two. He looked at his colleague and lately the bane of his existence, lifeless on the gurney, a new tracheostomy tube inserted into his neck. A hint of blood framed his mouth, and his color was pale, no longer blue. Dwyer felt the stress gnawing away at his gut. He had his clashes with Hunter, but he'd never wished him physical harm. He was a good cop, and Dwyer supposed, a good guy. He noticed Dr. Katz remove her gloves and knew she was coming out to speak to him. Motioning to Levine, they retreated to where Saintil stood, waiting for news.

Dr. Katz approached the threesome. "I'm Dr. Katz," she told Levine and Saintil. "We have Hunter stabilized. We put in a tracheostomy tube so he can breathe now. You said a prisoner attacked him?" She directed the question at Levine.

"Yes, during an interrogation. The suspect grabbed his throat and pulled hard. Hunter went down immediately, gasping for air."

"He's lucky to be alive," Katz said, meeting each of their eyes consecutively. "His attacker could have severely damaged the larynx and torn the vocal cords, causing him to bleed out. Hunter is going for a CAT scan now and then he'll have a laryngoscopy to further explore the damage. The surgeon will make any repairs. He has a group two, possibly three, fractured larynx. There's a lot of swelling, which is why he was having trouble breathing."

Dwyer needed the bottom line. "Is he going to be okay?"

"He should make a full recovery. He won't be able to speak for a few days and will need bed rest. The O.R. is being prepped and we'll admit him after the laryngoscopy."

"What about the trach?" Levine asked, unconsciously rubbing his own neck.

"We'll remove it once the swelling is gone. It may need a stitch or two, but most of the time, tracheostomies heal on their own. Any other questions?"

"How long will he be laid up?" Dwyer asked.

"I would say three to four days here. And then a few days at home. He shouldn't push his recovery, though. We don't want to risk permanent damage to his larynx. An orderly will direct you to a waiting room, if you want to hang around until after surgery."

"Thanks Dr. Katz," Dwyer said.

Levine shook his head, hands on his hips, the sleeves of his dress shirt rolled up, a blood stain on his shoulder from where Hunter's head had rested as they'd rushed him from the precinct. "I'll stay here and wait for Hunter to get out of surgery. I'll give his sister a call and fill her in on what's happened."

Dwyer's cell phone buzzed. "It's the commissioner. I have to take this," he said, as he started for the exit. "I'll meet you in the waiting room."

Levine gave him a nod and turned his attention to Saintil. "Do you want to stay or head back?"

"I'm glad to hear Hunter is going to be okay, but I really need to head home." She checked the time on her phone: 2:37 a.m. "Unless you want me to hang out or I'm needed at the station?"

"No. I'm sure Murphy and Barone have Maxine Hoyt under control. You go home, get some sleep. Tomorrow will be a long day."

"Thanks. I'll see you later."

Levine nodded. "Good night."

He watched as Saintil exited the hospital. A few seconds later, the ER team wheeled Hunter out into the hallway on a gurney, headed for the CAT scan.

Levine's keen eyes missed nothing—Hunter's feet hanging off the end of the stretcher, the white hospital blanket covering him up to the waist, the paleness of his skin, the bags of fluid connected to tubes going into Hunter's arm and the trach tube inserted in his throat.

How the hell did this happen? He had never had an interrogation go so wrong. And never had one where a cop ended up in the ER.

He heard familiar voices behind him. It was Murphy and Barone, walking ahead of a gurney and a couple of EMTs.

"What are you two doing here?" Levine asked.

Barone answered, "We had to bring Maxine in." He stepped to the side so Levine could see Maxine Hoyt sitting up, one hand cuffed to the gurney, the other holding an ice pack to her face. "The commissioner suggested it," he said, using air quotes. "The department can't afford any lawsuits or any claims of impropriety that could hurt the case. So, we have to have her face checked, you know, to see if anything is broken besides her brain."

Maxine lowered the ice pack, revealing her twisted, broken nose, and her glazed over, black and blue eyes. When she spotted Levine, she whispered, "Clara," and twitched an eye. Then she quietly sang again, "I picked an apple, I picked an apple..."

"Okay, Maxine, keep the ice pack on the face," an EMT said, bringing her hand with the ice pack back up to her face and holding it there.

Max pushed his hand away, her eyes wide as she screamed at Levine, "I picked an apple!" She laughed wildly, kicking her feet up and down and banging her head on the back of the stretcher. "I picked an apple!"

Levine was speechless as the EMTs rolled her away.

"I'm calling bullshit," Murphy said, anger turning his face red. "I bet that bitch is saner than any of us."

Levine couldn't help but wonder, *Is she?*

CHAPTER 21

Cameron

TEN DAYS AFTER MAX attacked Hunter, he was ready to visit Cameron. The doctor had removed the trach as the swelling decreased, and a fresh scar graced the base of his neck. Cameron gasped when he walked into the room. He had lost weight since the last time she had seen him, which was less than two weeks ago, and he looked gaunt and pale.

She'd expected to hear from Hunter the night the police staked out the piers, waiting for The Choker to attack his next victim, and when she hadn't heard from him, she worried that something had gone wrong. The next morning when John Mercedes came to her room and told her she had a visitor, relief swept through her, but when she went to the conference room and found Levine waiting and not Hunter, she'd nearly collapsed, certain Hunter was dead.

"Oh my God, Hunter!" she said, wrapping her arms around him, hugging him tightly to her. "Levine told me what happened. I've been out of my mind worried about you." She took a step back to examine his neck, which was still bruised. "Are you okay? Come here, sit down," she said, pulling a chair out for him. She sat down next to him, gripping his hand.

"I'm fine." Hunter's voice was a hoarse whisper. "I can't talk too much or too loud." He shrugged and squeezed Cam's hand. "I knew you had to see me for yourself...so here I am." He gave her a small reassuring smile. "Tell me about you. How are you?"

Cam shook her head and let out a deep sigh. "Better now. I've been so worried about you. I couldn't think about anything else. Levine told me you caught The Chelsea Choker, Maxine Jane Hoyt, and she did this to you?"

Hunter nodded. "She's a peach. At least she's off the streets. You?"

"Ok, Ok." She could see how exhausted he was and noticed the pain in his face when he spoke. "Um, well, let's see. What's new here at St. C's?"

"My sessions with Dr. Heisser have been going really well. We've postponed the hypnosis session to address the Jason alter. I wasn't up to it when you were injured, and of course, I wanted you there," she said, glancing at the scar and bruises on Hunter's neck.

She averted her eyes and continued. "I had another breakthrough though, which is good news... I guess. Dr. Heisser is pretty certain he has pinpointed when the alter who calls herself Charlotte Montgomery surfaced. It was when my mother died, which was when I was in college. I've avoided telling you too much about my past, mostly because it's painful and there's not a lot to tell, except the painful parts. I don't want to bore you."

Hunter held up a hand to stop her. "You could never bore me. I want to hear everything. And since I shouldn't be talking, you have the floor."

"Okay, you asked for it. As you know, I grew up just outside of Savannah, in a small town. It was just me and my mom. Are you sure you're okay?" She examined Hunter's face, looking for signs of pain. He nodded and grasped her hands between his. Cameron continued. "My parents were never married. My mother had me when she was only seventeen and her parents disowned her the minute they found out she was pregnant. She left home and never tried to go back. Anyway, it was tough for us. We never had enough money, and unfortunately, my mother had terrible taste in men. She attracted the rough ones. She married my stepfather, Kurt Duprée. You remember how that story ended, I'm sure. Mother shot him to death...to save me. It was during that time the alter known as Angel appeared."

Hunter shook his head and whispered, "It wasn't your fault. She did what she did for both of you. She made the right decision."

Cameron nodded. "She was a brave woman. We moved to another small town after that, and that was when she started calling me Cameron instead of Angela, mostly to protect my identity from the other parents. I started a new school, and everything was okay. Until I got to high school. Kids can be mean and they were. I didn't have nice shoes or nice clothes. But I had smarts. My grades were the only thing I had control over. I studied my ass off and was the salutatorian of my class. I told you I went to the University of Georgia, but I didn't mention it was on a merit scholarship."

"Good for you," Hunter said. "Smart and hard-working... not just beautiful."

"Thanks," Cam blushed slightly. "When I was a senior in college, I lived in the dorm as a resident assistant. It helped with bills because I received room and board as compensation, plus a small stipend. I was in my room one night when the campus minister and a police officer came to my room. I had no idea that something was wrong.

I learned the hard way if a cop and a priest knock on your door, it's not for tea and cookies. They told me my mother was in a terrible accident. A drunk driver pulled onto a highway into oncoming traffic and hit my mother's car head-on. She died instantly." A tear escaped, and Cam brusquely wiped it away with a finger.

"I'm so sorry, Cam," Hunter whispered.

"She was all I had in the world. I could feel myself spiraling out of control. It felt as though I were free-falling in slow-motion. I passed out, and the officer called for an ambulance. The officer told the ER doctor that when I came to, I was calm and matter-of-fact. Like a different person. Like a switch flipped, and I was no longer hysterical over my mother's death. It was all recorded in my chart. I have no memory of going to that hospital. I woke up the next day in my own bed wondering where the priest and the cop had gone."

"Charlotte Montgomery?"

"Yes. Charlotte emerged. My mother's death had no effect on her. In her mind, her parents were alive and well. She came from a beautiful, wealthy family. She was a debutante who lived in a mansion, and excelled at everything...school, work, family. Her world was the exact opposite of mine."

"Wow—that is incredible. How did Dr. Heisser discover this?"

"Hypnosis. Heisser coaxed her out, and they had a lengthy chat. He suspected that my mind fractured again when my mother died tragically. Dr. Heisser asked Charlotte if she attended the University of Georgia. She told him no, but she confirmed she found herself in a dorm room there once and didn't know how she had gotten there. He called the hospital and had my charts sent here. It all made sense after that."

"Jesus, Cameron, you certainly had a rough time growing up. I'm amazed by how much you've accomplished."

"Life gave me no choice," Cam said with a shrug. "I only had myself to rely on. My mother's parents came to her funeral. I'd never met them before. When they introduced themselves, I was shocked and didn't know what to say to them. They explained they'd made a big mistake turning their backs on her and had regretted the decision, especially after seeing how well I turned out. Can you imagine?

"They were wealthy people who lived in a mansion in Savannah. My grandfather had on a beautiful suit and my grandmother had on gorgeous pieces of jewelry. They wanted to get to know me, since I was their only grandchild. I looked at them, fat in their expensive clothes and fancy jewelry, and became so angry. I told them there were times when we didn't have enough money for food and on chilly nights we slept together, keeping each other warm because there was no heat. I wore hand-me-downs from the neighbors' children and the *only* reason I turned out so well was because I had a wonderful mother who would never have abandoned me!

"And then I told them they weren't my family. They were only the people who left my mother pregnant and alone when she needed them the most. And I walked away."

"I don't blame you," Hunter said, gently squeezing her hand between his. "Come here." He pulled her close to him and held her, rubbing her back.

Cam sat back, still holding Hunter's hand. "Dr. Heisser has been helping me work through that time in my life. I'm learning how to process my mother's death in a healthy way. Hopefully, we've seen the last of Charlotte Montgomery."

A knock on the door interrupted their conversation, and Grey Turner opened the door for Glen Levine.

"Cameron," Levine said with a nod. "I wanted to give you and Hunter a few minutes, but time is up. We need to get back to work." He looked back and forth between them as he pulled out a chair. "We need to discuss Maxine Jane Hoyt."

Hunter gave Cam a wink and reluctantly set her hand free.

"Detective, always good to see you. And I can't wait to hear what you have to say about Maxine."

"Since Hunter shouldn't be overly exerting his larynx, I'll do all the talking," Levine said, propping a pair of frameless reading glasses on the tip of his nose. He opened a thin manila folder and picked up the first page for Cam to see—a photo of Maxine. "This is The Chelsea Choker, aka Maxine Jane Hoyt. We captured her just inside the entrance to the piers when she attacked a woman who got the best of her. The victim's name is Angela James. When Maxine grabbed her, Angela laid her out with a right hook to the face and called nine one one. Murphy was fifty yards away and was the first one to arrive at the scene. Maxine had a blue ribbon in her possession that matches the ribbons used in all the Choker cases."

Cam examined the photo of Max. She was young, barely twenty, with dirty blonde hair, lifeless brown eyes encircled with purple and yellow bruising from an obviously broken nose, and a tight, thin-lipped smirk. It was her expression that struck Cameron—she felt as though Max was looking right into her own eyes with greedy pleasure.

"Did she confess?"

"Ha! She did everything but confess. She put on a real show. First, she acted like she was talking to the invisible man in the seat next to her. Then, when we confronted her about the deaths of her parents—"

"Her parents?" Cam interrupted. "How did they die?"

"Technically, it's her mother and stepfather." Levine flipped a page. "Here it is...Clara and Wayne Meyers. We have a report from Pennsylvania about a couple found murdered in their home and a missing person's report on the woman's daughter...one Maxine Jane Hoyt. Apparently, they had just cashed out a life insurance policy for Clara's mother, who died in her sleep at a nursing home. Twenty-five thousand dollars. The money and Maxine were nowhere to be found, and Wayne and Clara were dead...Clara was unrecognizable.

"Maxine allegedly took an ax to them and then threw the ax into the fireplace, destroying the murder weapon. When Hunter mentioned Clara to her, that's when things got really bizarre. Her eye started twitching, and she repeated the word Clara over and over. Then she attacked Hunter. Murphy calls bullshit on the whole thing. He thinks it's an act and I agreed. At first...but now I'm not so sure."

"Why? What is it that makes you doubt her sanity?"

"Everything. Everything about this girl is off. She's what, twenty? Instead of going to parties and dating, she's killing other women? And then the whole invisible man thing, and after she attacked Hunter, she was singing and...and cackling."

"Cackling?" Cam looked at Hunter and back to Levine with raised brows. "What do you mean—cackling? Like a witch?" Cam scoffed.

"Yeah. That's right. You weren't there—and I say she was cackling like a fucking witch!"

Cam looked at Hunter for his reaction. He shrugged. "I don't remember. I was too busy trying to breathe."

"Geez, I'd love to have a conversation with her." Cam held up a hand. "I know that's not possible, but it would be interesting."

"Actually, it is possible," Levine replied.

"What?"

"Maxine is being sent here. Today. Until the court sets her trial date. To be examined under the careful watch of Dr. Heisser and company... and you."

Cam looked at Hunter again. He nodded to Levine, saving his voice.

"We want you to interact with her. Make friends, win her trust and see if she screws up. Reveals something she shouldn't." Levine tapped the folder impatiently. "We need you. You have an upper hand as an established patient. She may know who you are and will hopefully find a kinship with another—" He broke off, leaving an awkward silence in the room.

Cam stared him down. She was nothing like Maxine Hoyt, who most likely killed for pleasure. Levine was unmoved. She understood he needed her, but didn't have to like her or respect her.

Cam broke the silence. "I just want to point out, one more time, that *I* am not a serial killer, even though I take responsibility for my subconscious actions. *I* would never hurt an innocent person, especially for pleasure or thrills or any other reason."

Levine ignored her. "So whaddya say? Are you up for a little undercover work?"

"You can do it," Hunter whispered.

She looked at Hunter, his handsome face haggard from the ordeal Maxine had put him through. Cam didn't want to disappoint

Hunter, and not-so-deep down, she wanted revenge. "Fine, I'll cozy up to Maxine and see what I uncover. But that means I'll need access to her. They can't sequester her. She needs to be out with the general population, which could be dangerous."

"I think you can handle yourself," Levine said with a stone-cold expression. "You're former FBI. She's just a kid."

"What if I need help? Will the guards know what we're up to?"

"No." Levine snatched Max's photo and put it back into the file. "We can't chance anybody tipping her off to what we're doing or your involvement. It needs to be business as usual around here, or Max will get spooked. We want you to interact with a relaxed and overly-confident Maxine Hoyt."

Levine stood, motioning to the eyes behind the camera that he was ready to leave. "Your mission is to determine if Maxine is indeed crazy or a cold-blooded killer. And to determine if there are any more bodies we need to find *and* if she has an accomplice. Good luck, Cameron. You have your work cut out for you with this one."

Hunter remained seated. When Grey Turner unlocked the door, Hunter motioned for Levine to go ahead. "I'll be along in a minute. Meet you in the lobby." Levine nodded and walked on. "Just a minute, Grey, okay?"

Grey gave Hunter a nod. "Take your time. I'll loiter in the hallway, minding my own business."

Hunter smiled slightly. "He's a good guy, isn't he?"

"Yes, one of the best here. I'm a little worried about this. What if it's too much too soon? Searching for information on a laptop and looking through files differs greatly from a face-to-face with an accused serial killer. What if the stress causes me to... regress?"

He took her hand in his. "If it's too much, you tell me. We'll find another way. Nothing is more important to me than your health."

Cam felt a slight relief in his words. She knew he meant it, but she didn't want to let him down. She also knew if she could break Maxine, it would help her going forward. "Okay. I'll do my best to take Max under my wing. I hope she's the talkative type."

Hunter stood, pulling Cam up and into the warmth of his embrace. He kissed her on the forehead. "Don't listen to Levine. You're not alone. John Mercedes and Dr. Heisser are both aware of the plan. You can turn to them if you need help. Be safe."

She was eye level with the healing incision at the base of his throat. *The bitch will pay for that.* She looked up into his tired eyes. "You, too."

Forgetting himself and where they were, he kissed her on the mouth with a tenderness and intimacy that made Cam melt into him, pressing her body to his and wishing for more.

Grey Turner cleared his throat as he stood in the doorway. "You're going to get me in trouble, kids."

Hunter and Cameron hugged tightly before he turned for the door. "Call me if you need me."

"I will," she said, following him into the hallway. They parted in opposite directions as Hunter headed out into the free world and Cameron went back to the bleached white room and barred windows of her daily existence.

CHAPTER 22

Cameron

CAMERON PACED THE FLOOR in her small room until she could no longer take the anxiety of anticipation. She needed to get her mind off Maxine Jane Hoyt's arrival.

She followed the blue linoleum in the hallway past the common room, where many of the patients were currently playing games and watching television, and headed down to the cafeteria. It was too late for lunch and too early for dinner, but the staff would be in the kitchen prepping the evening meal. She had befriended them, preferring the conversation of those who had access to the outside world and all its wonders and troubles to those incarcerated for being—well—like her.

Sometimes she would sit at one of the small Formica-clad tables reading a book or writing in a journal Dr. Heisser had given her. A younger woman named Dannisha had approached her one day with a cup of cooled tea. "It's not too hot," Dannisha said. "I don't want you to hurt yourself."

"Thank you." Cameron appreciated the gesture. "I'm Cameron," she'd said, holding out a hand.

"Dannisha." She looked around cautiously as she lightly shook Cam's hand, but seemed a little afraid of her. The kitchen staff wasn't supposed to come out into the open, but Cameron had noticed Danisha watching her and assumed curiosity had gotten the best of her when she finally approached Cam and said, "I see you in here a lot. What are you doing?"

"Writing in my journal. Dr. Heisser said it's a good way for me to work through…" She was about to say "the voices in my head," but instead said, "my feelings."

Dannisha nodded. "Sounds reasonable. You're not like the other patients, are you?"

"I'm not as loud, that's for sure," Cam said with a sigh before she took a sip of her tea. "I suppose I stand out in this group. I think I'm a bit more in control these days. We have different problems—the other patients and me. And since I'm a psychologist, I think I have a better understanding of what I need to do to get well. That's all I care about…getting well."

"Well, good luck to you, Cameron. I hope you do get well and get out of here someday."

After that day, Cameron and Dannisha had slowly begun to form a friendship of sorts. They'd kept the conversations superficial—the weather, the meal of the day, and the like. They both loved to read and would often discuss the current books they were enjoying. Dannisha's seal of approval was all the other employees needed to treat Cameron with a little respect and a lot of kindness.

Cam sat down at her favorite spot—a square table next to an iron-barred window. From that spot on the ninth floor, the world sprawled out in all its majesty, just beyond her reach. She could see the expanse of the park that the hospital oddly sat in, and the fat, inky East River, which separated her prison home on an island from the rest of the city.

In the fall, she watched as the leaves turned from green to rust and red, yellow, and orange—one last act of beauty in their doomed lives before they floated down and covered the ground in a multicolored quilt. The sun was lower on the skyline now, casting a golden hue on the world below, reminding her shorter days were on the horizon. Sometimes, she would spot a soccer game taking place at the far end of the island, beyond the chain-and-barbed-wire perimeter fence that kept her and her roommates in and the rest of the world out.

And the city. She had the perfect view of the Upper East Side and its towering buildings, guardians standing strong and tall, shielding the smaller buildings and their occupants against the wind, rain, snow and terrors of the impending night. She longed to wander the streets and avenues again, to dine alfresco on a warm summer's night, and to stroll through Central Park with Hunter at her side.

Dannisha sat down across from Cam, breaking the spell of her daydream of Hunter and freedom. She placed the usual cup of warmish tea on the table in front of Cameron before she dug into her apron pocket and produced two warm chocolate chip cookies wrapped in a paper napkin.

"I heard the cops were here today talking to you and thought you could use some medicinal sweets," she said, smiling. "What did they want? Were they harassing you?"

"Thank you!" Cam beamed. The cookies at St. C's were unexpectedly delicious, and Cam loved a good cookie with her tea. "They were just asking me more of the same. They're waiting for me to become 'normal,'" she said, using air quotes around the word, "so they can send me to a real prison," she lied.

"Is that a possibility? You transferred outta here and into an actual *prison* prison?"

"Yes, of course. The judge ruled if and when I'm deemed sane enough to stand trial, I would. Which would mean a maximum-security prison. No more reading books in the caf at my leisure." Cameron shrugged, biting into a warm cookie. "Mm-mm, that is good."

"Wow, I had no idea. Is that what you want? To be, you know, declared sane, so you can go onto max and get on with this?"

"No. No way." Cam waved a hand, as if to brush the idea away. "What I want is to get better. And to prove I was not culpable of the crimes committed. It may have been my hand holding the knife, but it wasn't my conscious mind committing the crime. Dr. Heisser and I are working on purging the alternate personalities — the alters, so the only one left is me." She paused at Dannisha's confused expression. "I'm diagnosed with dissociative identity disorder."

Dannisha's eyes had grown wide. "Uh-huh..."

"It means multiple personality. I have voices in my head that have minds of their own. I can only hear one of them clearly, though. A child named Angel. She's my guardian. She warns and protects me when there is danger. It's complicated. There's no reason for you to be afraid, though, Dannisha, okay? I would never hurt you."

"You wouldn't, but what about whoever else is roaming around in there?" She pointed at Cameron's head. "And how do you know that you're you? And not an *alter*? That you're really the one who was here first?"

Cam laughed out loud at the premise, but halted when she caught Dannisha's concerned look. "Don't worry. I'm the original."

"Isn't that what the others would say? That *they're* the original?" Dannisha forced a smile. "Okay...well I should get back to work." She rose from the chair, watching Cam over her shoulder as she walked away.

Cam sipped her tea and relished the last morsels of her cookie. She smiled to herself, thinking about Dannisha's question: What if she was an alter? *What if I am? I guess Dr. Heisser will purge me and I'll never know*, she surmised.

A ruckus in the hall brought Cam out of her thoughts. Dannisha and the cookies had distracted Cam from the impending arrival of Maxine Jane Hoyt.

She's here. Loud voices and a shrill laugh traveled the length of the hallway and into the cafeteria, as if they were meant to penetrate directly into her ears. She approached the doorway with caution, moving her head just enough so that she could peek out to see what was happening.

At the far end of the corridor, the guards struggled with a young woman who Cam recognized from the mug shot Levine had shown her. Maxine was tall and slender; her dull hair swung across her face as she thrashed against the guards' grip.

"Calm down or we'll sedate you," Grey Turner commanded.

"No. Nooo. Don't put me in there. There's a monster! Don't you see him?" She screamed as they dragged her into an unoccupied room.

Grey's baritone voice warned Maxine again. "I don't want to restrain you, but I will."

Another gut-wrenching scream emanated from the room and traveled throughout the floor.

She watched from the doorway as the two guards assisting Grey backed out of the room, followed by Grey himself. He closed the door, ensuring he locked it before he walked away.

"She's a live one, huh?" Petey Johnson nudged his fellow guard as they followed Grey down the corridor. "We're going to have to stay alert around her."

Cam ambled toward Maxine's room. She paused at the door and looked through the window to see if she could spot the crazed prisoner she was supposed to spy on.

Max suddenly appeared in the window, startling Cameron. Her mouth curved into a tight-lipped grin as their eyes locked. She blew Cam a kiss. Frozen in place, Cam stared into Max's pale brown eyes. Max slammed both hands on the door and pressed her face against the window, cackling and screaming, her eyes bulging, "I'm heeeerrre...I'm heeeerrre..."

Cameron jumped back and observed Max a few seconds more before she managed to move herself away from the spectacle. She retreated to her own room, right next door to Max.

Cameron slumped onto her bed, unnerved by Max's display. Adrenaline rushed through her body, causing the hair on her neck to stand on end, her heart to beat faster, and a chill to run through her, as if she were standing in a freezer.

Pain spiked in her head. She instinctively closed her eyes and rubbed her temples. It was the pain that served as a warning for an oncoming migraine. She knew it well and controlled it—most of the time.

A migraine was also the catalyst for her alters to spring to life. She couldn't risk it. She couldn't risk a full-on migraine brought on by the stress of Maxine Jane Hoyt and the consequences that it might cause. Not now. Not when she'd made so many positive steps towards recovery...toward purging her alters. If she became too stressed, it could bring out Angel, or worse, if she felt threatened, Jason might emerge.

What am I doing? I need my meds. I can't risk an alter taking over and undoing all of my progress. Cameron went back out into the hall, the overhead fluorescent lighting glaring down on her, and made her way to the nurse's station. The woman behind the safety glass, Loretta Cromby, looked her up and down.

"I need my meds."

Loretta was the head nurse on the floor. She was nearly six feet tall and built like a linebacker. She maintained a serious expression at all times, and only smiled when she was jamming a needle into someone's arm, or thigh, or wherever it was easiest for her to stick it. *"There now. That didn't hurt, did it?"* She would coo, showing off her yellow-tinged, crooked teeth. Her prematurely gray hair was worn cropped short to her head. A personal alarm was always in view, but she hadn't used it once.

Loretta had explained to Cameron on her first day at St. C's that in order to get herself through nursing school, she boxed for prize money, and was a champion in her weight class. Her record was ninety-eight knockouts, one technical. Her right hook was a sledgehammer and the only alarm she needed. Cameron understood the message and went out of her way to be professional and pleasant with Loretta.

Loretta stopped what she was doing. "Why do you need your meds?" she asked, serious and direct, as always.

"I feel a migraine coming on."

Loretta tilted her head as her eyes penetrated into Cam's. A few strokes of her keyboard and she was reading Cameron's chart. "What do you think is causing the migraine?"

Cameron knew she was fishing for information, not just a trigger. "Maybe the fluorescents. You know they're a trigger, right? Not great for me, but I guess having them all changed out just for me is out of the question."

"You never seemed to have an issue with them before," Loretta countered.

"Well, I don't know, maybe it was something I ate." Cameron was getting annoyed; she needed her meds, and she needed them now. "Can I just have them, please? I really don't feel well." That was the truth; nausea was making its telltale crawl through her.

"I'll get them and bring them to your room. It'll just take a minute. You can go lie down."

After Loretta had administered her medication, Cam lay on the bed in her darkened room, waiting for the pills to take effect. A faint tapping on the wall between her and Max pierced the quiet. Max was sending a message—she would never let Cam rest.

CHAPTER 23

Cameron

Nightmares and restless legs caused Cameron to toss all night. Max's arrival was more stressful than Cam had imagined it would be. The woman in the room next door had wormed her way into Cam's brain. She was either an award-worthy actress and a maniacal psychopath, or desperately ill. It was Cam's task to ascertain which one.

At the crack of dawn, John Mercedes, one of two aware of the plan for Cam to get close to Max, woke Cam. He told her to follow him. Confused and half asleep, she shuffled behind him as he led her to the guard's desk, where he handed her the phone.

"It's for you," he said, annoyed that the NYPD forced him to play along with the game of cat and mouse. He took a few steps back in a show of faux privacy.

"Hello?" Cameron yawned.

"Cameron. I'm sorry to wake you." Hunter's voice was still hoarse. "Are you okay? Did you meet Maxine?"

"Hi...I'm okay." It was a white lie. She turned her back on John Mercedes and spoke in a hushed tone. "I haven't really met her yet. We had a .... moment yesterday after the guards put her in her room.

But we haven't had a conversation. She was wild when they brought her in."

"I'm glad you're okay. We have something really important to discuss. I'm putting Glen on so he can tell you the plan. It's still too much for me to talk a lot, okay?"

"Yeah, okay."

"Morning, Cameron." Levine's all business attitude was clear as a bell even over the phone. "We've arranged with Security Chief Mercedes to give you and Maxine a little alone time today. You'll go to the cafeteria at eleven-thirty this morning, where Maxine will already have her lunch. The two of you will have a chance to get acquainted before the rest of the inma..., uh, patients come in. We want you to cozy up to her. Make like you're trying to befriend her. Hunter and I will be there in the guard's room, watching and listening over the cameras. If anything goes sideways, a guard will be ready to step in."

"Just one? I think you may need a few. She's out of her mind!"

"I think you can handle yourself. But we'll be ready if you need backup."

"Fine. Is there anything specific you're looking for?"

"Just do your thing without tipping your hand. That's all."

Cameron yawned again. Her back ached, and she was still tired from not sleeping well. "Put Hunter back on."

Before Levine handed the phone to Hunter he added, "Cameron, I *know* you can do this."

The next voice Cam heard was Hunter's.

"Cam?" Hunter coarsely whispered. "Are you okay with this?"

"Yeah, I guess so. She's... more than what I expected."

"What do you mean?"

"I don't know. She's just more," Cam said, exasperated. "Either she's trying way too hard to look crazy or she's completely off the hinges. I'll do my best to get her to open up. Levine said you're going to be here. Can I see you afterwards?"

"Probably not a good idea. We don't want Max to suspect anything. I'll try to call you later on. Okay?"

"Yeah...okay. I'll talk to you later."

"Good luck."

Cameron sighed. "Yeah, thanks."

She hung up the phone. Over her shoulder, John Mercedes snorted, shaking his head.

"I hope you know what you're playing with here."

"So do I."

Cam hurried back to her room and laid down, hoping for some more sleep. She dozed off and when she awoke again, it was nearly eleven o'clock.

Desperately in need of a hot shower and a strong cup of coffee before she could face Max again, Cam quietly entered the women's shower room, checking for other patients before proceeding. She didn't want to encounter Max when she was naked and alone while bathing.

The only other person showering was Murder 'Em Mindy, aptly nicknamed because her solution to every problem was to "Murder 'Em." Cameron had won Mindy's favor when she'd defended her from an aggressor. She was a good person to have on one's side. Mindy wasn't big or strong but she could, and did, bite the finger off of another patient's hand. She was capable of defending herself and would come to Cam's rescue if needed.

Cam and Mindy nodded to one another and continued about their own business. Mindy wasn't much for conversation and preferred painting and drawing alone over socializing. Cam quickly showered, cognizant that Max might walk in at any moment, although it was unlikely. Still, she wasn't taking the chance.

She dried herself and dressed, leaving the wet towel in the designated bin. The rules did not permit towels beyond the showers because another patient had proven they were good for strangling people.

Back in her room, Cam combed through her wet hair and pulled it back into a ponytail at her nape. Her dark roots crept out of her scalp, giving the effect of a skull cap with a blonde tail hanging in the back.

It was almost eleven-thirty and time to meet Maxine Jane Hoyt, aka The Chelsea Choker. The staff wouldn't serve lunch to the other patients for another half hour, which would give Max and Cameron thirty minutes to get acquainted in private.

She practiced a few self-defense moves before leaving her room. Her body had softened. Laziness was infectious in the hospital, and she was not immune. *It's time to get back in shape,* she told herself. *Especially with someone like Maxine in the next room.*

Cameron walked as slowly as she could toward the cafeteria, going over in her mind how she would approach Max, what questions she had, and what answers she needed. If Max was faking her psychosis, she would eventually slip up. And Cameron would be ready to attack.

Cameron stopped in the cafeteria's doorway and surveyed the situation. Max sat at the third table in on the right, eating her lunch off an orange cafeteria tray. Their eyes met, and Max smiled coyly at Cam. She kicked the chair across from her out from the table.

"Hi. I'm new here. Care to join me?" Max said.

Cameron felt her body warm, and a light sweat form along the back of her neck. She looked over at the guard, who seemed disinterested. Taking her time, she moved toward Max and sat down on the white plastic cafeteria chair facing her.

"Chocolate pudding day," she said, nodding at the cup of dark brown goo on Max's tray. "It's a real hit around here."

"I'm Max. What's your name?"

"Cameron. I saw the guards bring you in yesterday."

"Oh right. You're the lady in the hallway. Sorry about my... outburst. I was a little frustrated with the way they treated me," Max said, in between bites of a ham and cheese sandwich on white bread. "So, it looks like we're neighbors."

Cameron and Max analyzed one another. Cameron noticed every detail about Max. She didn't look like a monster. She was, at best, plain. The kind of person you forget right after meeting them.

Her hair—natural dark blonde, no artificial color, hung limp around her angular face and fell just above her shoulders; her very fair skin was freckled, and a tattoo on her wrist displayed letters written in another language as well as what looked like a small bird.

Her build was slim, bordering on underweight, but strong—the defined muscles of her arms flexed through the thin fabric of her hospital-supplied shirt. She was about the same height as Cam. Dull eyes matched her hair, but Cam recognized their inquisitiveness. They were eyes that examined her back, looked her up and down as Max seemed to draw her own conclusions.

Max smiled, staring Cam down. Her chin tipped toward her chest, and her eyes shifted upwards in their sockets, giving her an ominous appearance.

She's trying to shake me, Cam thought, *trying to claim the dominant position between us.*

"How long have you been here, Cameron?"

"Just over eighteen months. It's not so bad once you figure out who to steer clear of and which orderlies to stay on guard with."

"What'd you do to end up in a place as nice as St. Christina's?"

Cam smiled slightly. *Should I tell her the truth?*

"Oh, you know, the usual... I unwittingly killed somebody. Or somebodies, as it were. But you don't need to worry about me." Cam leaned in and whispered to Max. "I didn't do it. It was the guy up here," she said, tapping the side of her head. "Jason did it, and I'm being punished for it. You know what I mean?"

Max whispered back, "I do. I really do. I thought you looked familiar last night. You're the FBI agent who killed a bunch of cops, right?"

"Well, they weren't *all* cops," Cam responded, playing along. Maxine couldn't suspect that Cameron wasn't insane. "One was a doctor, one was... it doesn't matter who was who. All that matters is I didn't do it. Like I said, it was the guy in here." She pointed to her temple again.

"I'm being punished too for something I didn't do. They say I strangled people *to death,* but I would never do such a thing. It was this guy I got involved with. It was all his idea. And now the creep has left me here to rot in this...what is this place, anyway? Is it a hospital or a prison?" Max directed the last part at the guard, who shrugged, uncaring.

"It's a hybrid. Hospital and prison combined into one groovy place. The good news—the meds here are the best! You'll forget all your troubles and you won't care about them even if you don't." Cam laughed a little. "And let's not forget, it could be worse. They could have sent us to max security. This place is a country club compared to that. Right?"

"I wouldn't know," Max said, holding her gaze steady with Cameron's. "This is my first time incarcerated. You?"

"Yep. Me too. But I guess I've learned to live with it. You will too."

"No... I don't think so. My boyfriend is very rich. He promised he would get me out of here. He loves me and he can't wait to take me away. We're going to be a family."

"I thought he was a creep who left you here to rot," Cameron retorted, her first catch in Maxine's pitched lies.

Max stared at Cameron, expressionless, before laughing it off. "You know how men are... one minute you hate them and then you remember you love them. Right? I seem to recall you had a man of your own. A detective? Has he stood by you, or did he walk away when they locked you up in here?"

Now Max had taken Cameron off guard. Her relationship with Hunter was not public knowledge. As far as she knew, there was no mention of it in any of the news stories.

"There's no one. No man, detective or otherwise. Just me. So, how is your rich boyfriend going to get you out?"

"I'm sure he has a fancy lawyer ready to defend me. Or maybe he'll just break me out."

"Unless the cops catch him first. You said he did the killing. They're most likely zeroing in on him right now."

"I never said that." Max pushed her chair back and stood. "It was nice meeting you, Cameron. I have an appointment now with Dr. Heisser and I mustn't keep him waiting on my first day. I'm sure you and I will see a lot of each other, and we'll have plenty of time to play. Here, have my apple... as you may have heard, I prefer the fresh-picked kind. See ya later."

She placed the apple on the table in front of Cameron, started for the door, and stopped just a few feet in front of it. Then she looked up at the camera, smiled broadly, and continued on her way.

CHAPTER 24

Max

Max paced within the confines of her new living accommodations. It wasn't what she expected, but when she really thought about it, she didn't know what to expect. It was clean, sparse and private—no roommate.

She was fresh off her first meeting with Dr. Heisser, and was left unimpressed. She'd had fun playing insane, talking to an invisible Nash on the couch next to her and feigning disbelief that her mother and stepfather were dead. If the doctor thought he was going to get an honest peek inside her head, he was wrong. Dead wrong.

At the moment, she couldn't believe that Nash's plan to get her into St. C's had gone so smoothly. He'd mentioned it like it was no big deal, but Max had thought long and hard about the conversation they had had just a month ago. Nash had predicted everything that had happened up to this point when they'd sat one night on his dainty couch, him sipping brandy, the fire's flames dancing in front of them, and discussed the possibility of her getting caught.

He'd gone over various scenarios with her as to what she should do if she were arrested. He'd said the most important aspect of getting caught would be not going to prison. Not even if it were to await trial.

"But won't you bail me out?" Max had asked, her naivety getting the best of her once more.

"No. Bail will most likely be denied. Besides, they'd recognize the connection between us and I'd be arrested as well. Then who'll rescue you?"

"But how would I avoid going to jail? If I get caught, isn't that the only option?"

"No, sweet Max. You'll have an ace up your sleeve. If you give them enough breadcrumbs, they'll follow you wherever you lead. All you have to do is put on a show."

That was when Nash had given her the tutorial on acting crazy.

"Why do you want me to act crazy?"

"So that they send you to a psychiatric hospital for evaluation. And the hospital the city uses for such services is St. Christina's."

"And why do I want to be sent there?"

"Number one, I'll have access to you there. Number two, that's where my girl resides."

"Your big prize works at a hospital for the criminally insane? And you want me to get myself sent there? You're insane," she'd said bluntly.

"I said 'resides.' She's a patient."

"Holy shit! This chick is criminally insane? Like, I-kill-people-and-eat-them, insane? And you want me to...what? Buddy up to her?"

"Language, Max. You will befriend her, and you will do exactly as I say if you want to finally get your way...move away from here with me and Sammy."

He'd explained what she would need to do once inside St. C's in order to win his undying love, affection, and gratitude.

"Once you're admitted to St. Christina's, Max," he'd said, "you need to cozy up to Dr. Cameron Cooper. She's going to be your special playmate. You have a lot in common—like twin planets orbiting the same sun."

"She's a doctor and a patient?" Max had asked. "Why is she in there?"

"Dr. Cooper claims to have multiple personalities and one of them likes to kill women that look like her. Tragic, isn't it?"

"But why do I need to cozy up to her?"

"We're going to prove she's perfectly sane and you'll be a hero, Max. Wouldn't that be nice? Maxine the hero. You and I and Sammy Cat will celebrate together. Cheers to the hero!

"With her out of the way, my vendetta fulfilled, we can move on with our lives. I will make all your dreams come true. Once we get to Georgia, I'll take you to my favorite jeweler and perhaps we can select matching wedding bands."

He'd smiled slyly at her, swirled the reddish-brown liquid in his glass, and took a sip.

Her mind had jumped. It wasn't a proposal, but the suggestion of one. A hint at their future together.

"It seems like you have it all worked out that I get caught. Are you setting me up? Because I don't want to go to jail, and dangling a wedding band in front of me isn't enough to get me to agree to get caught. I could get the death sentence."

"Max, Max, Max," Nash had said. "This is a 'just in case' scenario. I have other ways, of course, to get you into St. Christina's without you being arrested. But if the police capture you, I want you to be prepared. Keep in mind that if they arrest you and you're placed in

St. Christina's, that I also have a plan to get you out. Don't forget, Max, I have friends everywhere."

His hazel eyes shined; his cheeks glowed from the cognac and the heat thrown by the fire.

"What is it, exactly, that you want me to do to this chick once I'm on the inside?"

His lips curled under their hairy frame. He inhaled a deep breath, slowly releasing it out, and his pupils expanded. Devil Nash was swirling around, trying to make an entrance.

"I want you to torture her," he'd hissed.

After the conversation about playing crazy, Max had Googled Cameron Cooper and was astonished when she found over twelve million results. The Cameron she was interested in sat at the very top.

There hadn't been much to read on the internet until recently. She'd been involved in some high-profile cases that had gotten media attention when she was still FBI, but nothing compared to when she was found out to be The Stealth Stalker. That's what she was famous for, or was it infamous? Either way, it was why she was in the news and plastered all over social media.

Nash had explained to Max that some people with multiple personalities could hear the voices of the others, but there were cases where the primary personality had no clue their mind had fractured. Apparently, that had been the case with Cameron.

Widespread coverage of the former FBI profiler-turned-serial-killer had answered questions Max never could have imagined.

She'd read how Cameron had been working with the NYPD to solve a serial killer case, a guy the press called The Stealth Stalker. When Cameron was attacked on the job and hospitalized, she reportedly told the lead investigator on the case that her name was Jason Jonette. The investigator, one Detective Hunter Finnegan, put the pieces together, and she was arrested for being the very killer they were hunting.

News articles in the search had led to conspiracy theories claiming Hunter and Cameron were lovers and co-conspirators living double lives—working as upstanding crime fighters and throwing authorities off by day, and killing by night.

Hunter was exonerated and was the department's spokesperson when Cameron was sentenced to life at St. C's.

Max had wondered what all of that had to do with Nash. How had she hurt him? Did she kill someone he loved? She couldn't find a connection after multiple search attempts.

Ready to give up, she'd made one last search. Jason Jonette.

And she had hit pay dirt. She found several articles about a serial killer in Georgia, Jason Julius Jonette, aka J-Bird. *Interesting*, Max had thought.

Even more interesting, he had kidnapped a young woman named Lisa Allen and an FBI agent—one Cameron Chadwick—and had tortured them for several days before they'd escaped and he disappeared.

All of it had only left Max more confused. She'd discovered that Cameron had changed her name, and that Nash and Cameron both had ties to Georgia, but how did they connect to one another? And why would Cameron have another personality with the same name as the guy who'd tortured and nearly murdered her?

Max had realized the answer was in her question. Nash had also explained that often, when someone had a split personality, it was due to trauma. In a very sick way, Cameron had become the guy she feared and or hated the most.

Max had watched old news videos covering the manhunt for the J-Bird. During one of the newscasts, when an FBI artist sketch of Jonette appeared in the corner of the screen, Max had paused the video and enlarged the picture. She'd sat for a long time staring at the image.

Finally, she'd had her answer.

And now she was incarcerated in a forensic hospital.

She sat on the lumpy bed with her back leaning against the wall and her legs crossed as she went over the details in her mind. It was all coming together for her. It wasn't luck or fate that Nash had approached her that night in the alley and invited her to dinner.

Nash had sought her out.

He must have heard about her parents' murders in Pennsylvania, Max reasoned. It had been national news, and to use his analogy, he'd followed the breadcrumbs she had unwittingly left.

He'd taken her in, given her the love and attention she'd craved. And knowing what she was capable of, and what she desired more than anything, he'd drawn her in. Played on her weaknesses. Made promises.

Or more accurately—lied.

Max realized now that Nash wanted her in St. C's all along. He'd left his own breadcrumbs and she'd followed them like a hungry dog. He'd set her up.

No! Max didn't want to believe that Nash would do that to her. He'd told her he loved her and she was sure he meant it. He'd let Sammy stay to prove it to her. He'd *chosen her* over the countless followers who begged to be at his side. He needed her on the inside to finish their work. He may have set her up without telling her the full plan, but he'd also promised he'd get her out and reward her.

She just needed to finish what they'd started and they would be together. A family like he'd promised. She needed to be patient. It was the first thing he'd taught her—patience.

A bell rang out, indicating the cafeteria was open for dinner and she heard murmurs in the hall as the residents moved toward their next meal. She'd just wait for his instructions. Nash had made it clear that he had friends, or more accurately, followers, everywhere. Someone would make contact soon. She knew it.

Pushing herself off the bed, she headed for the cafeteria. If nothing else, she had a room to herself and three meals a day. And it was ice cream day.

"What flavor ice cream do you think it is, babe?" Max asked the invisible man next to her as she walked past the guards. "Well, I hope it's chocolate."

CHAPTER 25

Cameron

"Cameron, please, come in," Dr. Heisser said by way of greeting. "It surprised me when Nurse Cromby said you requested a special therapy session today."

"Yes, thank you for seeing me. I'm sure you're busy, especially with the new girl on the block."

"Ah, yes, Maxine Jane Hoyt. I assumed you'd want to discuss your first meeting with her today. I watched, along with Detectives Finnegan and Levine, as you and Maxine became acquainted. Sit down, please. Tell me your thoughts on Max."

Cameron sat on a navy-blue club chair identical to the one Dr. Heisser was already sitting on. His office was one of the most calming places Cameron had ever been in. Instrumental music played softly in the background. The walls were a soothing, pale gray-blue, the carpet a darker shade of the same color, and the furniture was modern and comfy. Fresh-cut lavender in a crystal vase sat on top of a black-stained coffee table, releasing its calming spell into the air.

Cameron sighed as she leaned back, relaxing into the comfort of the club chair.

"Maxine is a character. I saw the guards put her in her room last night. She was wild, screaming and laughing. I peeked in as I passed and she... she blew me a kiss. And then today in the cafeteria, it seemed like she was waiting for me. Like she knew I was going to walk through the door at any moment."

"I suppose she could have seen on the news that Corrections transferred you here last year. Do you think she's an admirer? A groupie?"

Cam shook her head. "No, I didn't detect admiration. It was more like...she was taunting me. Probing me for information. And there was the way she looked at me, with what seemed like anger, or resentment. I sensed she had a purpose in meeting me."

"Are you saying a purpose to meeting you specifically or another patient? Someone who could empathize with her?"

"It seemed personal. You heard her ask me about a boyfriend. She specifically said a detective. How could she know about Hunter? Our relationship wasn't public."

"Perhaps she wasn't referring to him as a romantic relationship. It's possible she knew you were working together, and she referred to him as a boyfriend sarcastically. He was the one who briefed the press when you were arrested and revealed as The Stealth Stalker. And the press did point out that he was the one who hired you in the first place and how closely the two of you worked together before you were injured, hospitalized and diagnosed."

Dr. Heisser always delicately phrased the most egregious element of Cam's incarceration: the fact that a cold-blooded murderer roamed within her subconscious.

"I suppose... but she also said we would have plenty of time to play. Isn't that a strange thing for one adult woman to say to another? And she said her rich boyfriend is getting her out. Either by legal avenues or possibly an escape. I need to call Hunter about that one."

"The play thing is odd, but our patients have wound up here because of their eccentricities. You're right, though. It sounds personal. As for an escape, no one has ever escaped from St. Christina's. Next time you're alone with her, try to get her to open up more about the boyfriend. The detective implied he could be imaginary. See if you can get her to screw up regarding who he really is, if he really is."

"Okay, I can handle that. What about your session with her? How did that go?"

"Even though you're working with the police, my sessions with Maxine are still privileged. My goal is to determine if she is faking insanity or if it's real. So far, I would say she seems intelligent and somewhat normal if it weren't for the fact that she's a killer."

"She could be both. A sane killer. There are plenty of cases throughout history of people who seemed perfectly normal, but they were serial killers on the side. Driven by different motives, ideologies, and invisible monsters. We can't brush aside the idea that the boyfriend is real and not made up. There could be a dangerous person still free who helped Max commit these murders. The police need to keep looking."

"You have a point. Better to assume he's real and dangerous than imagined."

"And we need to keep probing her. If there is a real man out there, eventually she will slip up."

"Agreed—the talkative ones always do." Heisser nodded as he jotted notes down.

"There's one more thing," Cam added. She wrung her hands nervously. "I'm not sure I should work with Maxine. I'm afraid it might be too much for me, getting close to a serial killer. Isn't a serial killer the reason I'm here in the first place? I've made so much progress in the last several months. The alters have been nearly nonexistent. And last night, I felt...on edge. Max did that to me."

"I was told you requested your meds last night. Unusual for you to request medication before the scheduled time. Is that why? Because of Max blowing you a kiss and her interest in you?"

"Yeah... not just that, though. It was her entire demeanor. The thrashing, the possessed laugh, and the way she looked at me... like she wanted to take a bite out of me. It was more than I wanted to deal with. My goal is to get well here. I don't want to jeopardize my sanity and wellness for a case, and I shouldn't have to. The law enforcer in me wants to nail the bitch, but for the first time, I want to put myself first, meaning I want to heal and overcome my fractured mind. I want to help catch her, but I don't. Do you understand?"

"Yes, I get it. You're afraid the stress of getting close to Max will cause the need for the alters to resurface. But you've made too much progress for that to happen. You weren't aware what was happening before—that your mind had fractured and developed alters. Now you are. You're fully aware of the triggers and, more importantly, you now understand the why of it all—the traumas you suffered from childhood and beyond were the root of the problem. You've made incredible progress in healing from those traumas. Jason hasn't manifested in a violent manner since the altercation with Myra Gordon. Which brings up another point—we've put off addressing the alter known as Jason long enough. Don't you agree?"

Cameron didn't answer. Dr. Heisser had patiently waited for Cameron to say she was ready to be hypnotized and face the alter known as Jason Jonette, but she didn't want to face the horrible crimes that Jason had committed when he'd taken over. She didn't want to see and hear what he heard and saw—the cries for help...last words...life evaporating into death.

"Cameron?" Dr. Heisser said gently. "I know you're afraid, but I want to assure you that you can do this. I admit it won't be pleasant, but it is necessary for your healing. We can't purge Charlotte and Angel completely until we've purged Jason. You understand that, don't you?" Cameron didn't move. "You also put it off because of the attack on Detective Finnegan. He's fully recovered, and he asked me about the hypnosis session this morning. He wanted to make sure I was aware he was ready to help, but if you're not ready, then we'll wait. I get the feeling he's not going anywhere."

Cameron stared out the window as if she were in a trance. After a few seconds, she nodded slowly. "I'll consider it," she said with a sigh.

Dr. Heisser made another quick notation before changing the subject back to Maxine Hoyt. "If you're willing to continue to work with Maxine, and if we monitor you closely, we'll be able to handle the stress of the situation and keep you on track to recovery. If it ever becomes too much, or if we sense an alter is on the brink of returning, we stop. We reevaluate and we rest. Does that sound acceptable?"

Tension crawled through Cameron's body, leaving every muscle and fiber tight, and as it made its way up her spine, a sharp pain spiked within her skull. "I... I don't know," she said, squeezing her eyes closed and inhaling deeply before blowing the air out slowly.

"Relax, Cameron. You're safe here. And you don't have to do anything you aren't ready to do," Heisser said as he pressed the intercom button and requested Loretta to come into the office.

"Yes, Doctor?" Loretta loomed behind Cameron, stressing her out even more.

"Please get Cameron's Valium. She's over-stressed at the moment."

"Wouldn't it be better to see what happens when I'm stressed? See if any of the alters come out? How will we determine if I'm getting better if I'm always medicated?"

"The medication isn't keeping the alters away. That's the therapy. The medication helps you manage the stress until you can do it on your own. You're doubting yourself right now. I'm not sure why. You can handle Maxine and all the psychobabble she throws at you, but for some reason, you are questioning your own ability. Why is that?"

"I... I'm not sure.... Maybe it's because I'm desperately afraid I'll become an alter permanently. What if I turn into that monster Jason Jonette and I—me," she said, patting her chest, "I never resurface? He gets permanent control, which is what he wanted...to be in control." The conversation Cameron had had with Dannisha about how she knew she was the original obviously had had a bigger impact than she realized.

Heisser put his pen and paper down on the table and studied Cameron as she wrestled to stay calm.

"Cameron, look at me." He waited for her eyes to meet his. "That will never happen. *You* are in control and you always have been. The alter known as Jason Jonette is a manifestation of traumas. Traumas we have worked through. He will never be the victor because we are purging him, if we haven't already. But I can see how upsetting this is to you. I want you to take time today to write in your journal, meditate, and do some yoga. Tomorrow morning, we will meet again. If you still feel that working with Maxine is detrimental to your recovery, then I'll call Detective Finnegan and tell him I can no longer allow you to take part in the case. How does that sound? Fair?"

Cameron nodded, pulling her cardigan tightly around her body and hugging herself. Loretta appeared with the meds, which Cam greedily swallowed. She made her way back to her room, and as she passed Max's open door, Max called out to her in a singsong, *"Hi Cammie. Do you know how I picked an apple..."* Max's cackling laughter followed Cam into her room as she closed the door and lay down.

Why did it feel so personal?

CHAPTER 26

Cameron

Mellow yellow sunlight shone in through the small window of Cameron's room, waking her. She stretched in her bed, taking a moment to clear her head before rising. Cam had spent the earlier part of the night pondering Maxine Jane Hoyt, a barely twenty-year-old who was more kid than adult, and who, for reasons yet to be determined, had gone on a killing spree.

Max had been at St. C's for only two days, but Cameron was already getting a read on her. Max wasn't a monster, but committing violent acts didn't seem to faze her. Cam had read the report on the gruesome death of Max's mother and stepfather. Pennsylvania law enforcement was waiting for their turn at Max for the double homicide of Clara and Wayne Meyers.

Cameron had studied the photos of the rage- and emotion-filled attack. It was clear to her that whoever killed Clara and Wayne had a personal vendetta. It was not a home invasion, as the police had concluded earlier. She knew there was more to the story. A young woman didn't wake up one morning, grab an ax and kill her own mother, and in such an extreme way, for no reason.

There was also an interesting side note to the report, which stated that Max's grandmother had died unexpectedly in a nursing home.

Did Max kill her too? Whoever killed Clara and Wayne had burned the murder weapon to ash in the fireplace—only the steel head of the ax remained—and tossed the house. So it would be hard to prove Maxine Jane Hoyt had killed them without a confession. And Max did not seem like the confessing kind.

Cameron had observed that Max was cleverer and smarter than anyone had most likely given her credit for. She would have to move ahead slowly with the young woman-turned-serial killer if she was going to get her to open up. The information that Levine had supplied stated that Max referred to a boyfriend and Max herself had also told Cameron she had a wealthy boyfriend. Cam couldn't help but wonder if he was indeed real and most likely a participant in The Chelsea Choker killings. If he was real, he was still out there and a threat to anyone and everyone he might come across. With Max incarcerated, an already unstable partner could have a meltdown and start killing at random.

Swinging her legs over the edge of the bed, Cam stood, stretching again. Hunter had called just before the nightly lockdown and informed Cam that he and Levine would be at St. C's in the morning to discuss the case. The notion of seeing Hunter left her rejuvenated and feeling excited, even as the thoughts of Max and an alleged partner weighed on her mind.

She gathered clean clothes, and the moment her door unlocked at eight a.m., she made a beeline for the showers. Once she finished dressing, she inched open her door and peeked into Max's room. Max appeared to be asleep with the blanket pulled over her head. A guard would be along any moment to change that situation. Cameron made a quick trip to the cafeteria, where she grabbed coffee and some eggs before heading to the guard's station to pick up the laptop Hunter had brought her.

John Mercedes led her to the conference room where she was scheduled to meet Hunter and Levine.

"You're a little early, aren't you?" John asked.

"I want to be ready when the detectives get here."

He unlocked the door, flipped the light switch for her and stood watching her prepare her workspace.

"You really enjoy this, don't you?"

"I do," she agreed with a nod. "I look forward to meeting with the detectives, even if it's about Maxine. I wasn't expecting her to be so... forceful. And loud. Damn, that girl can scream. But she's just a kid, and she's going to be easy to manipulate and crack."

"In my experience in here, I've learned you never underestimate the ones you perceive as easy and never, ever, even for a second, assume anyone here won't stab you in the gut given the opportunity. That's how you stay alive here."

"Good advice. I'll keep that in mind. Thanks."

The sound of the key in the lock caused Cameron to look up. The door opened and in walked Glen Levine, followed by Hunter. His eyes crinkled in the corners as a smile lit up his face. Petey Johnson, who had unlocked the door, hung back in the hallway, avoiding eye contact with Cameron.

"Good morning, Cameron," Hunter said. His voice sounded stronger and not as hoarse.

"Good morning, Hunter," she replied, beaming at him.

"Yeah, good morning. Let's get started, okay?" Levine tore through their connection with the ease of a machete slicing through an over-ripe mango. "What's your take on, Max? Is she crazy or not?"

Cameron answered, "I just finished typing up my notes on Maxine Jane Hoyt. Did you hear our conversation clearly yesterday?"

"Yes, the video and audio were clear. She seemed a little aggressive to me. What did you think?" Hunter asked.

Cameron nodded in agreement. "Our conversation disturbed me somewhat. Initially, I felt as though she was interested in me personally. Now, I think I was just overreacting. She's new here and she's perhaps a little scared and just trying to act tough in front of the guards and whatever patients are within earshot. She was asking questions, which isn't unusual when you first meet someone and you're feeling them out. There was one thing that bothered me, though. She said she heard I had a boyfriend who was a detective. I didn't think that there was anything about us in the news. Was there?"

Levine and Hunter exchanged looks before Hunter answered. "No. The chief made it clear there was to be no mention of you and me having anything more than a professional relationship. Sounds like it was just a lucky guess, or she just assumed, since you were working with us."

"It made me hesitate. I have to admit, I was uncomfortable with the task of analyzing her after she came in screaming and then, after we spoke, I felt like I wasn't up for this. But then I spent the entire night remembering my training, and I realized Max is not the worst thing I've had to deal with. This is a controlled environment and I have the upper hand here. I'm okay with this now, but as I said, the conversation yesterday felt personal to me. She knew who I was and why I was here. What are the chances of that? She's from Pennsylvania. How long do you estimate she's been in the city?"

"P.A. police suspect she's the one who killed her mother and stepfather in August last year, so about fourteen or fifteen months, depending on how quickly she fled P.A."

"That's after the judge remanded me here. It just seems odd to me that she knew who I was, and she guessed I had a... friend who was a detective." Cam smoothed imaginary wrinkles from a yellow notepad. "She's either much more perceptive than she appears, or she's done her homework. And if that's the case, why? Why would she want to know anything about me? It's not like she knew she was going to end up here and would come face-to-face with me."

Hunter and Levine exchanged a quick look.

"What?" Cameron asked. "Are you hiding something from me?"

"Max is young," Hunter said. "She might have seen something on social media about you."

"Social media?" Cameron's mouth hung open as her eyes darted back and forth between the two men, looking for more information. "What do you mean?"

"You know how it goes, Cam. Whatever the latest is in the news makes its rounds on social media too," Hunter answered.

"Like what?"

Hunter shot another quick glance at Levine. "Just more of the same. Whatever they're talking about on the news, they talk about on social media, with some exaggeration. People love to comment on that stuff. Next thing it blows up the internet, or some shit. It's not for me...I don't have any social accounts. How about you, Levine?"

"Nah, I don't have time to scroll through that shit." Levine shrugged, looking bored.

"Maybe she's interested in you because of the crimes you're linked to," Hunter said. "You said she could be a groupie of The J-Bird. She could have an admiration for Stealth as well."

Cameron didn't like the way the conversation had turned. She was being lumped into a pile of serial killers without exception, and it wasn't fair. She changed the subject before things became unbearably awkward.

"Max mentioned a wealthy boyfriend. She said he was going to hire a lawyer or break her out. I know you two have your doubts about the boyfriend's existence, but the suggestion needs to be taken seriously. If she has a partner, he's still out there, and could strike out on his own. Which means the NYPD cannot relax and consider The Chelsea Choker a closed case just because Max is in custody. Until we determine if she's making him up or not, we need to treat this guy as a very real and deadly person."

"We've taken that into consideration," Levine said. "The commissioner has agreed to an extension on our surveillance until we can gather more concrete evidence against Maxine and determine if she worked alone or not. But if we're waiting for the pattern to continue, we're looking at sixty-four days from when we caught her. The commissioner most likely won't allow that. The best we can hope for is to determine if the boyfriend is real or not *now*, or amp things up again as we get closer to the sixty-fourth day." Levine sat back, rubbing his bald head. "When we had her in interrogation, and she started talking to the invisible man next to her, I thought it was an act, but after she attacked Hunter, I wasn't so sure."

"Why?" Cam asked.

"I've been at this a long time, and I've seen a lot, you know? To me, if I had to guess at that moment, I would've said she was schizophrenic. It was the way she lunged at him and started screaming. And the laughter. If all of that was an act, then she deserves an Oscar."

"Maybe someone coached her," Cameron offered.

"What do you mean?" Hunter asked.

"I mean, what if the guy she claims is her boyfriend is real and they're working together? I told you Max is clever. What if they prepared for all probable outcomes of their killing spree and they came up with a way to avoid prison if Max was caught...by acting crazy? Look at this place—it's huge! A lot of prisoners are sent here for evaluation before they go to trial. And that's exactly what has happened with Max. She was brought here to determine if she's mentally fit to stand trial. I've visited state penitentiaries many times, and I've got to say that this"—she held her arms out, motioning around herself—"is a helluva lot better than any super-max facility, which is where she would've been transferred to await trial if it wasn't for the fact that she went nuts in interrogation."

Hunter and Levine were quiet, Hunter with an index finger pressed to his lips, a tell that he was digesting and reasoning Cam's theory.

Cam continued. "Look, you said yourself, Glen, that you thought she was faking it right up until she attacked Hunter and started singing and laughing. Murphy said her behavior was BS and nothing but an act. He thinks she's faking it. From what I saw yesterday in the cafeteria, Max is not schizophrenic. She's cunning. She was trying hard to intimidate me and dominate. I think she also has a plan to get out of here. Or she thinks she does, and we need to keep a close watch on her."

"Nobody has ever escaped from St. Christina's. Ever," Levine said, echoing Dr. Heisser. "Even though we don't label this a maximum-security prison, it is. She's allowed visitors on Saturday. We'll be here watching her, and if by some slight chance she has a visitor, we'll pick them up and bring them in for questioning."

Cameron flipped open Max's file and scanned the pages. "Does she have any family besides the ones she's accused of killing?"

Hunter answered, "Max has no siblings. Her father, Jackson Hoyt, lives in Arizona. An uncle in Florida said he hadn't seen his sister, Clara Meyers, in over fifteen years. He's had zero contact with Max and didn't seem surprised when we told him she's accused of multiple murders, including her mother and stepfather. He said, 'Not my problem.' Max's father, Jackson, also took the news that we'd arrested Max for multiple murders with extreme indifference. He said that he wasn't 'surprised that she had it in her.'"

"Did he elaborate as to why?"

"No. He said that her mother was trash and a psycho, so the apple hadn't fallen far. He won't be visiting."

"Any more information on Clara and Wayne Meyers?"

"It's suspected Clara and Wayne killed Clara's mother, Alma Wilkes, who lived in a nursing home, for life insurance money," Hunter said. He leaned in to the table and flipped a couple of pages in front of Cameron, then stopped at the photograph of an elderly couple tagged Alma and Henry Wilkes.

Levine continued, "The nursing home staff found Alma deceased in her bed and assumed she'd died in her sleep. But the doctor who'd examined her and declared her dead noticed her eyes were bloodshot and asked for an autopsy. The coroner's report ruled her death asphyxiation from smothering.

"When the cops went to inform Clara they suspected someone in the nursing home had killed her mother, they found Clara and Wayne's remains. The police then discovered that the Meyerses were behind on their mortgage and the bank was about to foreclose. The life insurance policy was for twenty-five thousand dollars. That's motive.

"They didn't find the money, and the mortgage was still in arrears at the time of Clara and Wayne's demise. The bank foreclosed on the house six months later. P.A. authorities suspect Max killed Clara and Wayne Meyers and absconded with the money. We're still trying to figure out where Max was living. Barone is searching street and subway cams to see if any of them caught Max after she killed Tonya Nathan. Twenty-five thousand may be a lot in rural Pennsylvania, but it wouldn't last long in New York City."

"She could be homeless. Have you checked the shelters? Asked around on the streets?"

"We have," Levine answered. "Nobody remembered seeing Maxine. But we're still working on it."

Cameron examined the photograph of Alma and Henry. Max looked nothing like her mother; she was the image of her grandfather. She had his dull brown eyes, thin, drawn-out lips and angular jaw. Plain. Forgettable. "No one remembered seeing Max because she's so unremarkable. If she had kept to herself and didn't cause any trouble, she would have been invisible."

Cameron placed the photo back into the file labeled *Maxine Jane Hoyt, aka The Chelsea Choker,* and closed it. "If Max was close to her grandmother and knew that Clara and Wayne had killed her, that would have been the catalyst for her vicious attack on them. I studied the crime scene photos. That wasn't a home invasion, but a savage attack. It was personal...very personal.

"The coroner's report on Wayne Meyers states he only had two wounds—one to his chest and one to his groin. Judging by the very explicit attack to the groin, coupled with the interviews of neighbors and friends, I would say it's probable that he was abusing Max. Whereas Clara was completely unrecognizable. Max unleashed her fury on her mother most likely because her mother never protected her, and neglected and abused her in her own way. Abuse and neglect were horrors she'd learned to live with, but when her abusers killed Alma, that was the breaking point for Max. But it doesn't explain why she continued to kill once she arrived here."

"The boyfriend," Hunter said.

"The boyfriend," Cameron agreed.

CHAPTER 27

Cameron

"Hi, *Doctor Cooper*." Cameron was in the cafeteria, seated at her favorite table when Max interrupted her. "What are you doing there?"

"I'm journaling."

"Journaling..." Max repeated in a mocking tone. She gently slid the chair across from Cam out from the table and sat, crossing her legs and folding her hands demurely in her lap. "Aren't you fancy? What exactly do you journal?"

"Whatever comes to mind. Thoughts about life, what got me here, my dreams for the future."

"Dreams for the future! Hah!" Max snorted, then laughed at Cam. "You don't have a future sweet pea. I'm your future—you and me. We're going to grow old together right here in St. Christina's."

"You and I are nothing alike. My future and yours do not entwine and never will. Besides, I thought your rich boyfriend was working on getting you out of here."

"That's true, he is. But for the foreseeable future, it's you and me, sister. We have more in common than you might guess. A bond that ties us for eternity."

"A bond? What might that be?"

A sly smile turned Max's face impish. "I don't want to give away all my secrets. Yet. Once we get to know one another better, you'll see that we are twin planets orbiting the same sun."

"Hah!" Cameron reacted naturally to Max's audacious claim. "Twin planets. You don't know anything about me, Maxine. For starters, I don't have any imaginary friends I talk to."

"No, of course not. You don't talk to them, but you have imaginary friends who talk to you, don't you? And one of them likes to kill for fun, doesn't he?"

"Yes, that's true. There is a killer that lives within me. I already told you that, but I never said there was anyone else or that they talked to me. I don't know what you've heard about me, Maxine, but you shouldn't listen to rumors. Especially in here, of all places. There are mentally handicapped patients here who suffer from a multitude of disorders. Sometimes they outright lie and other times they imagine their delusions are real. Do you believe your delusions are real? That you can somehow read my mind and know who I am before I even tell you about myself? Or that your rich boyfriend actually exists?"

"He does exist," Max retorted, and then caught herself. "It's not my fault those idiot detectives couldn't see him when he was sitting right there." She pointed to the chair next to her.

"Is he sitting there now?" Cam asked, mocking Max.

"Of course not. He's not here," she said. "I told you—he's working on getting me out."

"Yeah, okay. I'm sure that's what he's doing right now." Cameron shook her head and continued writing in her journal. The best way to get Maxine to talk was to ignore her, which would ignite her hard-to-control temper.

"You're being rude," Max hissed quietly at Cam. "We're having a conversation, so put the pen down."

"No. I don't follow your orders. You follow mine. There's a pecking order here, and you are at the bottom. So, back the hell off. Now would be a good time to go play with your imaginary boyfriend."

"But I would rather play with your imaginary friend...what was his name? Oh right, Jason..." Max grinned at Cameron and then she snatched the pen out of her hand. "Jaaasssooooonn," she repeated in a deep, doom-filled voice, eyes wide. "Come out, come out, wherever you are..."

Cam folded her hands together and rested them on top of her journal. "You're not very mature for a killer."

Max flicked the pen at Cameron. It bounced off her and onto the floor. "I'm mature enough for Nash, and he's older."

"Is Nash your boyfriend? And what's he older than?" Cameron asked, as she bent down and picked the pen up.

"Older than you. Or the same age as you. How old are you, anyway?"

"Old enough."

Max sighed. "Ok. I have another question for you—what's up with Broadway Joan? She's kind of scary, right? Has your other personality, the doctor, diagnosed her as really that crazy or faking it? Because I think she's fucking nuts."

"First of all, *I am* a psychologist, or I was, until the state revoked my license. And second, we don't use terms like 'crazy' or 'nuts,' Max. It's offensive. Joan has mental health issues and a very low IQ."

"So...you're saying she's stupid?"

Cameron was getting annoyed. "No, that's not what I'm saying. I'm saying she has mental health...you know what? I don't want to talk about this. Go bother someone else."

"N-n-n-nope. I enjoy talking to you. What did Broadway do to get in here? Rumor has it she killed homeless people and then *ate* them! Can you believe that?"

"No, I can't believe it because it isn't true. She didn't eat anyone, for God's sake. Why don't we talk about you, Max? I'd like to hear more about your boyfriend. If he's going to break you out, maybe I could tag along? I've got money stashed away—I could pay."

Max leaned in to the table. "Yeah? How much?"

"Enough that I'm sure we could work something out."

"Wouldn't it be easier for your boyfriend, the detective, to get you out? I'm sure he could arrange something with the guards. Sneak you out in the laundry. That's happened so many times on TV that these prisons probably think it could never happen, or they cattle-prod the shit out of the laundry before it leaves here." Max slapped her hand on the table and laughed.

"They do the laundry in house, so if someone were to hide in a bin, they'd go nowhere."

"Oh. How come on TV it's always sent out? Weird." Max tilted her head, frowning, and seemingly in deep thought about television prison laundry. "Tell me some more about Broadway Joan. Have you ever talked to her?"

"Why are you so interested in Joan? Does she remind you of your momma?"

"Ha! Good one, Cameron. Glad to see you've kept your sense of humor locked in here all this time. But, no, she's nothing like my '*momma*.' She's interesting…that's all. Who do you find interesting in here?"

"Well, Max, if Joan is so interesting, why are you bothering me?"

"Because…you're pretty…interesting too. I was kinda hoping that while we talked that one of your other personalities would join the conversation. I read it's called switching. Can you switch on demand? Can you do it now? Who would you switch to? You told me about the serial killer, but who else is in there?"

"Where did you read about switching? And why do you care so much about me?" Cameron asked, leaning forward and mirroring Max.

"Are you kidding? You're the star of St. C's. You were like a fucking celebrity for a while. On the TV every day…the FBI agent turned murderer. People were arguing everywhere about if you were for real. It was blowing up Twitter. Psychos were making videos about it and posting them on Insta and TikTok. One person dressed up with a blonde wig and a badge and was talking normal-like into the camera, about arresting bad guys, and then they twirled around really fast, yanked the wig off, revealed that she was a he, and pulled out a knife threatening to kill everyone. That one had over a million views. It was crazy…oops, I mean, it was…yeah, crazy. It was crazy! Like nothing else was happening in the world."

Cameron sat back, stunned. Hunter had deceived her. He'd played down the role of social media in her case. He'd told her it was over in five minutes, as the attention span of today's youth equaled the length of a reel on Instagram before they moved on to the next one. According to what Max had just said, that wasn't true. It hadn't died down in just a few days or was largely ignored.

Because she didn't want Max to know how much of what she'd just said bothered her, Cameron continued fishing for more information on Max's alleged partner.

"Tell me some more about your boyfriend. Where'd you meet?"

Max's eyes scanned Cameron carefully before she answered. "We ran into one another on the street. He asked me if I wanted to have dinner with him, so I said, sure."

"Did you know him already?"

"No. That was the first time we met."

"So, you run into a stranger on the street, he asks you to dinner, and you say yes?"

"Yes." Max sighed in what Cameron perceived to be annoyance.

"Where'd you go?"

"A diner that was right around the corner. I know what you're thinking. You think I shouldn't have gone anywhere with a stranger. Right? Well, it was fine. He didn't attack me. We had a nice dinner in a very busy diner."

"And then what happened?"

"He kept asking me out, I kept going, and finally he asked me to live with him."

"Where?" Cameron had to get as much out of Max as she could, while she was in such a chatty mood.

"He has a gorgeous brownstone. At first, it was strictly platonic, you know what I mean? Just friends. I had my own bedroom. But eventually we grew closer. I could always see his attraction to me...I mean, just obsessed with me. I was the one who wanted to take it slow. Rich, older guy—I saw a couple of red flags, but as I learned more about him, I became more attracted to him. He was very patient with me, gentle. Now, he's not just my boyfriend. He's my everything. My best friend, my hero...my mentor."

"Mentor? How is he a mentor to you?" Cameron felt like she was finally getting somewhere.

"He teaches me things."

"Like what?" Cameron watched Max as she spoke. She watched her eyes and her body movements. It appeared as if Max was telling the truth.

"How to achieve results with patience, skill and most importantly...no remorse. After all, what we do is good. We help people."

"How do you help people?"

"By setting them free." Max sat still as she answered Cameron's questions, her boney hands clasped, resting on the Formica-clad table, her dull eyes steadily meeting Cameron's.

"What do you mean, Max? How do you set people free? You break them out of prison or places like this? Is that why you're here? You want to break Joan Namath out? Is she a relative?"

Max laughed out loud, tossing her head back and startling Cameron. Their quiet talk was suddenly interrupted. She glanced over to John Mercedes, who'd wandered by and was leaning against the doorway. He was watching from the corner of his eye, hand on his taser.

"No, that's not what I mean." Max snorted. "We set them free from these rotting, dying bodies that have entrapped our souls, and keep us pinned down here. We free souls so they can go to their reward rather than suffering here another minute. It's good."

Cameron processed Max's interpretation of murder before she spoke. "Okay. I just want to clarify, because I don't fully understand.

You set a soul free by strangling someone with a blue ribbon, but what does your boyfriend—Nash—do?"

"He chooses the lucky soul to be sent to paradise."

"How? How can he choose one person out of millions to receive such a...gift?"

"Interesting question, *Doctor Cooper*. I never asked him how he chose, so I can't answer it."

Max seemed sincere to Cameron. She wasn't any more than a weapon of destruction; not part of the planning. "What's in it for you?"

"What was in it for you when you went around killing innocent people?" Max retorted.

"I wasn't in control. I told you, the guy in my head did it, so I got nothing but locked up in here for the rest of my life. But you...you had a choice. You could've said no. Why didn't you?"

"Said no to what?"

"To killing those women."

"I don't know what you're talking about. I didn't kill anyone. That's your thing, not mine."

"You just said that you set their souls free. Those women are dead and you did it."

"I never said I killed anyone."

Cameron was starting to catch on. It was all a game to Max. Now the game was a game of words. She never admitted to murdering anyone. She said she set them free. Did them a favor. As Cameron processed, Max slowly closed the distance between them by bending forward across the table, her head tilted down, eyes up, in what Cameron had come to recognize as Max assuming a position of threat. To Cam, she looked more like a scrawny cartoon vulture.

"Stop trying to analyze me, *Doctor Cooper*," Max said in a low voice. "I don't like you poking around inside my head, and I don't want you creating another personality based on me this time."

Cameron straightened up at Max's last words. "What does that mean?"

"You know what it means. I'm going to find Joan now. I heard she doesn't have a lot of friends. Maybe she'll be mine."

Max pushed her chair out from the table and stood, eyes locked on Cameron, before turning and walking away. As she slunk past John Mercedes, she stood up on her toes and yelled, "Boo!" into his face.

Unfazed, Mercedes stood like a large, menacing piece of granite, unblinking. "Is that the best you got?" He looked down at Max, smirking. "You keep moving along now, before I show you what scary really looks like."

Cameron watched Max as she swayed down the corridor, singing to herself, and wondered why she'd been asking so many questions about Joan. If Joan Namath was some kind of target for Max, or if they became friends, formed an alliance, the outcome could be catastrophic. Even worse, if Max antagonized Joan, really pissed her off, the larger woman would snap her scrawny neck with little effort. Cam reasoned Max was too smart to put herself in danger. She was up to something, and the idea of Max and Joan left Cameron feeling anxious.

CHAPTER 28

Max

MAX LAY ON HER bed, staring up at the stark white ceiling and the rectangular light fixture attached to it. She had requested to make a phone call every day, multiple times a day, since she'd arrived, and was told no each time, *when* she got an answer. She desperately needed to speak to Nash about what he was doing to get her out of the loony bin. While she was having fun with Cameron Cooper, she also worried about some of the other patients. She figured the crazier she acted, the more likely they'd be to stay away. She hoped.

Her door was half-open when she heard a whistling sound getting closer. It was the orderly named Shane—in her mind she called him Humpty, because she thought if Humpty-Dumpty came to life as a person, he would be Shane. Same egg shape, same boring face, and just as clumsy. She pictured Shane sitting on a wall, having a great fall—because she had pushed him—and breaking into pieces. The thought amused her momentarily.

He nodded at her as he pushed the door open all the way.

"Fresh sheets. Stand against the wall," he ordered, motioning to the wall to his left.

Max stood and stretched, taking her time. She leaned against the wall next to the toilet, under the mounted camera, a feature found only in the most aggressive patient's rooms. The location of the camera provided privacy. From that angle, the guards could see the bed and most of the room, but not the toilet or sink. If the patient was out of the camera view for more than a few minutes when they were supposed to be in their room, an alarm would sound on the monitor at the guard's station. Two minutes was all the time they had to use the toilet and wash up. Any longer, and two guards would come to inspect, allegedly.

As Shane walked into the room with clean sheets, he quickly held out a hand to Max—in it was a cell phone. "You have until I change the sheets. He's waiting for your call."

Max quizzically examined the ancient flip phone Shane had slipped her. Her mother had one when she was a little girl, so even though it was an antique to her, it was not unfamiliar. Shane had already cued a number up on the screen labeled Mr. Wonderful. She tapped the number on the screen, but nothing happened. She hit it again, harder. Still nothing.

Shane watched her from the corner of his eye. Shaking his head, he mumbled, "Press the button with the green phone icon on it. That's how you connect."

Max did as she was told and after one ring, a familiar voice answered.

"Hello, Max."

Shane was the contact that she'd been waiting to materialize.

"Nash! Oh my god, I'm so happy to hear your voice! This place sucks! When are you getting me out? Have you called a lawyer? Because the guy the state assigned me is a moron. I'll end up on death row for sure if he represents me. And by the way, I'm mad at you! I know you set me up. How could you?"

"Shh...easy Max. I need to do the talking; you need to do the listening. Understand?"

"Yeah, okay..."

"First off, how are you doing, Max? Settling in?"

"I just told you—this place sucks! I want out."

"Relax, Max. It won't be much longer. This is what I want you to do. Our friend Shane, the man who just handed you the phone? He's going to be our inside helper."

Max looked the egg-shaped man up and down. "How is he going to help?" She imagined him trying to smuggle her out, tripping and falling, and once again breaking into a hundred pieces.

"When I need to communicate with you, he will be our go-between. If I need to get anything to you, he will be my mule. If you need to get a message to me, he will be your carrier pigeon. For example, tonight, after lockdown, Shane will leave a lovely present for Dr. Cooper to find in the morning. And you're right. I set you up, but only because it's time to get our revenge. But remember, Max, you are not to physically harm her. If you do anything to her before I say it's okay, I will walk away and leave you there forever. Understand, Max?"

"Got it. Don't touch the crazy doctor. What *do* you want me to do?"

"Mind games, Max. Just like we discussed."

"How long do I have to stay here? When will I get out?"

"You'll know when it's time and I promise, Max, it won't be long now. Remember everything we rehearsed. The sooner you get her to crack, the sooner you leave St. Christina's. Take care now, Max. Our time is up."

The line went dead just as Shane picked up the dirty sheets and shuffled his body in her direction. She discreetly handed him the phone back, and he slipped it in his pocket. Nash must be paying him a bundle, Max thought, as she watched him waddle out the door.

She sat back down on the freshly made bed and noticed how the sheets smelled like bleach and were somewhat crispy, just like the towels in the shower room. Not like when MeeMaw did the laundry and everything was fluffy and flowery, and not like the luxury sheets and towels at home with Nash, which he spritzed with lavender.

She thought about her sweet grandmother. Right about this time, they would be snuggled together to watch Wheel of Fortune. It was MeeMaw's favorite show and every night they watched Pat and Vanna, and the contestants yelling out letters, and they'd laugh out loud when the dummies on TV couldn't guess the puzzle that was so obvious to the two of them. They would have bowls of ice cream as they watched. Max had loved that time with her grandmother.

Until Clara and Wayne killed her. Max could feel the rage building in her as her memories turned to her mother and her asshole husband.

God—I hate them! She slammed a fist into her pillow. *I wish I could kill them all over again....*

She glanced around the hospital room-cum-cell that held her captive. *MeeMaw would be so disappointed in me.*

A noise from next door caught her attention. She had momentarily forgotten about Cameron Cooper. She sat still as she listened for another telltale sound that Cameron was back in her room. Sometimes the disgraced ex-FBI-agent-turned-prisoner disappeared. Where could she possibly be going that Max couldn't seek her out? The only thing she came up with was sessions with Dr. Heisser, the resident idiot who was trying to crack her brain open. She hated it when he called her Maxine. She hated it when anyone called her Maxine. But she especially hated it when Cameron did.

Nash wanted her to play mind games with Cameron. He wanted Max to crack her...but how? They had talked about it. Nash had instructed Max to ask Cameron a lot of questions. Questions about her time with the FBI, about unsolved cases, about lives lost because of Cameron's inadequacies. And finally, about why she'd left the FBI. What had driven her from the job she loved so much? If it would get her out of the bleached asylum sooner, Max would come up with a thousand questions.

The small room filled with an orange glow. Max stood and walked over to the barred window, looking out as the shadow of the building that trapped her inside grew across the open land that surrounded it. The moon was already visible, hanging high in the sky. Another day wasted in the hellhole called St. C's.

She wished she were free.

If it wasn't for Nash, she would still be free. A missing person, presumed kidnapped or killed by the people who had killed her mother and stepfather. Instead, the police now presumed her to be Clara and Wayne's killer. They weren't wrong. Did the police think she'd killed her MeeMaw as well? If they accused her of her grandmother's death, she would set the record straight and make sure they knew those two assholes did it. She'd make sure everyone understood without a doubt that she would never have hurt MeeMaw. She loved her grandmother, and her grandmother loved her back.

How did I get here? Max wondered, as she stood watching the glowing orange sun dip lower, touching the horizon. *If Nash wanted revenge, he should have gotten it himself and left me alone.*

She leaned on the windowsill with her arms crossed, supporting her. *What if he can't get me out? What if he won't get me out?* These thoughts had occurred to Max before the police hauled her in that night in the dog park. She'd done her research and knew St. C's was a maximum-security hospital for violent offenders.

She heaved a sigh, pushed off from the sill, and turned to face her existence. The sun had set, and the fluorescent light attached to the ceiling of the small room flickered on, producing a low buzz. It was almost dinner time. Three meals a day, a warm bed, and a room of her own. Everything she'd had with Nash, but nothing the same. It was the upside of being imprisoned. The state fed, clothed and sheltered her in a warm, but not safe, environment. It was better than being on the streets in the middle of a New York winter, and yet, it was also the worst possible place.

Max reasoned that if Nash couldn't, or wouldn't, set her free, that there were worse places, like the super-max penitentiary where she could still end up. If she played it right, kept up the crazy act, her lawyer would argue she was unfit to stand trial and she would have a permanent residence at St. C's. Eventually, she'd start acting 'normal' again, whatever that definition was, and maybe be released under the guise of cured in the not-too-distant future. Or maybe she'd find a way to escape.

Then she'd have her own revenge.

She'd show Nash that life with Clara and Wayne had prepared her for his disloyalty. The abuse she'd suffered at their hands had made her resilient. She'd grown up with betrayal and lies, and if he left her in St. C's, double-crossed her after everything she'd done for him, she'd take pleasure in getting even. She knew how to find him if he was stupid enough to screw her.

He'd taught her well to always be prepared. She'd snooped through his house, his belongings, his safe. Max wanted to believe Nash was sincere in his love for her, but she'd planned for the worst. That's what happened when you were raised by a woman like Clara Meyers...you never fully trusted or believed anyone. If Nash let her down, abandoned her, it would be the worst mistake of his life.

CHAPTER 29

Cameron

Through therapy sessions, daily yoga, and meditation, Cameron had learned to be more at peace in her own mind, even though there was nothing peaceful about her physical location. The inmates on her floor screamed, moaned and taunted the guards and each other all day and late into the evening. And then Max arrived along with her incessant scratching and tapping on the wall that separated them.

Cameron lay on her bed, concentrating on her breathing as her mind wandered to the beachside cottage of her imagination. She could practically smell the sea air as she envisioned seagulls squawking and hanging in the sky, the rush of the foamy salt water as it washed up the beach and then receded again, the ocean breeze pressing against her face and ears, blowing through her hair as the sun warmed her skin. She visualized her feet sinking into the warm sand and the sensation of the earth moving beneath her, the salty spray of the cool seawater dampening her warm face, and the sounds of the ocean bringing back childhood memories.

The beach was her happy place, and she longed to be near the sea. It was always her dream to live on the shores of the ocean, soothed by the motion of the waves as it transformed from minute to minute, day to day, never the same. She could gaze upon its beauty for an eternity and know she would never see the same thing twice.

*What could be better? S*he thought. *Hunter. If Hunter were with me, it would be better, it would be perfect, and I'd be euphoric.*

A faint smile reached across her lips as her thoughts consumed her, relaxed her. She was no longer in a forensic facility for the criminally insane. No, she was at her happy place with the man she loved. Life was perfect. In her mind, Hunter walked toward her, grinning, his tan linen pants rolled up at the ankles, his bare feet digging into the sand. He reached out to her, wrapping his long arm around her shoulders, and pulled her close to him, clinging to her. They'd walk along the beach, laughing, smiling, and gathering shells as the sea threw them to their feet.

In her mind, after their walk, they would sip wine under a brightly colored umbrella. Hunter would feed her cheese, a creamy Port Salut, and raspberry jam spread on a flaky cracker. She'd notice the new gray highlights shining at his temples and run her hand through his hair; he'd lean in and press his lips to hers for a tender kiss. She envisioned his eyes crinkling at the corners when he looked at her, the green in them deeper from the ocean's reflection. If given the opportunity to design a personal heaven, this would be it.

Cameron drifted off to sleep with the wish for her life playing in her head, and her dreams followed suit. It was a new sense of calmness, ironically gifted to her by the New York Detentions Department.

She would never have guessed that being sent to such a horrible place would have such a positive effect on her, leaving her more in control of herself and her mind, even though she really had no control over anything else. She had no freedom, not even to leave her room without someone unlocking the door each morning and granting her permission.

Cam was told what to do and when to do it every single day and had no choice but to comply; she was a prisoner, physically, and her body had been a prison for her sanity, but now...now she was experiencing freedom, maybe for the first time, if not physically, at least mentally, freedom from the horrors of her past that had tormented and fractured her. Was it too much to hope she would be free in body, mind, and soul some day? To have the dream, to live the dream? To be with Hunter in her happy place?

On good days, she thought it was possible, but that it would take time and hard work, and she would work harder than ever to make it happen. Her only fear was that it would be too long for Hunter to wait and he might move on before freedom granted her the opportunity to join him.

She slept peacefully all night, an accomplishment in the cinder-block structure with strange creatures howling at all hours. The meditation and visualization that led to peaceful dreams in happier places had a price; every morning it was a slight shock when Cam awoke to her cave-like room and she remembered where she really was. She had learned not to get upset about it anymore, but the disappointment she felt was profound. She reminded herself each morning that she was one day closer to freedom.

The sun peeked through the bar-clad window of her room, waking her from a deep slumber. Yawning, she stretched her limbs under the scratchy sheet and blanket. Her body had become accustomed to the daily ritual of St. Christina's, and she always woke up about a half hour before the guard would arrive to open her door, setting her free for the day. Free within the confines of St. C's.

Sitting up, she slipped her feet from underneath the warmth of the blankets and placed them on the cold tile floor. But suddenly, something on her beige, hospital-issued blanket caught her eye.

Her heart lurched as she picked up a long, blue ribbon and held it dangling between her fingers in front of her. She looked it up and down, her heart racing; someone had come into her room in the night and left the calling card of The Chelsea Choker.

She instinctively glanced around her, looking for any other signs that someone had been in her room. There was nothing that looked out of place. *Was it Max? It had to have been! But how? How did Max get out of her room and into mine?*

Then two thoughts occurred to Cam; if Max had been in her room in the middle of the night, then she could have easily killed her. The other thought—Max must have an accomplice inside the hospital.

Unconsciously, Cam put a hand to her throat as she stared at the ribbon. It must have been Max. Or was it someone else working with Max? The guards would have caught Maxine out of her room and entering another room in the middle of the night, not that she'd have access without a key. But if it were a guard, the other guards might not pay attention. Or an orderly.

Cam reasoned the idea of an orderly away; the guards would definitely note someone like that entering a patient room in the night and the orderlies were no longer privy to patient room keys after the Myra incident.

Her fingers released the ribbon onto her blanket, and she wiped her hand on her pajama pant like she'd been touching something dirty or vile. The blue ribbon coiled onto itself, a sharp contrast to the beige blanket. It was a threat, of that she was certain.

Max was showing Cam she could get to her at any time, and it was easy. She shuddered at the thought of someone in her room as she slept, standing over her, *stalking* her. It was creepy even for this place, and even worse, they could have attacked and easily killed her. If someone could get to her through a locked door in a high security place like this, then she knew she was in serious danger. The game had just taken a jagged turn.

She stood and backed away from the ribbon as if it were alive and would strike at any moment, wrapping itself around her neck and squeezing until she was dead. Cam reached for the door handle and tried opening it, but it remained locked tight. She pressed her face to the glass, looking up and down the hallway as far as the small square window would let her. There was no one.

Quietly, she approached the wall separating her from Maxine Jane Hoyt and pressed an ear to it. Silence. She looked up at the camera hanging over the sink in front of her, its small light blinking green as a sign of all systems working. She knew the night shift would still be on duty. As far as she understood, none of them were aware of her deal with Hunter and the NYPD to analyze Max. Only John Mercedes had been told about the plan to pump Max for information.

Cam opened the wardrobe and took out fresh clothes for the day, the same as every other day. Light blue elastic-waist pants, a light blue pullover shirt, and the cashmere sweater Hunter had given her. She peed, washed up and brushed her teeth, eager to get away from the ribbon of death.

The guard would arrive in a few minutes to unlock her door and check on her. She debated whether or not she should mention the calling card curled up on her bed. She decided she wouldn't, but would head straight for the phone at the guard's station and call Hunter pronto.

Trapped in her room, Cam was a sitting duck ready for the kill. The walls closed in on her with every second that passed. What if the guard who unlocked her door was Max's accomplice? What if the blue ribbon wasn't a warning but a foreshadowing as to what was about to happen, and whoever opened the door would use it to silence her forever? Her imagination ran wild as she protected her neck with both hands.

She stood back from the door and placed herself in front of the camera and its green blinking light. What was once an intrusion was now a lifeline.

One guard always stayed in the box, as they called the guard station, observing, ready to hit the alarm in case of any problems as the doors opened in the morning. If that alarm sounded, teams of guards armed with tasers and billy clubs would rain down on the patients on the ninth floor until they contained the situation.

Cam's imagination turned on her once more as she envisioned the guard at the station leering with pleasure as Max strangled her to death, and she pleaded with her eyes for help. She accepted she had a target on her back because of her association with The Stealth Stalker killings, and because of the beating her alter, Jason, had given to one of their own, Myra, that bitch. Yet, she'd never felt unsafe in St. Cs. Until now.

She stared at the clock as if it were counting down the last remaining minutes of her life. The guards would have changed shifts by now, and she desperately hoped a friendly face would come to the window and unlock her door. She knew it wouldn't be Petey Johnson. Not since the last time he'd opened her door to find Myra on the floor bleeding, moaning, and on the verge of being slaughtered by Jason.

Footsteps echoed in the hall outside her door, but she couldn't see who the feet belonged to. What if it was Merck the Jerk? If the money was right, that sadistic asshole would work with someone like Max. But wouldn't Max want to do it herself?

And then Cam remembered...Max sedated her victims before she killed them. She needed them incapacitated to overcome them. What if Merck was about to weaken her so Max could come in and finish the job without a fight?

Cam braced herself for the worst. She watched as the door handle turned, still unable to see through the small window who was on the other side. When her heart rate picked up as panic and fear washed over her, she recalled her FBI training and stood ready to fight off any would-be attacker.

Suddenly, the door pushed open with a thud as it hit the wall and Cam stood ready to fight for her life. She recoiled her arm, her hand closed into a tight fist, ready to strike, as a large, hulking figure stood before her—it was Grey Turner. She didn't let her guard down as Grey put his hands on his hips.

"What are you playing at?" he asked.

"What do you want, huh? You come in here to hurt me? Well, I'm not going down without a fight."

"Cameron? Is that you?" Grey asked. His hand moved to his taser. He'd witnessed what she'd done to Myra Gordon and didn't want any trouble.

"Yes, of course, it's me," Cameron snapped at him. "Where's John Mercedes? I need to speak to him...now!" She glanced up at the camera, still blinking green. "Tell him to come here." She still held her fight stance, as if it would do much good against a man who was at least twice her size.

Grey pressed the radio strapped to his chest and spoke. "I need Security Chief Mercedes to a patient's room, ASAP. Room 921—Cameron Cooper."

A voice answered back, "Roger that."

"Back out of here, Grey, and stand in the hallway, please," Cameron demanded.

Grey did as she wanted, but kept his eyes trained on her. After what was less than a minute but seemed like several to Cameron, John Mercedes appeared at her door. He nodded to Grey Turner. "What's up?"

"Cameron demanded to see you." Grey shrugged and nodded his head in Cam's direction.

John Mercedes peered into Cameron's room, taking a step closer to the threshold. "What can I do for you, Cameron?"

"I need to make a phone call."

CHAPTER 30

Hunter

HUNTER COULDN'T GET TO Cameron fast enough. Levine was driving, blue lights flashing on top of the unmarked black SUV.

"We were supposed to be setting Max up, gathering info about her, but it looks like she was the one gathering info and setting up Cam. How did she get the ribbon into the hospital? How did she get into Cam's room? She must have help on the inside. *Damn it*!" Hunter snapped, frustrated and frightened for Cameron.

If anything happened to her, it would be his fault. He'd asked her to do this, get involved with a serial killer case, when she wasn't sure she was ready. He'd dropped Max, a violent criminal, off at Cameron's feet. Cameron wasn't violent, and even though she'd been a trained FBI agent, it was a long time ago. She might not be able to defend herself against a much younger, psychotic killer like Max.

"Stop the car. Pull over." Hunter commanded.

"What? Why?" Levine asked as he pulled the SUV in front of a fire hydrant, the only open space on the street.

"If we go in there all gangbusters, Max might figure out Cam can contact us and that Cam is working with us. We have to think about this for a minute."

"She'll think the guard called us. The Chelsea Choker made a move on The Stealth Stalker. We're there to investigate. Makes sense, doesn't it?"

"Yeah...I suppose. I still feel like we need to take our time. Act like we don't care that one psychopath tried to kill another, or Maxine will be on to us."

"Okay," Levine agreed. He turned off the blue light. "I'll drive over like it's any other day. We're in no rush. After all, there was no blood drawn. Cam's not physically hurt. We're just two detectives following up on our cases."

"Good."

Levine pulled back onto Thirty-Fourth Street, heading toward the FDR and Wards Island. He took his time, occasionally glancing out the window at the East River, glimmering beneath the morning sun.

Hunter's mind was on fire with visions of Max strangling Cameron to death or smothering her with a pillow. He would douse the flames just to have a new scenario ignite where Cam died by Max's hand or by whoever Max had helping her. "There has to be somebody on the inside. Who do you think it is?"

Levine rubbed his thumb along the steering wheel as he drove and contemplated the question. "Could be anyone, but it would have to be someone with access to the patient rooms."

"That's right. A guard, a nurse, or an orderly."

"The orderlies don't have keys anymore, remember?"

"Right—the Myra Incident."

"The Myra Incident." Levine nodded. "That narrows it down. And it would have to be someone on the night shift."

"Right. Cam said she hadn't told anyone about the ribbon, not even John Mercedes. She's trapped in there and doesn't know who she can trust."

"She, we, can trust Mercedes. Don't you think? I mean, he's not on the night shift and he likes Cam. I've caught him giving her the thumbs-up when he thinks no one is looking, encouraging her. And she's mentioned she likes him. He's a decent guy. Takes his job seriously, and isn't he a former Marine? I feel like we can trust him with this, don't you?"

Hunter stared out the windshield ahead of him. Traffic wasn't heavier than any other day in congested New York City, but it was slowing them down and making him more anxious. He had the urge to jump out of the car and run for the pedestrian bridge that led to Wards Island instead of sitting in a car crawling in traffic.

"Throw the light back on. Let's get out of this mess."

Levine did as Hunter demanded, and as the cars in front pulled to the side for them, he maneuvered through the traffic at a faster pace. By the time they arrived at St. Christina's, Hunter's back hurt from the stress. He jumped out of the SUV before Levine had it in Park and, with long strides, rushed for the front doors of the hospital.

"Hunter," Levine yelled. "Slow down. We're just investigating, right?"

Hunter stopped and waited for Levine to catch up. "Right. No rush. Just another day." He took a deep breath, blew it out, twisted his head from side to side and tried to release some of the anxiety turning his muscles rigid. "Any suggestions as to how we go about this?"

"Yeah, I think we should go into Dr. Heisser's office. And then have Mercedes bring Cameron in there to meet with us. We'll have all the important players in one place to discuss what happened and what needs to be done."

"Okay, sounds good to me," Hunter said as he pushed the call button for the elevator.

When they arrived at the ninth floor, Hunter spied John Mercedes at the guard's desk and made eye contact. "We're here to see Dr. Heisser."

John stood, his expression clouded with concern. "He didn't mention it."

"We don't have an appointment."

"I'll check in with him while you two secure your weapons."

Hunter and Levine placed their guns in the lock box and waited for the other guard to buzz them through. When John put down the phone, he nodded to them. "You boys got lucky. Dr. Heisser is in his office and has time to talk. Follow me."

The door buzzed and Hunter and Levine walked through, following John through the maze of corridors that led to Dr. Heisser's office.

"Does this have something to do with Cameron's urgent need to make a call this morning?" John looked back and forth between the two detectives. "Don't lie to me. She had me put her in the conference room you always meet in and made sure I locked the door behind me when I left. You two want to tell me what's going on?"

"It does," Hunter answered. "Can you get Dr. Heisser? We'll head to the conference room. We'll explain everything to you then."

When Hunter and Levine entered the conference room, Cam sat alone at the long table, pale, nervously tapping her foot, a blue ribbon splayed out on the table. Hunter's breath caught momentarily.

"Are you okay?" His eyes locked on Cameron's. He could tell she was anything but okay, but he had to ask.

"I...I'll be fine." Cameron shook her head. "But this is serious. Someone was in my room last night. They could have killed me. Max is not alone—"

Cameron stopped talking as John Mercedes and Dr. Heisser entered the room. She eyed Hunter and tilted her head to the side.

"It's okay. We can trust them."

"Trust us with what?" Reid Heisser said.

"Have a seat," Hunter said.

Levine and Hunter sat across the table from Cameron, the ominous blue ribbon a dividing line between them. Dr. Heisser sat at the head of the table and John Mercedes took the seat at the opposite end.

Levine reached for the ribbon and then pulled back, as if it might rear up and bite him. "We should bag this and get it to forensics. If we're lucky, whoever put it in your room didn't think to use gloves." Levine reached into the inner pocket of his suit jacket and produced a small plastic bag. He pulled a pair of vinyl gloves from his pants pocket, slipped them on, and placed the ribbon into the baggy.

"What's that?" Dr. Heisser said, watching Levine.

Hunter nodded to Cam.

"I found that on my bed this morning when I woke up. Someone was in my room last night *while I slept.*"

"That's impossible," John Mercedes said. "No one can get into a patient's room at night without a key."

"Right." Hunter slapped a hand on the table. "So, who has keys? The guards, the nurses, and you." He pointed to Heisser. "So, who was in her room? Who dropped a blue ribbon, the calling card of The Chelsea Choker, aka Maxine Jane Hoyt, on Cameron's bed?"

The men remained silent, looking at one another as Cameron's face flushed. She looked at Dr. Heisser. "They could have killed me."

"I...I don't know how this happened. Chief, what do you have to say about this?" Dr. Heisser appeared baffled.

"This is the first I'm hearing about this. When Officer Turner unlocked Cameron's door this morning, she didn't mention a ribbon on her bed or that she suspected anyone had entered her room. She demanded to see me. He called for me and I went straight to her room. She asked to use the phone and then to be brought here. That's all the information I have about any of this. I can view the overnight footage of Cam's room. Hopefully, we'll be able to identify who left it there."

"That's a good place to start," Hunter said. "Can you do it now and be discreet?"

"Yeah, yeah, of course. I'll go right now. I'll get to the bottom of this. Don't you worry, Cameron. You're safe." John Mercedes pushed his chair back and rose, shaking his head. "I don't know how anybody could expect to get away with something like this, but not everybody knows there's an observation camera in Cameron's room. I'll find him."

As the Security Chief left the room, Dr. Heisser leaned forward. "Cameron, are you okay? Do you need to talk about this?"

"It freaked me out at first, but I've calmed down. The ribbon is an obvious message. Maxine is telling me she can get to me whenever she wants." She paused. "Oh, no! I just realized...she's obsessed with

Joan Namath. Somebody should check on her and make sure she's okay."

"I'll do it," Dr. Heisser said. "I'll come back as soon as I'm done." He walked out of the room, leaving Hunter, Levine, and Cameron alone.

"Are you sure you're okay?" Hunter asked. He wanted to push the table out of the way and hold Cam to him, protect her, assure her he would never let anything happen to her. More than that, he wanted to walk out of St. C's with Cameron, never to return.

"I'm better now that you're here. I felt so...vulnerable this morning. I didn't know who I could trust. Leaving the ribbon was a threat. I'm lucky they didn't attack me. You see that, right?"

"We do. That's why we came right away. We can have you put into a secure room tonight if that'll help."

"I think we should wait and see what John finds in the video footage before we make any rash decisions. While I was sitting here waiting for you to arrive, I've had time to move past the visceral reaction to the ribbon I first had, and think about the implications of it and what it means. I want to confront Max. See what she knows. See if I can get her to slip up and reveal how she got it into my room."

"Are you sure, Cam? Maybe that's what she's waiting for...for you to confront her and give her a reason to attack you."

"No, it's a game to her. She's trying to get to me. Maybe she wants to prove she's the superior serial killer by toying with me before she makes a move to kill me. That could be why she's also obsessed with Joan. She's also a serial killer. I'm sure you remember her—Broadway Joan Namath, who killed homeless people up and down Broadway one summer?"

Hunter and Levine nodded.

"Joan and I are the only ones on this floor labeled serial killers. It could be the ultimate challenge for Max. A 'kill the competition' thing. If she gets rid of us, she wins. In her mind, anyway."

Dr. Heisser returned to the conference room and sat at the end of the table again. "Joan is fine. Watching television as usual. I searched her room myself and found no sign of any ribbons. Knowing Joan, if she found such an item on her bed, she'd carry it around like a present or a prize. She would definitely have it with her so that no one else could steal it and she'd be paranoid about it. There was no sign of a blue ribbon on her person. I also checked the other patient's rooms. No sign of a blue ribbon anywhere else."

Hunter ran his fingers through his hair and leaned back in his chair. "Great. It appears she only targeted you." His eyes met Cameron's. He desperately wanted to take her home with him. Keep her safe. And send Maxine Jane Hoyt to super-max where she belonged. "Seems like Max is sending you a direct message."

John Mercedes opened the door and stepped back into the room. "I found something. Shane Reynolds, an orderly, entered Cameron's room last night as she slept, and left the ribbon on her blanket. That's all he did. Entered, placed the ribbon, and left. It was quick, and it happened while the guards were making their rounds."

Hunter looked up at John. "I want his personnel file."

"I can't give you that without a warrant, but I wrote the address he provided. My guess is...he won't be back." John held out a slip of paper with handwriting scrawled across it.

"I'll take that," Levine said, standing and snapping the paper from John. "I'll call this in and get a patrol car over there to check it out."

Hunter slammed his large hand on the table before standing. "Damn it! I thought a guard was always supposed to be in the box, watching the cameras. How the hell did this happen?"

John Mercedes looked from Hunter to Dr. Heisser, not sure of how to respond. "We were short a guard last night. Officer Burgos went home sick."

"So what? It's too much work for the other guards to pick up the slack and make the rounds without Burgos? Your people broke protocol. Is one of your guards in on this as well?"

"Look, Hunter, I'm just as concerned about this as you are. The people we watch in here are dangerous, more so than in an ordinary prison because of their mental handicaps and the fact that the state doesn't allow us to carry guns. We have to do everything by the book in here or everyone in here, staff included, is in danger. I'll find out what happened. I promise."

Hunter shook his head. It wasn't John's fault—he wasn't even in the building when Shane placed the ribbon. "Did you check if this Shane guy entered any other rooms?"

"No. I'll get Petey on it right now." John left the room and Hunter knew he wouldn't be back.

He turned to Cameron. "Are you sure you don't want to be moved? At least for the night?"

"No, that's okay, Hunter. I'm sure the guards will be extra diligent tonight, and I don't want Max to know she got to me. Now we know she had inside help—Shane Reynolds. I have a feeling if he's found...it won't be alive. Somebody gave Shane that ribbon and the orders on what to do with it. Which would indicate the boyfriend is real. I want to take a crack at Max. See if I can pry some information out of her."

"Maybe Shane is the boyfriend."

"Not according to the description Max gave you. I don't think she was lying about the way she sees him, real or not. If he is real, he could be just as deadly as she is. And that's where our priorities are right now—finding out if there's another killer out there waiting to strike again."

CHAPTER 31

Cameron

THE GUARDS MADE THEIR rounds, as usual at eight a.m., unlocking doors and demanding the patients rise for breakfast. Cameron stretched under the warmth of the blankets tucked under her on all sides. She usually slept better and felt more secure when wrapped tightly within her blankets. Out the window, the sun shone high in the sky, a sign she'd slept later than normal. Pushing herself up on one elbow to a sitting position, she looked around her small room before swinging her feet off the bed and onto the cold linoleum floor. Nothing was out of place. She'd tossed and turned most of the night trying to stay awake, fearful of another threatening message. Finally, she'd fallen asleep from exhaustion and now she'd overslept.

Cam eyed the blinking green light on the camera mounted out of her reach and made her way over to the toilet. It was the only place she had any privacy—sitting on the pot. When she was done, she washed up, brushed her teeth and hit the showers.

The hot water running down her back soothed her tired and tense muscles. She could have stayed under the spray of water for an hour, but that wasn't an option. After she dressed, she left her room to go to the cafeteria for breakfast. She'd had little appetite the night before, and now she was starving, so she filled her tray with coffee, scrambled eggs, and a mixture of diced apples and berries that had a slightly brownish tinge to it from sitting out all morning. When she finally settled in to eat, Joan Namath appeared before her with a strange, shit-eating grin, a rare occurrence for the usually tense and angry woman.

Joan was holding her hand out to Cameron. "For you, Cameron. Take it. Do you like it? Isn't it pretty?"

Cameron stared at the contents of Joan's large, rough hand, her mouth open, her breath catching. She carefully took the prize from Joan and held it up in the light to examine it more closely. It was the feather of a blue jay.

The beautiful, sky-blue feather with black bars was about four inches in length, and the sight of it sent a chill through Cam. Another message—this time the calling card of the J-Bird, Jason Julius Jonette, the lunatic serial killer who'd kidnapped Cameron and college student Lisa Allen over thirteen years ago. He'd promised he would hunt them down and kill them as they'd escaped.

"Where did you get this, Joan?"

"You like it? Right? He said you would. He said we'd be best friends if I gave it to you."

Cameron stared up at her. "Yes, Joan, I love it." She tried to sound sincere even as thoughts exploded in her mind that Jason Julius Jonette was back. *It can't be.* "Who gave it to you? Who told you I would like it?"

"The guy with the sheets, Shane. Can I sit here with you, Cameron, now that we're friends?"

"Yes, of course, Joan. Please, sit." Cam motioned to Joan to take the seat across from her as a chill ran through her body, touching every nerve and setting off a trail of tiny alarms. "Shane gave you this feather to give to me? How did he know I would like it so much?" Shane Reynolds had disappeared. When police arrived at the address he'd provided on his application for employment, they found an abandoned, rat-infested building that was scheduled for demolition. They'd searched the place anyway, as best they could, and found no one. Cameron knew Shane was nothing more than an inside man to help Max. Cam also knew it meant that Max's boyfriend was very real and was sending very real threats.

Joan shrugged. "I don't know. He said you would. And now we can be friends."

"Yes, Joan, of course we can be friends. I really like you and I'm so happy we're finally friends." Cameron knew Joan's mental state was more that of a child than an adult, but she was also a killer who could seriously hurt or murder someone without warning, using nothing but her bare hands. She had to be convincing when she talked to Joan, and it wouldn't hurt to have Joan on her side. "And thank you so much for this beautiful feather. I promise to keep it safe. I'll put it in my book, right here," Cam said, tucking the blue feather into her journal. "This way I'll see it every day and it'll remind me you're my friend. Do you remember when Shane gave you the feather?"

"It wasn't yesterday. It was the day before. But he said not to give it to you until today. He said today is your anniversary."

Cameron nodded as if in a trance. *Anniversary? What could Shane have meant by that?*

"Did Shane mention what it was the anniversary of?"

"No. Do you want to play a game with me?"

"Sure, Joan, after I'm finished with my breakfast. Okay? I'll meet you in the rec room. You go now and pick out a game."

"I'll pick out a good one and get it ready to play. Hurry up and eat."

Cameron nodded and gave Joan a thumbs-up as she hurried away to select a game. Gulping the rest of her coffee, and making sure no one was watching her, Cam made a beeline to the guard's box and the lifeline phone to Hunter with one thought burning through her brain—Maxine Jane Hoyt wasn't just another serial killer, she was a disciple, or copycat, of Jason Julius Jonette! Cam felt woozy—how could this be? Was Max really that sinister, that cunning, to kill those women and actually have it work out that the courts placed her in the same hospital as herself?

***

Hunter and Levine had raced to St. C's after Cameron's call. They met in the same conference room as always. Levine unfurled the large paper map Hunter had brought Cameron on the first day and spread it across the wooden table as Cameron paced the room. If it weren't for the blue feather that she clutched in her hand, she wouldn't have believed for a minute that Maxine Jane Hoyt had even heard of Jason Julius Jonette or his FBI-given monicker, The J-Bird.

Cam walked over to where the men stood, examining the map, held the feather out over it, and released it. They watched quietly as it drifted down to the table, landing softly on the paper. "Show me the exact spot where Maxine was arrested," Cam said to Hunter.

He searched for a moment before jamming his finger onto the map and tapping. "Right here. At the entrance to the dog run."

Cam pulled the cap off a red marker and drew an X, just as she had done with the previous murders. The map now had six red X's drawn on it.

She opened the folder, taking the photos of the women whom The Chelsea Choker had killed, and carefully laid them out in order of death date under the map. Then she connected the X's on the map by drawing a line with the same red marker through each one in the chronological order of when each woman had died, ending where Max had attacked Angela James right before the police arrested her. Finally, she stepped back to review the information.

"Show me the crime scene photos from the night you caught Max," she said.

Hunter flipped through a red accordion folder labeled "Chelsea Waterside Dog Park" and fished out a stack of color photos. "What are you looking for?"

"I'm not sure," Cam said, flipping through the stack. She stopped in mid-flip, her brows arching. "What's this?"

Hunter and Levine leaned in to see what she was referring to. It was a photograph of a large statue.

Levine answered, "That's part of an art exhibit. The city installed statues of different animals in and around the dog run. That's the one Maxine was hiding behind when she attacked Angela James." He nodded at the map. "You know, this looks like a fishhook. Do you think that means anything?"

Confused, Cam walked around the table to see what Levine meant by fishhook.

As she studied the map from Levine's perspective, she suddenly gasped. "No, not a fishhook...a J, as in the letter J." Her eyes darted from the photos of the women to the large letter J she'd inadvertently drawn on the map when she'd connected the X's. She grabbed the files of each murder victim, shoving them into Hunter's hands, and a fat black marker.

"Hunter, tell me the age of each woman in the order they died, starting with the first one killed, to the last."

Hunter flipped through the files. "Brittany Davidge was thirty-two."

Cameron jotted the number on a piece of paper, placing it under Brittany's photo, shaking her head.

"Jessica was thirty-five," Hunter continued. "Nicole was thirty-seven and Michelle was forty. Umm, Tonya Nathan was forty-three and Angela, who survived but represents the last X, is forty-five." He looked at Cam with a blank expression. "What's up?"

"Five murders with the sixth intended victim surviving...just like—" Cam slammed the marker on the table, shaking her head. "Shit! How could I have been so stupid? Look at these pictures. The women's hair! It starts out dark brown with Brittany and progressively gets lighter until Angela. Angela! Oh my God, Angela!" Cam said, covering her hand with her mouth.

"Cam, what is it?" Hunter stood, trying to see what she was seeing.

"It's not Maxine Hoyt who's behind the murders—I mean it is—she definitely committed the acts, but she was prompted. Taught. Groomed how to do this. The person behind all of this, her boyfriend, Nash? It's Jason Julius Jonette. The real Jason Julius Jonette. The J-Bird," she exclaimed, holding up the blue jay feather and waving it in the air. There was a reason the damn thing had given her the chills earlier.

"I was thirty-two when he kidnapped me and had dark brown hair, just like Brittany. And now, I'm forty-five with bleached blond hair and a wide, dark brown stripe down the center, just like Angela," Cam touched the top of her head where her natural color had been growing out for the past year and a half, leaving just the bottom half of her hair blond. Angela's hair was the same, probably by choice...a popular style, loved by celebrities, to have their platinum hair set off by dark roots.

Levine tapped the photo of Angela with a pen. "How could he have known about your hair? He couldn't have been inside the hospital. You would have recognized him."

"Shane. That little rat. He was already working here when I arrived. My profile of Jonette was that he came from money. He must have been paying him off, which means there could be others.

"And the name Angela...my real first name. And when we connect the dots in order to where each woman died, it creates a J. A giant J, drawn in blood, across the Chelsea Piers." She motioned to the red J she'd just drawn on the map. "That ends at the statue of a giant bird. The J-Bird."

She held her hand to her forehead, the puzzle sliding together easily in her mind. JJ Jonette was back and was playing games with her. He'd drawn the police in and left obvious clues as to where and when the next attack would occur. They'd been pieces in his game.

"What was it that Max said to me? Something about planets...that's it—she said we were twin planets orbiting the same sun! The sun is JJ. He wanted Max to get caught... she's in here for me. It's his way of getting to me." She paced along the length of the table. If Max wanted to kill her, it wouldn't be difficult. "When Lisa Allen and I escaped, he screamed that we should have killed him. That he would hunt us forever until he killed both of us. He's here. In New York City. He's here to kill me."

Levine stood. "I'll call this in." He motioned to the camera that he wanted the door opened.

Hunter leaned over the map and the photos of the women. "Son of a bitch. Levine, call Jeff Alexander, too. He was Cameron's partner in the FBI and worked on The J-Bird case with her."

Cam took deep breaths to calm herself, to no avail. Max was playing with her. But if Jason Jonette wanted her dead, Max would have killed her already. *Or maybe that's just it,* she thought. *Jason Jonette doesn't want Max to kill me. He wants to do it himself!*

Hunter's phone rang. "It's Barone," he said, making eye contact with Levine. "What's up?" He listened for several seconds before responding, "What? When did this happen?" His eyes traveled from Levine to Cameron and back again, his mouth hanging open. "Send it to me now."

Hunter grabbed his laptop out of his messenger bag and opened it, tapping at the keys until the screen came to life.

"What's going on, Hunter?" Levine asked.

"Someone sent an anonymous video to the station. Barone said it's indisputable evidence that Max is our killer."

The trio waited patiently for new mail to arrive in Hunter's in-box. As quickly as it popped up, Hunter tapped it, opening the email Barone had just sent. He clicked on the attached file and watched as it downloaded. "Come on, come on."

A video opened on the laptop screen, and Hunter clicked the play button. The image was clear, in color, and obviously taken with expensive equipment. They stood in silence, watching. A hooded figure appeared on the screen wearing a black coat and black pants.

The video footage was from inside a bar, taken from across the room. As the figure entered the bar, they pushed the hood back off of their head.

"It's Maxine," Cam gasped.

They watched as Max made her way to the end of the bar and found an empty barstool.

"She scratched her nose. Maybe a signal to someone," Hunter observed. "Look, now she's nodding. She's definitely signaling someone else. She's looking around...right there. Her eyes locked on something or someone."

Tonya Nathan appeared in the frame, swaying to the music as she spoke to the bartender. The guy sitting next to her stood and left, and Tonya slid onto the vacant seat right next to Max. The camera zoomed in tighter on Max and Tonya. They could see Max pour a clear liquid into Tonya's drink.

"Max just roofied her," Cam said and pointed to Tonya's glass. They continued to watch as Max followed Tonya from the bar and the camera followed Max. "She doesn't seem to know that someone is filming or following her."

The view of the camera followed a chain-link fence and through some bushes until it stopped and focused on a bench on the other side of the fence, inside the basketball court. Max and Tonya came into view, with Max helping Tonya lie down and Max climbing onto the bench next to her.

Audio erupted. They could hear Tonya gagging and struggling as Max strangled her. When Tonya stopped moving, Max pressed her head to the woman's chest, then tied the ribbon around her neck, stood and said, "I'm going to get a bottle of water—be right back, love." Cameron and the detectives could clearly see Max's face as she murdered Tonya Nathan.

"We've got her." Hunter slammed his hand on the table. "This is indisputable proof that Maxine Jane Hoyt is The Chelsea Choker."

"Yes, it is proof. But...where did it come from? Who was on the other side of the camera?" Levine said. "Do you think it's her boyfriend? Why would he do this?"

"Her boyfriend is JJ Jonette," Cameron said with a sigh. "He did this to show us how manipulative he is and that he can get anyone to do his dirty work. And to show us he was there the entire time, and we had no clue. This can work to our advantage, though. When I show this to Max, she'll know that he not only betrayed her, but that he set her up. She's going to lose it and, I'm hoping, she'll take her revenge and lead us right to Jonette."

CHAPTER 32

Cameron

CAMERON ENTERED THE RECREATION room where patients watched television, played cards, read books, or zoned out. She scanned the room, spotting Max sitting next to Broadway Joan watching *The Price Is Right*, one of Joan's favorite shows, and made her way to the back corner of the room and the faded green sofa under the barred window. No one else was nearby and Cam could observe everyone in the room from that vantage point.

After opening her journal, she started writing. Ever since Max had arrived at St. C's, she'd used the journal not only as Dr. Heisser recommended but also to keep track of her days with detail, in case anything happened to her. She'd told Hunter about the journal and that if she were attacked, it should be the first thing he looked for, even though she typed a nightly report before turning in her laptop at the end of every day. Her journal would have the most updated information. For anything urgent, she would call him directly.

Max and Joan remained in Cam's peripheral vision, and Cam was aware of any movements they made as she wrote. It concerned her that Max had taken an interest in Joan and that Joan didn't seem to mind Max hanging around. Max could easily manipulate such a volatile woman. They could prove to be a dangerous duo.

As expected, Max turned her head, looking over her shoulder, and stared in Cam's direction. Cam could hear her murmur to Joan before she stood and walked toward the green couch.

"What's up, Cameron? Not feeling sociable today? Don't want to watch TV with everyone else? Too good for us?"

Cam was all too aware of Max's tactics to incite a response. She looked up at the slight woman, tipped her head to the side as her eyes scanned Max from top to bottom and back up again.

"You look tired, Maxine. Are you not enjoying your new accommodations? It's only going to get worse when you're sent to super-max. You should enjoy what you have now, before it's all taken away." Cam smiled at Max and went back to her journal.

"I'm not going anywhere," Max said, before sitting at the opposite end of the couch and facing Cam, her feet up on the cushion and crossed at the ankles. Daylight illuminated her face. "I'm going to be your next-door neighbor for a long time."

"It's not going to happen. I overheard the guards talking. The police have you for the murders of those women. I heard there's video—crystal-clear video, showing you assaulting a woman with intent to kill. I also heard they like you for the deaths of two people in Pennsylvania, maybe three, and when New York finishes convicting you, they'll hand you over to the Pennsylvania district attorney. New York doesn't have a death penalty, but guess what? Pennsylvania does." Cameron closed her journal and shifted in her seat so that she was facing Max. "So, no, you will not be my neighbor, but you are going to live on death row until the day you die."

"That will not happen. I didn't kill anyone."

"By the way, Max, I found your gift this morning. A very pretty blue ribbon. Does it mean you want to be my special friend?

Maybe you want to braid my hair later and tie it with the ribbon. Although...it could make the other girls jealous."

"That wasn't from me. It was from Nash. And I'm pretty sure it's not meant for your hair."

Cam saw a shift in Max's expression. She'd gone from mischievous to menacing in the blink of an eye. "From Nash? Or do you mean Shane? That's right, I know it was Shane who left it on my bed. Is he your boyfriend? Because I doubt very much he's coming back for you."

"You mean Humpty?" Max let out the raucous laugh that Cam now associated with her. "That was a good one. No, Shane is not my boyfriend. I told you, like a hundred times...Nash...Nash is my boyfriend."

"So, how did Nash give the ribbon to Shane?"

"Like I told your boyfriend—Nash is everywhere."

"What does that mean, Nash is everywhere?"

"He has friends in low places, but more importantly, he has friends in high places."

"Are you saying Nash is friends with the Chief Medical Officer of St. Christina's?"

"I don't even know what that means. All you need to know is that *my boyfriend* got into your room, whereas yours can't even keep you safe at night."

"How did he do it? Did he pay Shane off?"

Max shrugged; her lips jerked with a smirk. Cam knew she was enjoying herself and it was time to give it back to Max and watch the sparks fly.

"Which brings me to the most pathetic part of the Maxine Hoyt story. Your so-called boyfriend will not only *not* rescue you, but he'll get away scot-free. I bet he already has a new girlfriend. Probably a lot cuter than you." Cam watched Max's face turn red.

"You don't know anything. Nash loves me. He promised he would get me out of here and I believe him."

"He promised he would get you out of here? It's unusual for prisoners waiting for trial to get sent here. How did he know you'd end up here?"

"Because he knows I have issues. I'm schizophrenic and need medical help. That's why they put me here, in a hospital, where I can get the help I need. Just like you."

"You are not schizophrenic." Cam sighed. "The cops know that. What you are is screwed. You did the dirty work for someone else and now you're going to pay for it, with your life, while he's out on the town using another stupid, needy woman to do his killing for him. Why doesn't he do it himself? Is he physically weak? Too fragile to take down an unsuspecting woman by himself?"

Max stared at Cameron, the muscles in her jaw twitching under its thin skin. Her nostrils flared. Cameron prepared to be attacked. She had learned from her mistake when Audrey Lloyd kicked her in the face for asking if she was okay and wouldn't be caught off guard again.

Max threw her head back and burst out laughing, a loud, wild noise that caused other patients to take notice. Cam watched her carefully, still ready for Max to lunge at her. She didn't inquire what it was that Max had found so funny, because she knew Max wanted her to ask. She sat, leaning against the arm of the couch, trying to appear at ease while she pressed Max's buttons.

Max finally stopped howling and looked at Cameron, who was casually examining her nails.

When Cam noticed Max staring at her, she commented, "I could use a manicure."

Max placed one foot on the floor and leaned forward, poking the green fabric of the couch with a skinny finger. "Nash is not weak. We are a team. A family. Something you don't know about, right? What it is to have a family? I heard you were an illegitimate little bitch whose mother killed her stepfather, and that you have no one. Well, except the detective. But it's only a matter of time before he gets tired of waiting around for you. A handsome guy like that probably has lots of women throwing themselves at him. I bet his new scar only makes him hotter."

Now Max was pushing Cam's buttons.

"How is Detective Finnegan? Is he all better? Any permanent damage?" Max cooed.

Cam mirrored Max, leaning in, "I hear things too, Max, like how you murdered your mother and her husband. And your grandmother. What was her name? Oh, right...Alma Wilkes. What kind of depraved person kills their own grandmother, who was so frail she was in a nursing home? I think that's the one that will ultimately land you on death row. And for killing an old woman like that, they'll speed up your time. You won't languish waiting for execution like so many prisoners do. They'll put you down within the year. *Like the rabid animal you are.*"

Max dug her nails into the couch cushion, squeezing it with a death grip. "Let's talk about you, *Doctor Cameron.* How many women are dead because of you? How many kids cry themselves to sleep every night because *you* killed their mothers and now...you're trying to get off with some split personality bullshit? It won't take long for Heisser to see through you and send you on to super-max."

"At least I didn't kill my grandmother."

"Let me ask you a question," Max said, regaining her composure. "Why'd you leave the FBI? How does Cameron Cooper go from being FBI super-agent to serial killer? Was it something to do with a case? Is that what broke you? How many people lost their lives because you couldn't save them or because you outright killed them?"

Cameron decided to change tactics. Max was asking questions she didn't want to answer or even think about.

"You know, Max, lethal injection isn't always painless, like they tell you. They use three different drugs, starting with a sedative. If the sedative doesn't do its job properly, and there's been cases where it hasn't, when they inject the vecuronium bromide, a paralytic, you'll feel like you're suffocating as your lungs are paralyzed. And then you'll feel the potassium chloride entering your veins, traveling up your arm, burning its way through your body like acid, until it hits your heart like a vice. You'll know the precise moment it hits the heart as you begin to struggle against death. But I wonder..."

Cam knew she had the young woman's attention as Max's eyes widened and she swallowed hard, released her grip on the cushion and crossed her arms over her chest, an unconscious reaction to protect her heart.

"What do you wonder?" Max asked, as concern washed over her pale face.

Cameron suddenly saw the child sitting across from her and she remembered Max wasn't a monster but a young, naïve girl; no longer a teenager, but hardly an adult. She'd been used, lied to, and manipulated. At that moment, Cameron saw the fear in Max's eyes.

"It's nothing."

"Tell me! What do you wonder?" Max fidgeted, glancing around the room at the other patients before her eyes focused again on Cameron.

"I just had a thought. Since I was law enforcement, I know how these things go down. If you gave up the boyfriend, if he exists, they might go easy on you. Sometimes cooperation yields leniency. It would be the smart thing to do. Self-preservation. You might just escape the death penalty...but, nah, someone like you—you'd never do the smart thing. You'll die protecting someone who'd never do the same for you."

Max seemed to digest Cameron's words. She sat motionless, staring out the window as a few flurries drifted past.

Cameron pulled the soft cashmere sweater around herself a little tighter, hoping it wouldn't get ruined if Max were to attack her. She waited for Max to respond, but when she didn't, Cam offered help.

"I could talk to Detective Finnegan. Put in a good word for you."

"Why would you do that?" Max's attitude had changed completely. She'd gone from aggressive to somber, and Cam knew she'd hit a nerve.

"Because I don't think killing those women was your idea. I think someone manipulated you to do it. Maybe they made promises that they never intended to keep. Or was it money?" Cam could see by her lack of reaction that it wasn't for money. "Was it for love?"

Max stood up suddenly, glaring at Cameron. *Bingo. We have a winner.*

Max screamed at Cameron, "I'm tired of you playing doctor around here and so is everyone else!"

Joan jumped up off the couch and swung around to see what was happening. The other patients silently watched as the low hum in the room quieted. The only sound came from the television.

Nurse Arante, who was busy distributing afternoon meds, placed a hand on her personal alarm before addressing Max. "Maxine, calm yourself down, now!"

Max swung around to face the smaller woman. "Or what?"

"Or there will be consequences."

"What are you going to do? Lock me up?" Max screeched.

Her voice reminded Cameron of Levine's words when he had described her attack on Hunter. He'd said she was singing and cackling.

Max closed in on the nurse, who stood her ground, placing the tray of medication on a table next to her. The entire staff was trained in self-defense, and even though Nurse Arante was petite compared to Max, she knew what to do to protect herself and take Max down. "Don't come another step closer, Maxine."

"Don't call me *Maxine,*" Max screamed at Arante, with fists clenched at her side. Just as she took a step closer to the nurse with her fist drawn back, Joan Namath stepped between them and shook her head. Max stopped in mid-strike, huffing, before she slowly lowered her arm.

Corrections officers Rosalie Diaz and Merck the Jerk came flying into the room, batons in hand. Nurse Arante had pressed her alarm, alerting security that she was in danger.

"What's the problem?" Diaz demanded.

Nurse Arante craned her neck around Joan so she could see the officers before stepping around her. "Maxine needs a time out."

The two officers grabbed Max by her scrawny arms, ready to drag her back to her room.

"Wait," Arante said. "Her meds first." She forced Max's afternoon pills into her mouth and watched as she swallowed them, checking her mouth to make sure they were gone. "Now you can take her. When you've placed her in her room, lock the door behind you."

Diaz and Merck led Max out of the rec room as a quiet hum returned, the excitement of the day only a fuzzy memory for most of the patients.

Nurse Arante made eye contact with Cameron, who was trying to remain as inconspicuous as possible.

"What did you say to her?"

"We were just chatting. You know, girl talk." Cameron shrugged.

"Girl talk, huh? I will report this little incident to Dr. Heisser. Keep it up, Cameron, and you'll be back on the tenth floor in no time."

It was Cameron's turn for some sobering words. The last thing she wanted was to go back to Ten. Her goal was to go down and out the door, not regress and go back up. She'd explain to Dr. Heisser later what had happened. Hopefully, her methods to pry a confession out of Max, which were more FBI than psychologist, wouldn't anger him.

It was right then that Max's words came back to taunt Cameron. *Why'd you leave the FBI? How does Cameron Cooper go from being FBI Super-Agent to serial killer?* The answer to that one was Jason Julius Jonette. *How many people lost their lives because you couldn't save them or because you outright killed them?*

Cam counted. *Jennifer Saunders, Linda Birch, Amy Larsen, Adrianne Schechter, Medina Montan.* The women her alternate personality had savagely murdered.

CHAPTER 33

Cameron

THE NEXT DAY CAMERON found Max in the empty cafeteria, sitting alone with her back to the door, as if she were waiting for someone or something to happen. Cam chose a seat at another table and placed her laptop in front of her. It was ready to go with the video Barone had sent Hunter of Max killing Tonya Nathan cued up. Cameron wanted Max to come to her. She wanted her agitated, emotional. *Mirror the feigned disinterest, let's see where this goes.*

Just as Cam predicted, Max sighed loudly, slammed her hands on the table, and shoved her chair back, the metal feet screeching across the floor. Watching the reflection of the room in the plexiglass shield that separated the kitchen staff from the patients, Cameron observed Max turn around to see Cam's back to her and heard Max grunt like an angry animal.

She walked over to where Cam sat, placed her hands on the table, and leaned down into Cam's face.

Cam looked up innocently. "What's up, Maxine?"

"You are being rude," Max said, striking her usual intimidation pose of chin tipped down, eyes up, and brows furrowed.

"No, I don't think so." Cam smiled and sat back in the chair. "I don't want to sit with you, Max. You're not interesting anymore."

Incensed, Max screamed, "I'm not interesting? Hah! You're pathetic. Do you know that? You—"

"Shut up, Max. I don't care what you think of me or what you have to say, especially now that I know that you're only a pawn. Someone to be used and discarded by someone else...another psychopath."

"What are you talking about?"

"I know Nash is actually Jason Julius Jonette, or JJ, as he once told me. And I'm not impressed that you worked with him. Or did he trick you? Promise you something he will never deliver?"

"His name's not JJ. It's Nash."

"His name is not Nash, or JJ, or Jason. He would never tell you his real name or anything else about him that's real. I know more about the real Nash than you'll ever know."

"You don't know anything about him." Max slammed her hand on the table again, her face flush with anger. "And you will never know him better than I do. I know what he does for a living, where he lives, where he grew up, and his favorite flavor of ice cream. What do you think you know?"

Cam played along. "Educate me, Max. What does Nash allegedly do for a living? Murder for hire?"

"He's a highly respected appraiser."

Cameron scrutinized Max's every word and body language. She saw a seething anger ready to explode as Max protected her man and played up his importance. "An appraiser?" Cam chuckled. "Could he have picked anything more ambiguous?"

"I followed him...to the museum. Nash appraises art and statues, stuff like that."

"He knew you would follow him. He led you to the museum, and then he stood back, watching you search for him in there, amused by your stupidity. He couldn't say he held a standard position like a dentist or a banker.... that would be too easy to disprove. But an appraiser—kudos. Kudos, JJ."

"You bitch," Max shrieked, fuming. "You will never know him because I'm going to kill you."

"Oh please, Max, you don't have permission to kill me. When you were longing to snuggle with him in what I imagine was his sparsely furnished contemporary apartment, and he was keeping you at arm's length, he made it clear I was off limits. I was all his. Don't you see?"

"So much you know! He lives in a gorgeous townhouse on the west side with fancy old lady furniture. And we snuggled plenty. We did more than snuggle. He made love to me."

Cameron shook her head. "Made love? Jason Jonette does not 'make love.' He doesn't need or desire that kind of intimacy. For him, it's the kill. That's what gets him off. And you played right into his hands. You killed for him—he watched every time, but you didn't know. He was close enough to hear the women take their last breaths. That's what excites him. He would only touch your skinny body to manipulate you further...or kill you."

Max lunged across the table at Cameron, reaching for her neck as Cam pushed her chair back in surprise and jumped up. John Mercedes, who'd been watching closely and listening from the hallway, rushed for Max and grabbed her by the shoulder, forcing her back into her chair. He clutched her under the jaw to the point of pain and said, "Stay put or next time it'll be the taser and the baton."

"I have something to show you, Max. You see, ever since you arrived here, I've been covertly working with the NYPD to gather information about you and your boyfriend. But it seems that your boyfriend thought we needed a little help," Cam said, glancing at the camera in the corner of the ceiling. Hunter and Levine were on the other side of that camera, watching, waiting. She sat back down across from Max, turned the open laptop toward her seething adversary, and clicked the play option.

"We can only assume that Nash was the creator of this video because the two of you worked together, and with that assumption comes the assumption that he was the one who sent it anonymously to Detective Finnegan. He's betrayed you, Max."

The two women sat in silence as the video ran its course. Cameron observed as Max first appeared confused, then her demeanor morphed to stunned. It was crushing when betrayal was served by someone you loved and trusted, even for a sociopath.

"You still think JJ loves you?" Cam said, almost feeling bad for Max. "Did he ever tell you about me? Why he's interested in me?"

Max stared at the video, frozen with her image straddling Tonya, having just strangled her to death.

"He and I met more than a decade ago, when you were just a child. That's how far back we go. He was killing back then as well. He's been a killer his entire life. Only he and the devil know how many lives he's taken. I was still with the FBI when he turned his attention to me. Do you remember you asked me why I left the FBI?"

Max continued to stare at the laptop's screen. A sadness seemed to overtake her.

"I left because another woman, about your age, almost died at JJ's hand because of me. We called him The J-Bird back then because he would leave a blue jay feather tucked in the hands of his victims. Just like this one." Cameron held up the precious feather Joan had gifted her that morning. She placed it on the table next to the laptop in front of Max. "Joan gave it to me this morning. Apparently, Shane gave it to her to give to me. A message from your friend Nash. Do you see how he bypassed you there?"

Max, eerily still, didn't flinch.

"We were closing in on him when he kidnapped me, and while he was having his fun with me, confident that I would die when he decided he was done with me, he told me his name was Jason Julius Jonette but preferred to be called JJ. He demanded that I beg for my life, and when I didn't, he kidnapped a college student named Lisa Allen. He tortured her in front of me, waiting for me to break down and start begging, but I didn't...couldn't. I knew the moment I started begging, he'd kill her. As long as I kept my mouth shut, no matter how hard it was, no matter how much Lisa suffered, he would let her live until it broke me. I couldn't let the monster win."

This was a part of Cam's life she hadn't explored yet in therapy and she needed to take a moment to collect her thoughts and herself. Her heart was beating a little faster recalling the days locked in a cellar, tortured by Jonette, and how much worse the mental torture was when he'd turned his monstrous attention to Lisa Allen. Cam kept reminding him she was the one he wanted, not Lisa. *Let the girl go*, she'd commanded. *Untie me, and you and I can fight this out to the death*. But he didn't.

"Obviously, we got away," Cam continued. "My guess is that we were the only ones ever to escape JJ, and he's been obsessed with finishing what he started—killing us both. Lisa and I left Georgia on different paths. I changed my name and moved around, remaining anonymous, until I was arrested, and as you said, blew up the internet. He knew where to find me, but he couldn't get to me in here. That's where you came in. The one thing I can't figure out is how he plans on getting to me himself. I know he would never let you kill me. That would be no fun and so unsatisfying, so how does he plan on getting in here so he can do it himself? Do you know, Max?"

Max lifted her eyes from the laptop screen and met Cameron's.

"JJ sent this video. Indisputable evidence that you were the one who killed those women. He was close enough to take a clear, close-up video as you strangled Tonya Nathan to death. And then he sent it to the police. Let me guess—he told you if the police ever caught you, he had a plan to rescue you. No, wait, not rescue... a plan to get you out. And this is it. You are getting out... of St. Christina's. You're getting out tomorrow. There's just a matter of paperwork. Good news, right? JJ came through for you...maybe he loves you after all." Cameron shook her head.

Tears rimmed Max's eyes, puddling and ready to spill over and down her sharp cheek bones.

"Except that you're going straight to Clairmont Correctional for Women. Yikes, that's a tough joint. You'll stay there until you get a trial date for capital murder. As I told you, New York does not have the death penalty, but the New York State AG is petitioning the governor for a special exception on the death penalty just... for... you. He doesn't want another state to have the pleasure of killing you. He wants to do it himself. History will forget you."

Pleased with herself, Cam sat back to assess Max, who was now visibly shaking, face red, eyes fixated on Cam, her hands white-knuckled and curled into tight fists.

Cam pushed more, wanting Max to lose control. "But none of that matters. Chances of you making it to trial are... not good," Cam said, shaking her head with a pout. "Serial killers don't fare well in prison. They freak the other prisoners out. They'll murder you before justice is served. It's a pity too, because the families of the deceased deserve closure."

A guttural scream emerged from Max. "Ah-h-h-h-h-h!" Her face contorted like a cornered animal ready to pounce. She lunged, aiming for Cameron's throat, screaming, "If I wanted to kill you, I could have. I didn't want to displease Nash—he loves me...he's chosen me. Not you."

Cameron shoved her chair back, swatting at Max's hands and struggling not to fall over backward. They wrestled until Mercedes pressed his Taser into the small of Max's back, sending her body into convulsions. Petey Johnson yanked her hands to her back, handcuffing her.

Max lay convulsing on the cafeteria table, drool pooling next to her face on the Formica, as Cameron straightened herself up. Mercedes and Johnson jerked Max back to her seat, holding her in place so she wouldn't fall over, and Mercedes radioed for a doctor and a sedative.

"Max? You still with me, Max?" Cameron asked. "Oh Ma-a-a-x," she called in a singsong.

Max lifted her head, her dirty blonde hair hanging on her face, saliva dribbling down her chin. Her body involuntarily shuddered, an aftershock of sorts.

"It doesn't have to be so dire, you know?" Cameron said. "If you help us, we can help you. You tell us where JJ Jonette is and the police commissioner will ask the D.A. to put you in solitary so you can at least get your day in court. Tell the world your side of the events."

"What about the families of your victims?" Max whispered. "Don't they deserve *closure*?"

Surprised, Cameron flinched at the question.

A grin slowly formed on Max's lips. "You and I are the same. Don't think for one minute we're not. You have as much blood on your hands as I do. People are suffering right now, missing loved ones, because of you. You claim insanity. I think you're brilliant. And we serve the same master. You even went so far as to use his name when you killed. Did you think that would please him?" Max chuckled and shook the hair from her face. "When Nash first mentioned you, I Googled your name. I found way more than I'd imagined I would. Cameron Cooper, the FBI agent who went on a killing spree and called herself *Jason Jonette*."

Cameron could feel Max's eyes boring into her as she spoke. Her words were unsettling.

"But I still couldn't put it together...why Nash was so interested in you. Until I Googled *Jason Jonette* and found an old newscast about a serial killer, Jason Julius Jonette. The J-Bird. And there it was, an artist's drawing of the man police were hunting. And do you know who that drawing looked like?"

Cameron had an inkling but wouldn't interrupt Max when she was feeling so chatty.

"It looked just like Nash. I had all my answers at that moment." Max glared at Cameron. "At first, I think it flattered him that you copied him. But then you stupidly got caught. Something that's never happened to him. How embarrassing. Now he's just angry that you dared to kill in his name without his permission. And as far as me needing permission to kill you, think again. He sent me here to give you a message—to prove you will never be safe from him. He can get to you even in a maximum-security shithole like this."

Max stood suddenly, forcing the chair away from her, and leaned over the table. "Don't go to sleep tonight, Cameron. I'm waiting for you."

Hunter entered the room and stood looming over the table. He nodded at John Mercedes, who pushed Max back down on her chair. "I have an update. Murphy and Barone used the street and subway camera footage to follow Max home from the dog park. That's the beauty of New York City—there are cameras everywhere, from the Lower East Side all the way to the Upper West Side. But since there's over ten thousand cameras in the subways alone, it took a while to go through it all. Knowing the exact time of the attack made it easier, but still, that's a lot of footage. And it paid off."

Cameron and Max exchanged looks and then turned their attention back to Hunter.

"I spent the morning on Central Park West in a very beautiful home that is now a crime scene. I have some digital pictures to show you just in case you don't believe me, Maxine." Hunter opened his bag and retrieved an iPad, which he held up for the two women to see. "The first picture is of the outside...nice place. Late 1800s brownstone, worth about eight million, most recently rented out to Nash Jones with the lease ending two days ago." Hunter locked eyes with Max for a beat before continuing.

Then he swiped the tablet's screen to a photo of an empty room that featured a fireplace. No dainty sofa or carved coffee table. He studied Max as she took it in, unblinking. He swiped the screen again and again, displaying pictures of every room in the house—each one void of furnishings, until he got to one last room.

"As you can see, the house is empty, except for one room," he said as he gave the screen one more swipe. "Your bedroom, Max. That one is still fully furnished. And look at this, Cameron...Max has a trophy wall." Hunter zoomed in on the solid wall to the left of Max's bed that had a photograph of each victim taped to it in a perfectly aligned row.

A deep red spread across the skin on Max's neck and face, flushing her cheeks.

"And if you look right here"—Hunter zoomed in tighter—"you'll spy a spool of blue ribbon that forensics is testing as we speak."

"Did you see an orange cat with green eyes?" Max asked quietly.

"Oh, yeah. We found a half-dead cat locked in the bathroom. One of the cops, who's an animal lover, took it to the vet, but honestly, it didn't look too good." Hunter shook his head and frowned. "Was that your cat, Max? It doesn't look like Nash was too fond of it. He left it there with no food or water. Didn't even leave the toilet lid up so it could get a drink that way. He just left it to die."

A tear rolled down Max's cheek and landed with a splatter on her shirt, leaving a dark stain in its wake.

"We also found a toothbrush and a hairbrush with several strands of hair the same color as yours that is also being tested as we speak." Hunter sat down at the end of the table with Cameron and Max on either side. He placed the iPad angled toward Max with a photo of Sammy Cat, limp and unresponsive, in her line of sight. "He's gone, Max. Nash set you up to take the blame, alone. He's not coming back, and he's not rescuing you from here. You're going to jail for a very long time. That is...*if* the Pennsylvania D.A. doesn't have enough evidence to hand you the death penalty for killing Clara and Wayne Meyers, and Alma Wilkes. You're facing several life sentences."

"I didn't kill my grandmother." Another tear rolled down Max's cheek. "I loved her and I would never hurt her."

Hunter leaned in before thinking better of it and straightened himself up and away from Max. "Is that a confession to killing Clara and Wayne? Did they kill Alma, and you got revenge?"

"It's a statement of fact, that's all. I didn't kill Alma Wilkes."

"Tell me what happened, Max. Tell me about Nash and I'll help you get revenge against him, too."

Max silently nodded. "It all started with dinner..."

CHAPTER 34

Cameron

With Maxine Jane Hoyt packed up and on her way to Clairmont Correctional Maximum, Cameron Cooper was enjoying the first sound sleep she'd had in weeks when a disturbance abruptly awoke her. Her eyes focused on the ceiling above her, not sure what had roused her from her dreams. She could tell by the amount of light in her small room that the sun was inching its way to the horizon.

A tapping on the metal door that kept her locked in through the night startled her. She rolled to one side, propped herself up on an elbow, and focused on the door, listening for the sound.

Someone was standing on the other side of the door, and they had just taken a step in front of the door's small window. When she heard the tapping again, she sat up to get a better look, but in the dim light; it was hard to see.

She pushed her blankets to the side and placed her feet on the floor, her heart beating a little faster at the early morning intrusion. Once she'd taken two small steps toward the door, wary that it would spring open suddenly and knock her down, a face came into focus and she recognized Elliot, the orderly who had replaced Myra Gordon.

She didn't know Elliot as well as some of the other orderlies. He hadn't been at St. C's that long. He nodded his head at her and motioned for her to come closer to the door, but, uncertain about what was happening, Cam didn't respond immediately. Instead, she looked up at the camera in her room. The green light was on, which meant someone should be watching; someone should be concerned by her unusual activity.

Elliot tapped again and motioned once more for her to come closer to the door. She knew he had no key and was sure he couldn't get in, but then again, in this place, it was best not to be sure of anything.

Reluctantly, Cam approached the locked metal door. She stopped, standing about a foot from it.

"What do you want?" she asked Elliot.

"I just thought you might be interested in the sunrise. It's a particularly interesting one this morning. You should go have a look." He smirked at her and walked away, whistling.

What the hell was that all about? Cam took a small step closer to the door and peered through the window on her tippy-toes, afraid he was going to thrust the door open on her. But she could see him walking away; the faint sound of his whistling traveled back to her. She backed up from the door and stood motionless, trying to understand why Elliot had woken her and wanted her to look out the window.

Something was wrong. Cameron's skin prickled, and she rubbed her arms, taking a few deep breaths to calm her heart.

As she turned, she could see through her small, barred window the pink and orange of the sky as the sun came up over the horizon. Her imagination ran wild at his suggestion that she look out the window. *Will someone shoot me through it when I come into view? Did Elliot just enjoy sunrises? What the hell?*

Cautiously, Cameron approached the window, straining to see if anyone was on the ground below or in the trees nearby. Then she scooted a bit closer to see what Elliot had wanted her to see.

Nine stories below, on the sidewalk that weaved around the property and in between buildings, she could see a man standing behind a person slumped over in a wheelchair. The man wore a black winter hat with ear flaps and a square brim that was slanted down, as if he were looking at the patient. His hands, clad in black gloves, gripped the wheelchair's handles. The person in the wheelchair had on a black baseball cap, the brim pulled down obstructing the face, and a black and red blanket with a large, oval, bright white 'G' in the center covered them from their feet up to their chin. There was a word printed along the bottom in white letters. Cam squinted but couldn't make it out.

Weird for this time of the morning. She looked all around as far as the tiny window would let her see. There was nothing, no one else in sight as the sun broke the horizon, casting long shadows across the frozen grass and painting the earth gold. None of the patients at St. Christina's were up this early and certainly were not out for a ride around the property.

As the shadows stretched with the morning light, Cameron realized how odd the two on the sidewalk below were behaving. They hadn't moved—at all. They stood as still as statues. While she stared down at them, the man behind the wheelchair looked up at her and waved. Then, he looked down at the person seated in front of him, embracing the shoulders at first, and removed the black cap that shielded the face from her view. A tumble of brunette locks fell free.

Leaning over, he took the person's face into his gloved hands and tilted it up to Cam, placing his own face next to it, and beamed. Finally, he stood up straight, removed his own hat, revealing both salt and pepper hair that Cam knew had once been black, as well as a face adorned with a mustache and goatee, and blew her a kiss.

Cameron gasped. It was JJ Jonette.

The large 'G' on the blanket suddenly brought the past screeching back to her and dumped it at her feet, as the memories of being kidnapped by him and barely escaping assaulted her mind. The 'G' on the blanket—she recognized it. It was the logo for the University of Georgia. The beautiful face of the co-ed Jonette had kidnapped and tortured to punish Cam for not obeying him rushed to her mind as panic bloomed.

The person in the wheelchair was Lisa Allen!

"No!" she screamed. "No! What are you doing? Stop! Somebody, stop him." She screamed again as she pulled at the bars on the window. Spinning around, she waved at the camera in her room, screaming and pointing at the window. "Help! Help! It's Jonette. He has Lisa! You have to stop him! Please help!"

Cameron turned back to the window, but now they were gone. She pressed her face up against the bars, trying to get a wider view, but it was too late. Jonette had disappeared. Lisa, apparently unconscious, in tow.

Grey Turner was the first to Cameron's door. He opened it and stood with his hand on his taser, and proceeded cautiously, not sure who he was dealing with.

"Cameron?"

Cameron, face still plastered to the bars on the window, spun around. "He's got Lisa Allen! You need to go after them—before he gets away. I just saw them down on the sidewalk—you need to run! Now!" she screamed. "Call the guards at the gate—he needs to be stopped! For God's sake, don't just stand there! Go!"

"Calm down, Cam. Who is Lisa Allen and who has her?"

"Jonette! Oh my God, get out of here and go after them. He'll kill Lisa and you're letting them get away!" She rushed at Turner to run past him, but he grabbed her by her arms and held tight.

"Call the guards at the gate," he shouted over his shoulder to the guards behind him. "Tell them to be on the lookout for a man and a woman." Then, turning back to Cameron, he added, "What do you mean, he has Lisa?"

Cameron shouted over Grey's massive shoulder, "It's Jonette...he's a serial killer. That's who Max was working with. Lisa Allen is the woman he kidnapped when he took me thirteen years ago. We escaped together." She looked up at Grey, shaking. "He has her in a wheelchair. He must have drugged her because she looked unconscious. Please, Grey, please, you have to do something! He'll kill her! He could be killing her right now!"

Grey Turner released Cameron's arms. "I'm going to check the cameras. You need to calm down, okay? I'll be right back."

It'd felt like an eternity before Grey came back to Cameron's room. She'd been pacing like a pissed-off caged tiger, praying that they got to Jason Jonette and Lisa Allen in time and had rescued Lisa.

Grey unlocked Cameron's door and pushed it open as she rushed him. "Did you find them? Is Lisa okay?"

"There was no one out there," Grey said, narrowing his eyes at Cameron. "Are you sure you saw people? Maybe it was an animal or shadows cast by the sun?"

"What! I know what I saw. Where's Elliot? He was in on it. He woke me up, told me to look out the window, and when I did, I saw Jonette. He fucking waved at me." Cameron motioned with her hand, imitating Jonette. "Then he held Lisa's face up to me so that I could see her. If she dies, it's going to be on you and every other fat-assed guard here for not doing your jobs!"

"Look Cameron, I believe it when you say you saw some-thing—"

"Not something. *Someone.* Jason Jonette, aka The J-Bird. A serial killer that Maxine Jane Hoyt was working with to murder women. He's also wanted in Georgia. You've screwed this up," she said, poking him with her finger. "And Lisa Allen is going to pay for it with her life. The grounds are fenced in. How the hell did he get in here without being seen, and how the hell did he get out? Did you even call the guards at the gate house?"

As if on cue, the radio in Grey's hand crackled, and a voice called out to him. "Chief, it's Vasquez. Do you copy?"

"Copy, Vasquez."

"You need to get down to the gatehouse. O'Reilly and Gomez...are dead."

Cam covered her mouth with a hand and stepped back from Grey. Their eyes locked. "It's too late...he's gone," she whispered. "Ask them if there's any sign of Lisa."

"Copy that, Vasquez. Any sign of a woman?"

"No. No one else here," Vasquez answered, his voice shaky.

Grey turned to Cameron. "We released the dogs. If they're still on the grounds, they'll find them."

"They're gone," Cam answered, as if in a trance. "He won't kill her, not yet. This was for me. He wants me."

"I have to go. I'll send for Dr. Heisser. You okay until he gets here?"

Cam nodded. She sat on her bed, staring straight ahead at nothing and at everything.

It was time to end the game. Cameron knew she had to be the one to face Jason Jonette. He had done all this for her. To get her attention. To drive her crazy. For revenge in interfering with his work more than a decade ago. She knew he would never stop until they were face-to-face. She had to be the one to stop him.

She should have listened to him thirteen years earlier when he screamed that she should have killed him. She should have. She should never have let him get away alive, but she was so terrified, more for Lisa than herself, that she'd let him live. Not this time. This time she would hunt him and kill him herself. There would be no trial, no jury, no prison to provide him with his constitutional rights as a human being.

Only death.

She was determined to find a way out of St. Christina's. If The J-Bird could find a way in, then she could find a way out. And once she did, she would track him and kill him. It's what he wanted. It's what she wanted. Lisa was bait for her and her, alone. The game had begun without her knowing it and there were no rules. She knew he wouldn't kill Lisa until she was there to witness it—the ultimate failure. But she wouldn't let it happen. She couldn't. He would die, not Lisa.

I'm going to kill that bastard, she grimly thought to herself.

Yes, we are, a voice whispered in agreement.

This time, it wasn't the whisper of a child.

Acknowledgements

To my husband, Kevin, thank you for being the first one to read my books and for your honest feedback. And for all of your support and encouragement—without it, I'd have to get a real job.

Thank you to my editor, Marsha Zinberg, not just for editing but for the education I receive every time we work together.

Many thanks to everyone who took a chance on a new author and read *Fractured: The Stealth Stalker* and has continued on with *Snapped: The Chelsea Choker*. You'll never know how much your positive and uplifting words mean to me. And to those who didn't enjoy it, that's okay. I don't love everything I read either, but I hope you don't give up on me. Maybe you'll love my next book.

To my family and friends who have been so enthusiastic with your support, I'm overwhelmed. I can't thank you enough for cheering me on as I pursue my dreams!

And, as always, a big thank you to my children, Colin, Kirsten, and Kyle. You are my sounding boards. I appreciate your feedback on blurbs and book covers. And your many, many friends who are avid readers! You are all awesome!

About the author

C.S. Dodds is the pen name of Christine Dodds. She is a member of International Thriller Writers and the Independent Book Publishers Association.

Christine was born in the West Village of New York City and currently resides in New Jersey. She is married to a man who was her first-grade crush. They have three children, who they are very proud of, and who certainly make life interesting.

Did you enjoy reading *Snapped: The Chelsea Choker?* If so, please send Christine an email at christine@csdodds.com She would love to hear from you.

Reviews are the lifeblood of authors. Please consider leaving a review or a star rating at:

www.amazon.com/author/c.s.-dodds

www.goodreads.com/author/show/22653778.C_S_Dodds

Check out Christine's website to get updates about new releases and to join her mailing list at: www.csdodds.com

Typos are the turf monsters of books. They hide from authors and editors but love to jump out at readers. If you spot one of these sneaky little monsters, please let Christine know at:

christine@csdodds.com

Thank you!

* 9 7 9 8 9 8 6 6 6 1 8 4 1 *